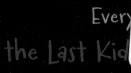

Every
the Last Kid

"TERRIFYINGLY FUN! Max Brallier's *The Last Kids on Earth* delivers big thrills and even bigger laughs." —JEFF KINNEY, author of the #1 *New York Times* bestseller *Diary of a Wimpy Kid*

★ "A GROSS-OUT GOOD TIME with surprisingly nuanced character development."
—*School Library Journal*, starred review

★ "Classic ACTION-PACKED, monster-fighting fun." —*Kirkus Reviews*, starred review

★ "SNARKY END-OF-THE-WORLD FUN."
—*Publishers Weekly*, starred review

"The likable cast, lots of adventure, and GOOEY, OOZY MONSTER SLIME GALORE keep the pages turning." —*Booklist*

"Jack is a fantastic narrator . . . Young zombie fans will rejoice in this new series that has all the oozing (by the zombies) and heroism (by the kids) that they could hope for."
—*Bulletin of the Center for Children's Books*

"HILARIOUS and FULL OF HEART." —*Boys' Life*

"*The Last Kids on Earth* is a BLAST."

—Powell's Books

"I would recommend *The Last Kids on Earth* for PEOPLE WHO LIKE VIDEO GAMES because it is equally as fast-paced."

—*The Guardian*

"It's hard to find something unexpected to do with zombies, but this clever mix of black-and-white drawings and vivid prose brings new life to the living dead."

—Common Sense Media

"The MONSTERS IN THIS BOOK just beg to COME ALIVE."

—Parenting Chaos

"One-part SWISS FAMILY ROBINSON, and one-part WALKING DEAD, Max Brallier and Doug Holgate's well-imagined book is sure to appeal to readers with big imaginations."

—The Reading Nook Reviews

"The NEXT HOT READING ADVENTURE for reluctant readers or for anyone looking for a fast-paced, humorous adventure."

—Guys Lit Wire

Winner of the Texas Bluebonnet Award

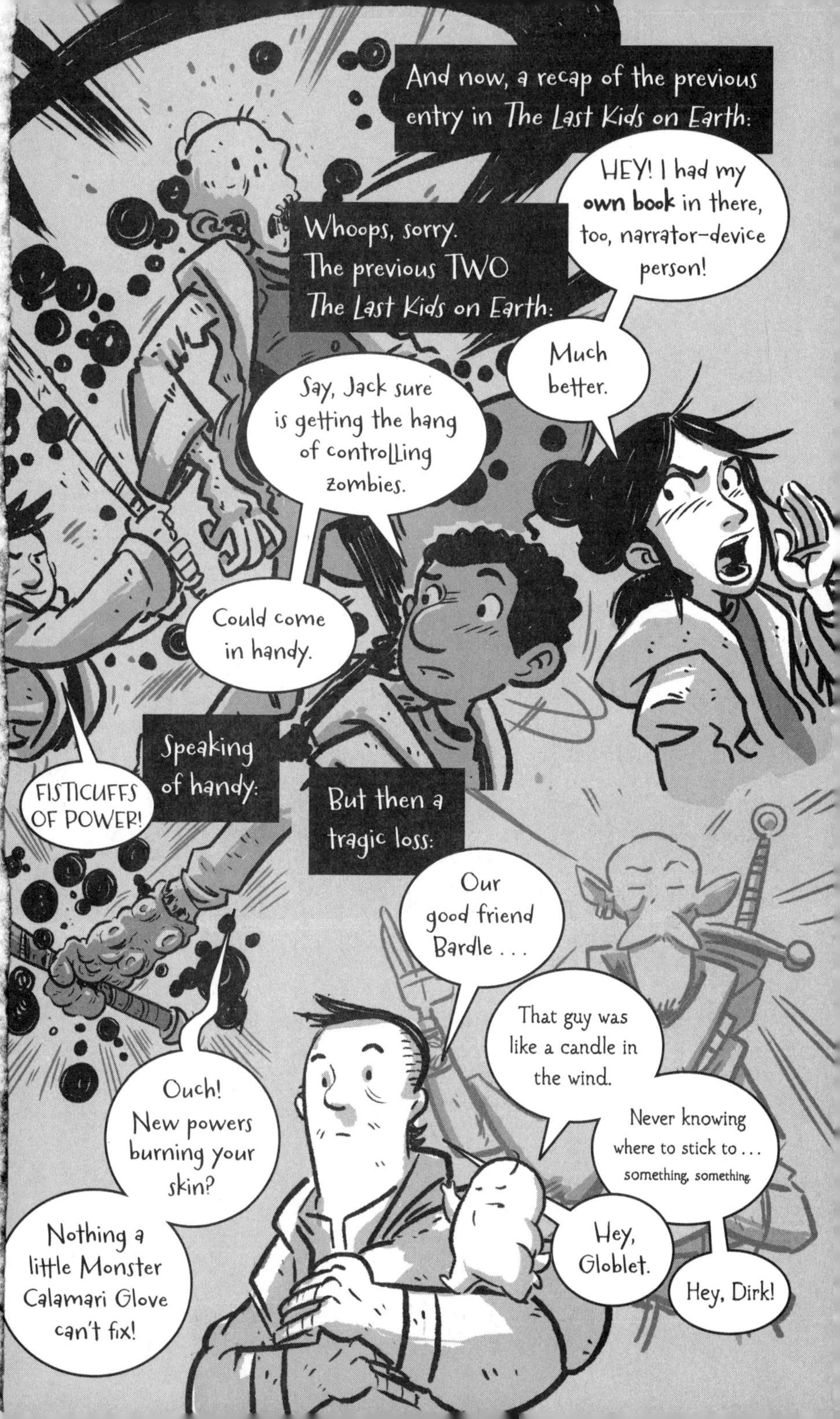

And now, a recap of the previous entry in *The Last Kids on Earth*:
HEY! I had my **own book** in there, too, narrator-device person!
Whoops, sorry. The previous TWO *The Last Kids on Earth*:
Much better.
Say, Jack sure is getting the hang of controlling zombies.
Could come in handy.
Speaking of handy:
FISTICUFFS OF POWER!
But then a tragic loss:
Our good friend Bardle . . .
That guy was like a candle in the wind.
Never knowing where to stick to . . . something, something.
Ouch! New powers burning your skin?
Nothing a little Monster Calamari Glove can't fix!
Hey, Globlet.
Hey, Dirk!

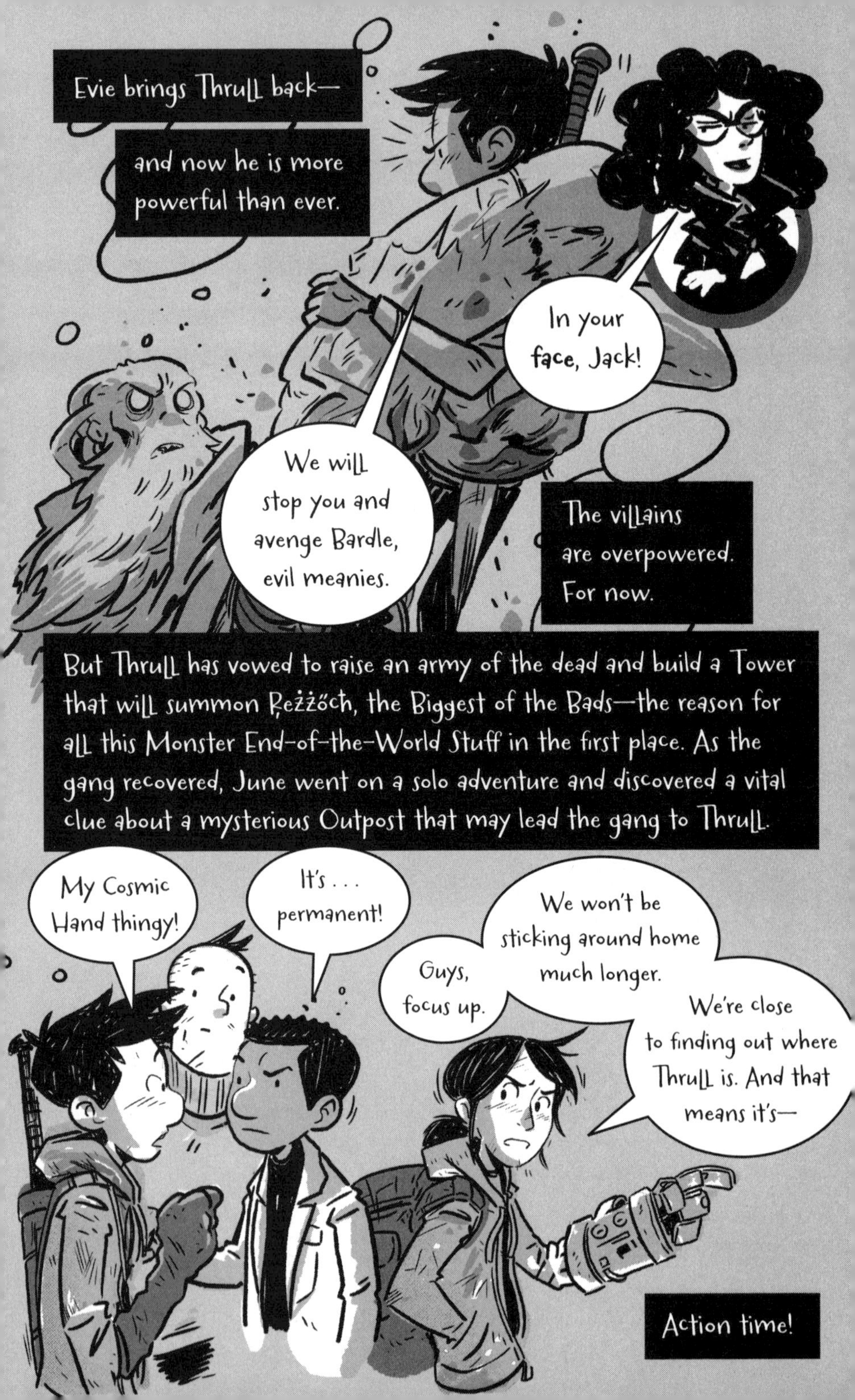
Evie brings Thrull back—
and now he is more powerful than ever.
In your face, Jack!
We will stop you and avenge Bardle, evil meanies.
The villains are overpowered. For now.
But Thrull has vowed to raise an army of the dead and build a Tower that will summon Ŗeżżőch, the Biggest of the Bads—the reason for all this Monster End-of-the-World Stuff in the first place. As the gang recovered, June went on a solo adventure and discovered a vital clue about a mysterious Outpost that may lead the gang to Thrull.
My Cosmic Hand thingy!
It's . . . permanent!
Guys, focus up.
We won't be sticking around home much longer.
We're close to finding out where Thrull is. And that means it's—
Action time!

THE LAST KIDS ON EARTH and the SKELETON ROAD

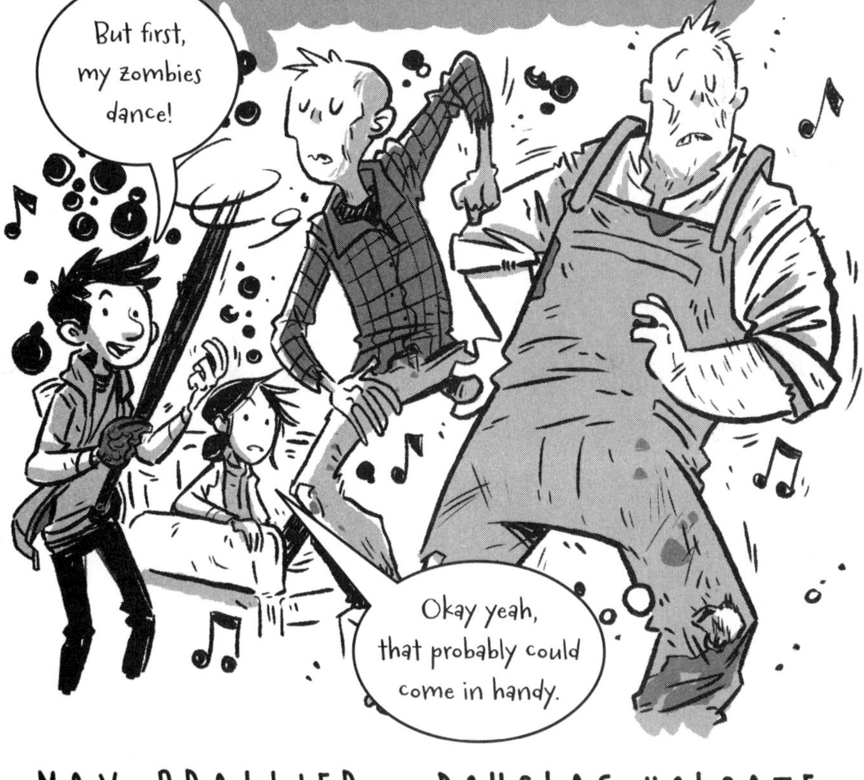
But first, my zombies dance!
Okay yeah, that probably could come in handy.

MAX BRALLIER & DOUGLAS HOLGATE

VIKING

VIKING
An imprint of Penguin Random House LLC, New York

First published in the United States of America by Viking,
an imprint of Penguin Random House LLC, 2020

Visit us online at penguinrandomhouse.com

LIBRARY OF CONGRESS CATALOGING-IN-PUBLICATION DATA IS AVAILABLE
ISBN 9781984835345

10   9   8   7   6   5   4   3   2   1

Book design by Jim Hoover
Set in Cosmiqua Com and Carrotflower

Printed in the USA

To Lila. Fist bumps!

—M. B.

For Merri, Tom, and Jack.

Welcome to the world, little man!

—D. H.

THE DECOMPOSING DOZEN

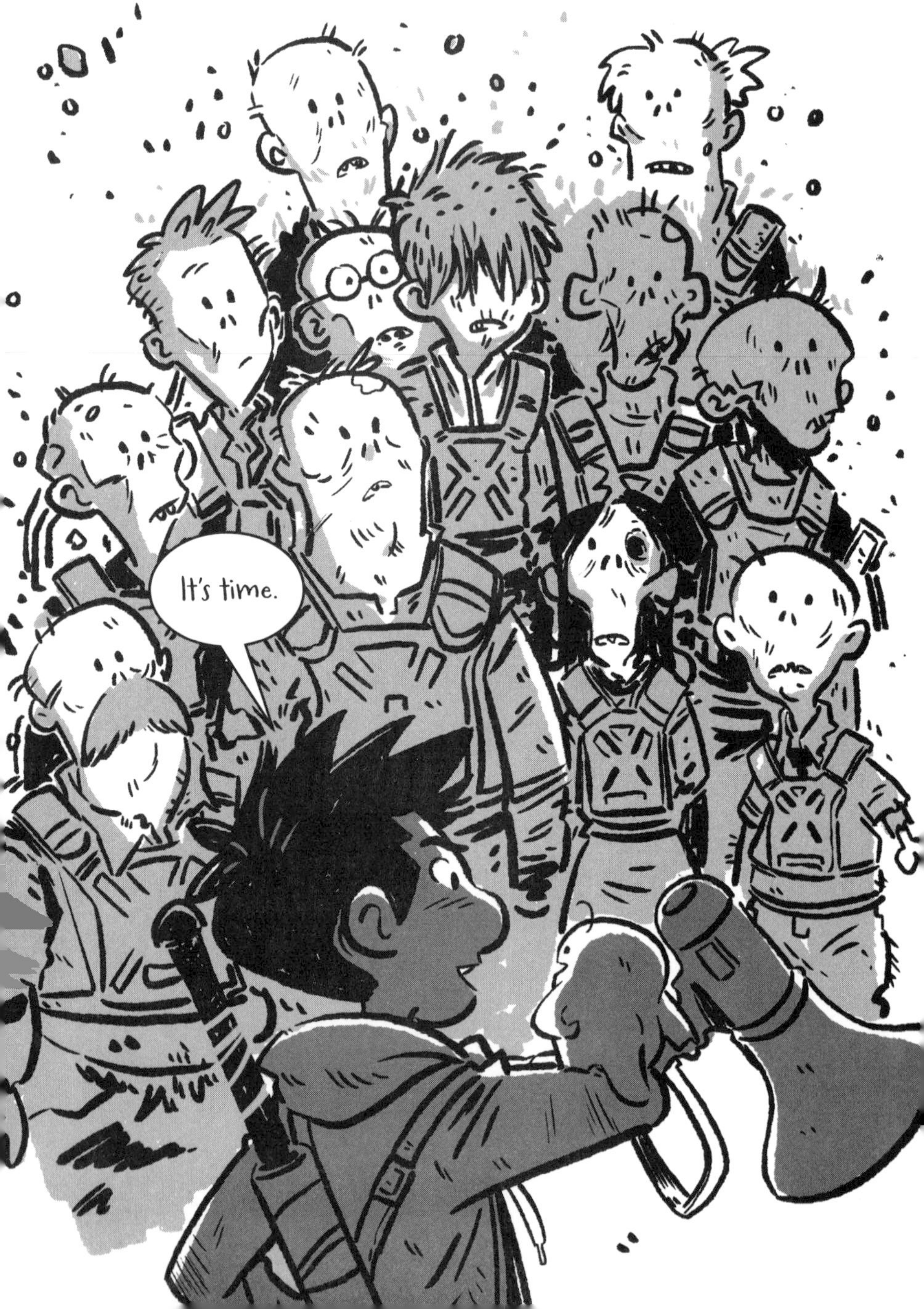
It's time.

chapter one

See these twelve zombies right here? I call
them the Decomposing Dozen. They are
the *elite*.

The best of the best.

The cream of the crop.

I know they're tough—but I'm about
to find out what they're *really* made of.
That's why I'm standing on top of an old
school bus, staring out at a bizarre series
of bone-shattering obstacles.

Tiny goo-ball Globlet is beside me,
clutching a bullhorn that's twice her
size. She squeaks: "ARE THE ZOMBIES
READY?"

A low murmur echoes in response:
"Ermmmm."

Globlet turns, then squeaks: "AND ARE
THE UNIVERSAL WARRIORS READY?"

My friends all shout back, "Yes!"

I grip the Louisville Slicer and *focus*. My heart rate slows. The Cosmic Hand trembles. Then, with a flick of my wrist, I command the zombies forward as I shout, "ATTACK QUINT!"

The zombies heed my command—and together they charge! The lumbering bodies are speeding up a ramp toward Quint.

He raises his new gripper-grabber pole, which is just a long stick with pincher jaws at the end. He opens the jaws! The zombies are nearly upon him! And then . . .

RUMBLE RUMBLE RUMBLE RUMBLE RUMBLE RUMBLE RUMBLE

Y'know what—HOLD ON, TIME-OUT. You're probably wondering what's going on—you might be curious *why* I'm ordering a horde of zombies to barrel headlong into my best friend.

Yeah, it's time to hit you with a little recap action. . . .

INITIATE RECAP ACTION! STUFF THAT HAPPENED AND STUFF YOU MISSED!

See, for the past few months, Quint, June, Dirk, and I have all been pretty busy. June even got into a crazy adventure that ended in a showdown with a villainous monster pirate: the Boss Rifter.

And June learned a *lot*. Like: (1) Thrull is getting stronger; (2) the Tower is gonna be catastrophic if he finishes it; and (3) there's a place where we can discover more about the Tower and its location: a mysterious Outpost. Find the Outpost, find the Tower.

Problem was, the Boss Rifter got away before we could learn *where* this Outpost is. So, our crazed monster warrior buddy Skaelka ventured out into the wild, searching for it.

Yep, one day, Skaelka simply saddled up onto her Carapace (it's like a monstrous hermit crab, with a car for a shell) and rode off. It's been weeks and she still hasn't returned. . . .

And me? My life? I've been busy polishing my zombie-controlling powers. Total Jedi-like training. Our monster friend Warg has been helping me develop my skills and better understand the capabilities of the Cosmic Hand.

That's what I named the sucker-covered monster-tentacle-glove-thing that is now *forever* wrapped around my wrist and hand.

See, we chopped off Ghazt's tail so he wouldn't have the ability to control zombies, but we didn't anticipate *Thrull* stealing the tail and taking the ability for himself! But then Thrull didn't anticipate *me* siphoning it away from him!

It was a lot of back and forth, but it amounted to me having one pretty cool suction glove Cosmic Hand thingy and—with the power of Ghazt's tail inside the Louisville Slicer—the rad ability to command and control zombies, yay!

With Warg's help, I've made serious progress: I can actually make zombies *do* stuff. I mean, I'm like, two steps shy of being a legit necromancer now. . . .

I quickly realized that the more time I spend training with *any one particular* zombie, the stronger the connection between me and that zombie becomes.

"Just like Dungeon Loot Hunter: Crawler of Tombs 3!" Quint said when I explained it to him.

"Exactly!" I replied. (Dungeon Loot Hunter: Crawler of Tombs 3 is our favorite RPG.) Anyway, in RPGs, you gotta pick one or two characters and really focus on leveling them up. If you keep flipping between different characters, you just end up with a bunch of, like, average dudes. And I do *not* have time for average dudes.

My powers aren't, like, unlimited though. I'm only able to control a few zombies at a time. For example, I *cannot* lead a legion of zombies into battle, but I *can* stage super-epic zombie lightsaber fights. And I do. . . .

C'mon, zombies—get 'em! Then June and I will have infinite hang-out time!

So, what I have to do is clear: treat this like an RPG. I'll pick a few zombies who are *already* naturally combat-capable—and level them up! Bottom line: I'm forming a super-elite group of undead warriors. Jack Sullivan's Zombie Squad.

But finding good zombies has been tough. Up at Warg's tree-farm home, where the zombies stay, I put them all through a bunch of tests. It did not go well, although it wasn't really their fault. . . .

Rover, NO! The zombies are not toys!

GLURRRRMMM . . .

Then one day, when I was out on my usual Wakefield walkabout, searching for zombies to add to our army, I spotted an old friend: Alfred! The zombie who helped us find Ŗeżżõch and the Tree of Entry!

Previous adventure with Alfred!

Alfred was trying to cross from one rooftop to another via a toppled water tank when he slipped and fell right into my outstretched arms. It was like a delightfully awkward first meeting in a romantic comedy. . . .

Seeing Alfred trying to navigate a water tank balance beam gave me the big idea! I was like: YES! THAT'S HOW I'LL CHOOSE MY RPG ZOMBIE WARRIORS! With an elimination game, like those obstacle course shows on TV. Y'know the ones: *Gladiator Wipeout* and *Extreme Ninja Obstacle Hero* and *Toddler vs. Piranha*!

So, my buddies and I put together our own elimination course. We built it at Laser Extreme Adventure Zone—the place has everything: trampoline park, laser tag arena, rock-climbing wall, churro stand, and tons of other rad junk.

Dirk got *super* into building the course. I think it's 'cause these sort of combat competitions are in his blood.

See, Dirk let slip that his dad was on the old TV show *Universal Warriors*. Man, that show was *the best*. Each week, a bunch of regular 9-to-5-type folks would face off against super-jacked, spandex-clad "Warriors"—and the Warriors would just straight-up *destroy* the normal people.

Dirk told us his dad was a Warrior named the Big Dagger. To be honest, I don't remember the Big Dagger, but there were *a lot* of Warriors on that show over the years.

Anyway, Dirk has built an awesome Zombie Squad Elimination Course. It started off pretty bootleg—kinda like one of those local haunted houses where random people from town dress up and try to scare you. But it's never that scary because the crudely costumed werewolf that pops out from behind a hay bale is clearly your math teacher.

Anyway, *now* our Zombie Squad Elimination Course is rad—and finally ready! I've chosen the top twelve zombie warrior prospects—and I will do my best to get them through the course.

The rules are simple: any zombie that reaches the finish line makes my squad. Get to the end—and they shall be deemed worthy!

Sounds simple, but it won't be easy: Quint, June, Dirk, Rover, and some of our monster buddies like Biggun and Fern are going to try to stop 'em.

We gathered at the Elimination Course early this morning. My friends took positions across the course while I directed the zombies to the starting line. It was time to find out just how tough my Decomposing Dozen was. Time to find out if I could get them to the finish line. . . .

I took a deep breath, then—

SLICE! I swung the Slicer and the zombies rushed forward! The competition had begun! Quint readied himself as they streamed toward him. And with that, now. . . .

BACK TO THE ACTION!
WILL QUINT SURVIVE? OR WILL
HE BE DEVOURED BY THE UNDEAD?!
SPOILER ALERT: HE'S A-OK!

Not today, zombies!

Quint spins, swinging his staff, and a second zombie tumbles off the ramp. "You'll need to do better than that, Jack!" he shouts.

He's right. I gotta *focus* if I plan on any of my zombies reaching the finish line. I snap the Slicer, and the remaining zombies pick up speed.

To control the zombies, I concentrate *in the*

extreme, thinking *hard* about what I want them to do, then I shout that command while swinging the Slicer. That's how I can control them; it works, since me and the blade are now, like, *one*.

"FORWARD!" I bark, and swing the Slicer twice more. The remaining zombies speed through the next wave of bone-shattering obstacles. . . .

I'm high up on my school bus platform, trying to get three zombies across a swinging bridge, when I hear the sound. . . .

It is a terrible noise—and it sends a horrible shiver shooting straight down my spine.

Globlet, still on my shoulder, grabs my shirt. "Jack, what was that?" she asks quietly.

"Not sure, Globs," I say. I turn, searching for the source of the horrifying sound. Then my eyes catch movement in the parking lot.

It takes me a moment to understand what I'm looking at. But when I finally see what's making the awful, deafening sound—my heart begins to slam.

Skeletons.

Skeleton *soldiers*.

Hundreds of them. Marching toward us.

I suspected this was coming. Still, I'd hoped I was wrong. . . .

This is like my nightmare. The vision I had, months ago, when Quint and Dirk and Warg came to show me what they'd found in Evie's Cabal of the Cosmic *book . . .*

Not just skeletons.

Thrull's skeleton army.

chapter two

"It's Thrull's skeleton army!" Quint cries out from atop a rope bridge.

"Be back, Globs," I say, and then I'm leaping from the bus and speeding across the course.

When I finally reach my friends, the skeletons are swarming toward them.

"They're *armed*!" June shouts.

"Wearing some pretty wicked armor, too," Dirk says, sounding half impressed. "I mean, not as cool as ours. But still . . . cool."

The skeletons' weapons and armor are built from bone. They swing Dozer spike swords and they wave war hammers sharp with Wormungulous teeth and they twirl daggers of twisted Wretch talon. Some wear helmets carved from Carapace horns. Others carry shields of sliced monster scales.

"They're fast!" Quint notes. "On the plus side, we don't need to fear their bite."

"You sure about that?" Dirk asks.

"Of course! These aren't zombies, they're skeleton soldiers!" Quint says. "Like old-school Ray Harryhausen–style warriors."

"I don't know what Ron Henry-Homer old-school warriors are," Dirk says, spinning his gladiator jousting pole. "But I know I'm gonna bash these boneheads like old-school-style *Universal Warriors*!"

We assume our most intimidating action poses. Biggun assumes an even more intimidating action pose—

Biggun's meaty paw smacks aside four
skeletons. Globlet peppers skeleton soldiers with
a Blow Dart Blaster she nabbed from a Rifter.

"Guys, I actually think we got this," I say,

happily surprised. "These dudes are *weak*!"

"They are only bone," Quint agrees.

"We can just smash them!" Dirk yells.

"Come on!" June orders as they charge into the horde. I'm about to follow my buds, when—

SMACK!

Rover knocks me right on my butt as he eagerly hurls himself into a wall of skeletons. "Go, buddy!" I shout, sitting up.

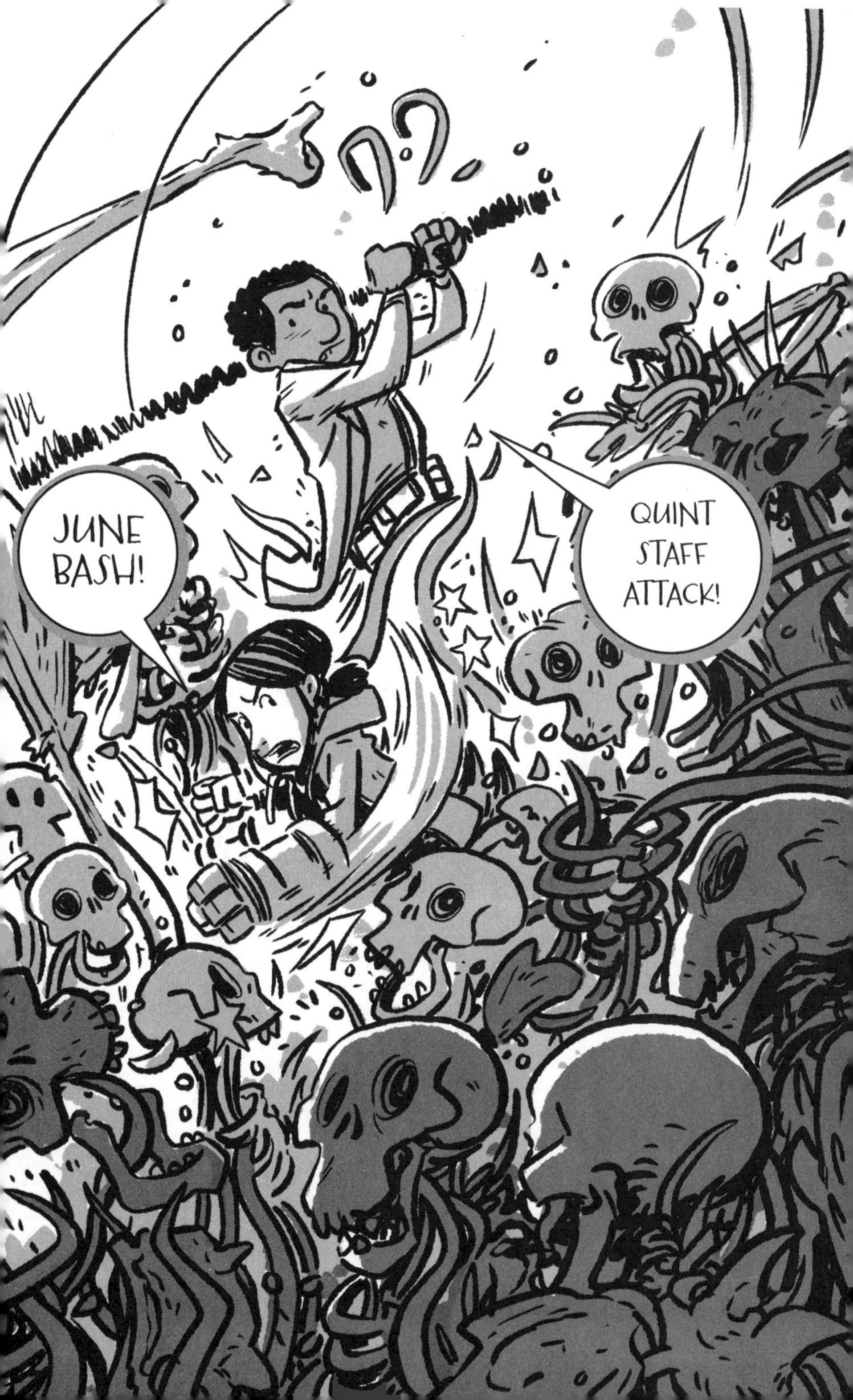
JUNE BASH!
QUINT STAFF ATTACK!

Thrull's skeletons burst apart like Legos. I watch my buddies dismantle a squad of skeleton soldiers in *mere seconds*.

I'm feelin' good. We've destroyed gigantic beasts, fought the undead, and taken down villainous overlords. But these skeletons? One hard hit and they crumble! I could beat these dudes in my sleep. . . .

Suddenly, one skeleton comes screaming toward me. *Finally*, I think. *I was getting jealous watching my buddies have all the fun.*

The skeleton leaps onto the hood of a car. Its bony feet sprint up the windshield, then across the roof—*TAK-TAK-TAK-TAK*.

It launches off the car, sailing toward me like a big ol' meatball.

I swing the Slicer *hard*—like I'm trying to whack a wiffle ball to the moon. There's a loud *KRACK*. Sounds like a homer, all right—definitely hammered that dude into the cheap seats.

But then I stop.

Something's happening. The skeleton's skull *snaps* to the side, and—

GROSS VINE SOUNDS!

SCHLURP!

What the huh?

A tangled, interwoven thread of *Vine-Thingies* runs through its entire cage-like body. The vines coil in and out, like tangled TV wires. Then—

TWANG! The skull *snaps* back into place.

The skeleton smiles . . . something I didn't even think was *possible*. It is a hideously toothy, vile grin.

I stagger back—and now I see the enemy in its entirety. . . .

TWANG! TWONG! THUNK!
All around us, the skeletons are snapping back together. Pulling up from the ground. Rising like puppets plucked by Thrull's terrifying strings.

The skeletons we thought we'd just defeated are piecing themselves together again. One jams its arm back into place.

"Guys!" I say as we regroup. "It's the vines! They're running *through* the skeletons!"

"The vines must be giving the skeletons their power!" Quint adds. "Reanimating them! I was wrong. These skeletons are not—"

"Ron Henry-Homer things?" Dirk asks.

"*Ray Harryhausen things*," Quint says with a sigh. "But YES. These *are* different!"

"Hold up!" June says. "Remember the Tendrill? We needed goo-slime to stop it! I bet that's what'll stop these vines, too. And luckily," she announces, "I've got just what we need."

She pulls one of Quint's goo-slime grenades from her action fanny pack and begins loading it into Blasty (that's her wrist-attached, Swiss Army–style, everything-but-the-kitchen-sink gadget-cannon).

"Uh-oh," June says, struggling.

"Uh-oh?" I say. "I don't like uh-oh. What is uh-oh?"

"It's jammed," June says.

The skeleton army is fully reassembled. Back on their feet, ready to rumble . . .

More skeletons appear—dozens, coming from all sides. My Zombie Squad Elimination Course is completely overrun!

"Hey, Jack," Dirk says. "You say you can control zombies? Might be a good time to start doing it . . ."

"Right, duh!" I say. "My zombies! Now, where are they . . . ?"

I scan the course, searching for any still-standing zombies. Unfortunately, the Decomposing Dozen didn't exactly ace the course. I spot one zombie dangling upside down from the rock wall, two others tangled in the ropes course, and a few rolling around on sweaty old gym mats.

Not good. It looks like every single one has been knocked out of commission.

"Jack! There!" Quint says, pointing.

Spinning, I spot three zombies milling about near the finish line.

Nothing about this day went like I'd expected— but in the end, it looks like I've found my squad after all.

They are the only three standing. They are—

- MY SQUAD -

I summon them with a quick Slicer swing,
bringing them shuffling toward us. It's like a
video game—and they're my little minions.

"The skeletons keep coming!" June shouts,
finally giving up on loading the goo-slime

grenade. "We gotta get to the BoomKarts—and get outta here!!"

She's pointing to where they're parked, across the obstacle course, beyond the laser tag arena.

"Alfred," I say to my old zombie butler. "You're gonna lead the way, buddy!"

I swing the Slicer, little flicks and twists that translate to zombie commands. Glurm charges straight into the skeletal horde blocking our path, and Lefty and Alfred follow.

KRAK!

SKELETONS SHATTER!

We follow the zombies, but a fresh skeleton horde appears, blocking our path to the BoomKarts.

"Into the laser tag area!" I shout.

We rush inside—only to discover the labyrinth-like laser tag course has become a glow-in-the-dark death trap. . . .

Skeletons surround Biggun, Rover, Globlet, and Fern. More pour in, speeding down the halls, leaping over cover, bursting around the zigzagging turns.

"Stay together, gang!" June barks.

"Don't gotta tell me twice!" Dirk replies as he yanks two skeletons off Biggun's back.

Spinning around, I see Globlet and Fern now fight from land and sky, tag-teaming a pack of skeletons. Rover is using his teeth to rip the vines out of one. Biggun picks more skeletons off himself and is now using his body to block one entrance.

But more skeletons march toward us. Their faces are still locked in those awful, toothy grins. They don't get tired or fatigued—and they never have to stop to catch their breath. Guess that's one benefit to not having lungs.

"It's about to get real, guys," I say.

June growls, "Let 'em bring it."

And they do.

Three of them SPRING AHEAD and tear toward us. Dirk and Quint whirl around, directly in their paths.

All I can do is watch in terror. Dirk has no weapon—his jousting pole is now in pieces. And Quint only has his staff.

But together—

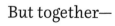

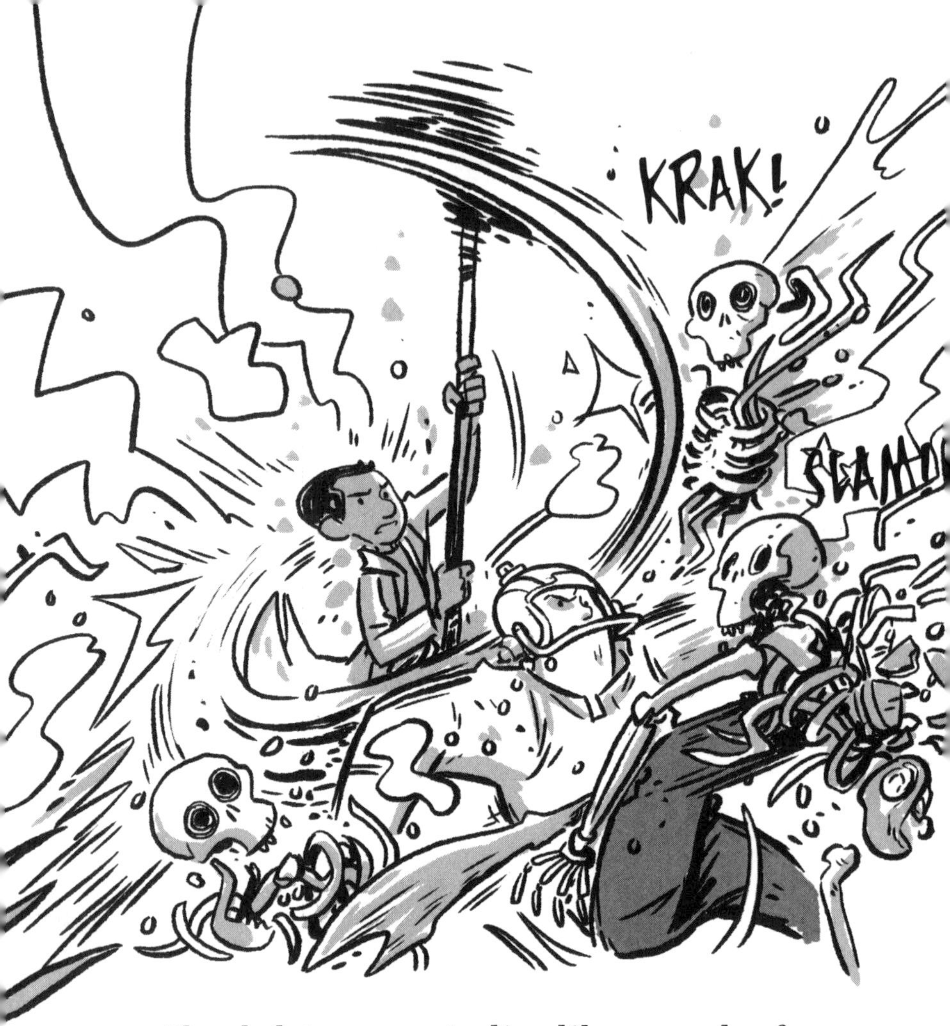
KRAK!

The skeletons are sizzling like a couple of burgers plopped onto a hot grill.

One opens its mouth in a silent shriek. It has a Dirk-boot-sized hole in its rib cage—and for some reason, this hole isn't reassembling. The skeleton looks down, confused. Sizzling vines dangle from its center.

The skeletons that Quint cracked aren't reassembling, either.

Quint glances at the butt end of his staff. Dirk looks at the bottom of his boot. It takes a minute for them to realize what just happened.

Then Dirk's face lights up.

"My boots," he says to Quint. "They're covered in goo-slime! From Project Day-Glo!"

"And I've been using the bottom of my staff as a stir stick!" Quint says.

"Wait, wait—Project What-Now?" I ask. I'm suddenly more concerned that I've clearly been left out of something *massive* than I am about a bunch of bone-soldiers.

"Not now, Jack!" Dirk snaps, and I follow his eyes upward, to a skeleton flinging itself at us, hands gripping a battle-ax. Seconds before it cleaves us, June jumps in, using Blasty to block the blow—

Dirk grabs the skeleton and shot-puts it across the laser tag arena.

"Guys, good news!" June exclaims. "Jack's fear of ever missing out on anything ever might have just saved the day. That block totally unjammed Blasty!"

She cocks the loading mechanism and slides the goo-slime grenade in. Totally ready to rock.

Fear seems to have settled into the skeletons, something we never saw happen with the zombies.

They all take a slow step backward. . . .

"Catch!" June says cheerfully, and she fires the goo-slime grenade directly into a group of thirty skeletal soldiers.

Here today . . . gone to-marrow!

KAAA

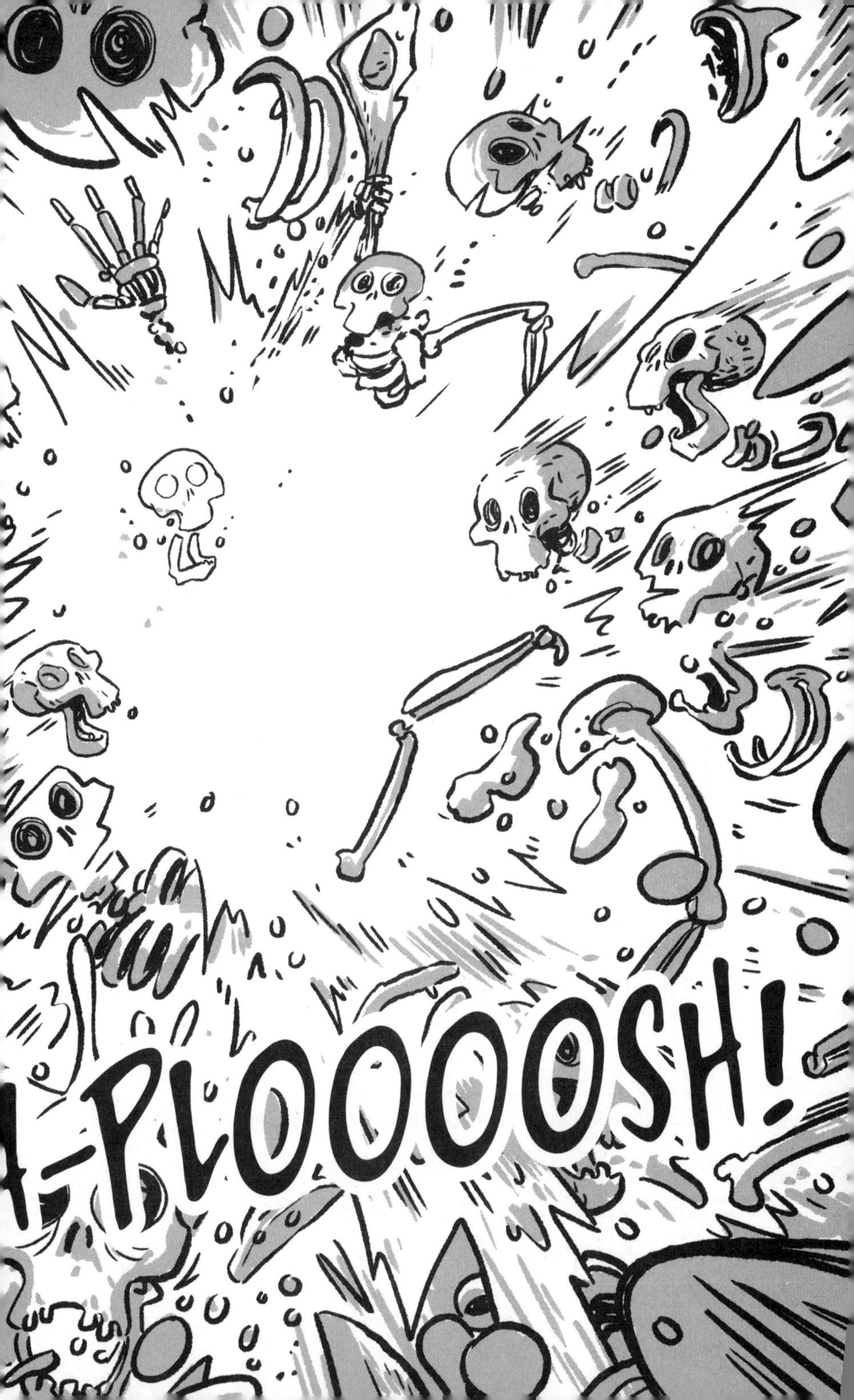
-PLOOOOSH!

There's an explosion of greens and pinks, which mix together, creating a swirling fog.

"You need a better catchphrase," I tell June as the fog clears.

"Oh, you mean like 'fisticuffs'?" she asks with a teasing grin.

"HEY!" I exclaim. "THAT WAS A WORK IN PROGRESS! THE APOCALYPSE HAD JUST STARTED, THINGS WERE CONFUSING, AND I THINK IT WAS DAYLIGHT SAVINGS TIME MAYBE!"

Just then, Globlet comes hopping over. "Whoa, June! *You did that?* Right on, girlfriend! Rad."

Globlet's right—rad indeed.

June's goo-slime grenade completely blew apart two dozen enemies. The vines have melted away to nothing and smoke coils off their chalky remains.

A few injured skeletons stagger around. One raises a bone-ax high in an attempt to attack. But the weight pulls it backward and it flops onto the ground.

"Whoa, whoa," Globlet says. "Those sizzling vines smell straight-up *nasty*."

"Uh-huh," Dirk grunts. "And I'm not sure the party's over yet."

As the smoke clears, we see dozens more skeleton soldiers approaching.

I swing my blade, bringing Alfred, Lefty, and Glurm shambling forward. The zombies stare down the skeleton squad. Biggun looms behind us. Rover strides forward until he stands beside me.

The skeletons pause. They might not have *brains*, but they *do* know enough not to get beaten and broken on *purpose*.

"Let's see just how smart they are," June says. She reaches down and pops open the side of Blasty. Then, empty-handed, she mimes sliding in another goo-slime grenade.

"You want some more?!" she barks, and points the cannon at the skeleton horde.

They sway back and forth.

My heart pounds—if they don't buy it, we'll be overrun. Then—a loud *HISS*—and, at once, they turn and go, scurrying away, into the parking lot, into the distance.

"AND STAY OUT!" Dirk shouts.

"The goo-slime worked quite well, friend," Quint says. "But they'll soon be back."

"And in greater numbers," I say.

Quint grins. "Like Tusken Raiders!"

"Hey, speaking of—we need a name for those dudes. Skeleton soldiers? Bone battlers? Vine villains!"

Dirk groans at the Star Wars nerd conversation. As we make our way through the crumbled course and toward our BoomKarts, my mind is racing.

I guess, sure, *technically*, we won that fight. But it doesn't *feel* that way. That was close. Too close. And the size of that fighting force was, like, I dunno—an appetizer! No doubt Thrull's got something bigger planned for the main course.

chapter three

OK, so I'm officially calling that the First
Battle of the Skeletons, 'cause it sounds epic
and historic. And during that epic and historic
battle, Alfred, Lefty, and Glurm proved
themselves the zombies most worthy of joining
my ZOMBIE SQUAD.

And right now, they're the only ones keeping
me company, because Quint, Dirk, and June
went MIA *immediately* after our skeleton brawl.

Quint and Dirk left to work on "Project Day-
Glo," though they won't spill the beans on what it
is. And—not gonna lie—that's super frustrating
for a person like me, who likes to know what his
buddies are doing at all times because *that's the
type of thing buddies should know*!

And June ran off with Globlet and Biggun to
fortify the town's defenses, now that we know
Thrull's soldiers are within striking distance.

Which leaves me and my zombies for a
skeleton battle debrief. Sure, we were victorious,
but I gotta be sure they know who's in charge.

An ear-shattering SHRIEK interrupts my
dramatic speech. I shove my head out the
window: it's Phyllis, the pelican-monster who
keeps watch on the town wall. This is a big deal:
a Phyllis shriek is the signal that someone—*or
something*—is approaching town.

"Uhh—talk amongst yourselves, zombie buds!"
I say, and I send them shambling away.

Moments later, I'm at the edge of the Town Square, squeezing my way through the gathering monster crowd.

I find June up front, peering through binoculars. Globlet is perched on her shoulder.

"What is it?" I ask excitedly. "Bad guys? Good guys? Average guys?"

June lowers the binoculars—and I see that her eyes are wet with joy. "It's Skaelka!" she says.

"She better have brought me a snow globe," Globlet chirps. "She promised!"

I grin. Skaelka's return is a huge relief. We've all been on edge since she ventured out in search of information about the Outpost.

Skaelka's riding her Carapace like a horse down Main Street. She bobs and sways in the car's saddle seat. A hood covers her head. Her ax glints in the bright afternoon sun.

The Carapace scuttles slowly down the road, claws stabbing the ground awkwardly, like one of those dogs wearing shoes. I realize that the Carapace is hurt. Its outer shell—the car—must have gotten torn off in battle, and one broken cannon trails limply off the back of its body.

"Looks like they saw some action out there," I say grimly.

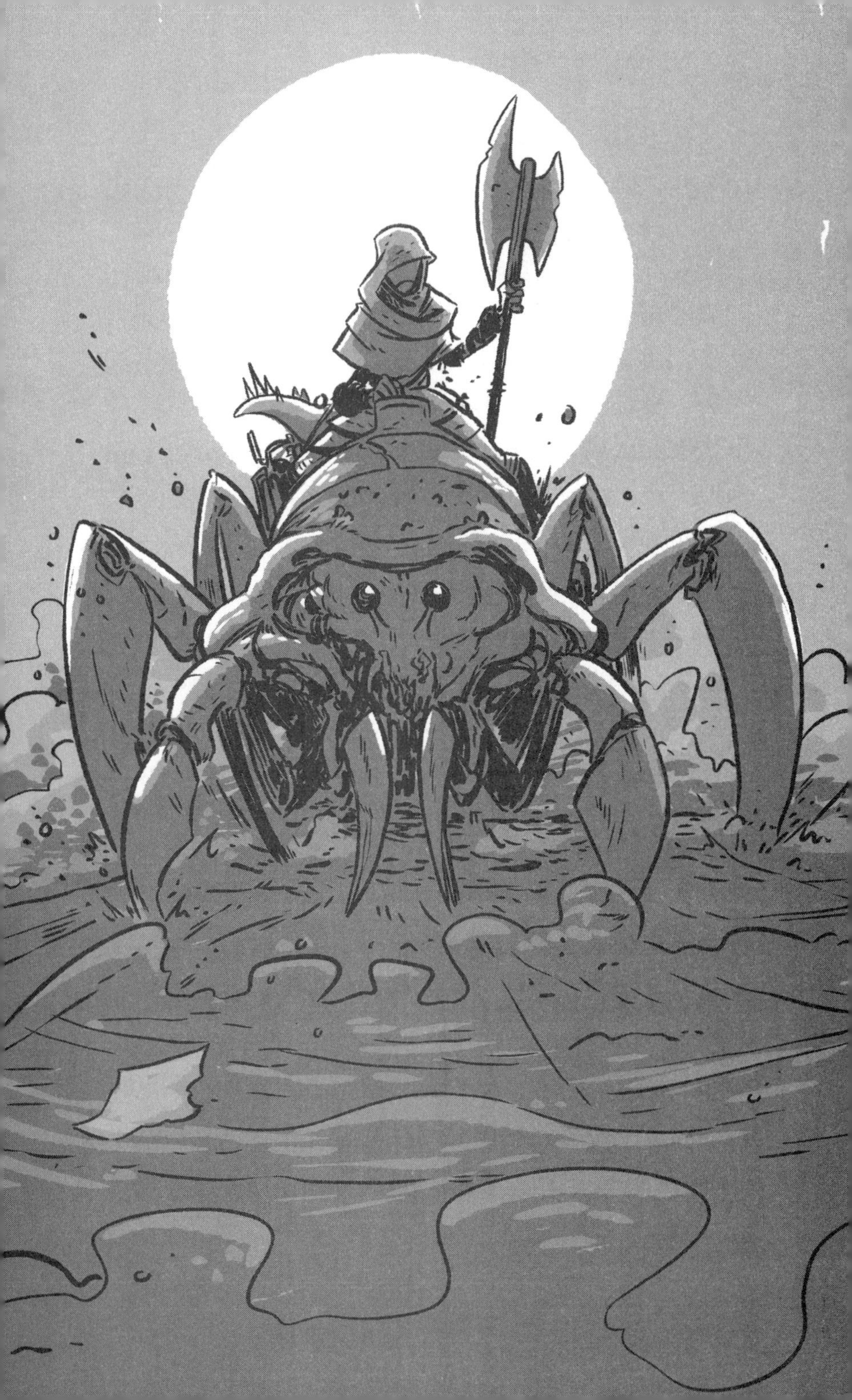

"YOU'RE BACK!" June shouts as Skaelka brings the Carapace to a stop. Skaelka's barely out of the saddle and June's launching a full-blown interrogation. "Where have you been?? What did you find out?? What took you so long?"

"And did you find an Arbys?!" Globlet demands. "Was it true? DID they have the meats?"

Skaelka's silent. She pats the Carapace, and the creature hobbles off toward its sleeping hole, where it'll nap until needed again.

Skaelka removes her hood—and that's when I see that her Carapace isn't the only one with battle scars. Her skin is horribly sun-beaten and marked with cuts and raw bruises. Her armor is dented, her sash is torn, and her lucky Dozer-whacking cudgel is gunk-splattered.

"Yeep," Globlet says. "You look crummy."

Normally, Skaelka would punt Globlet for a crack like that. But not now. I see none of that usual frenetic Skaelka energy we've come to know and love and—on occasion—fear.

Skaelka's voice is raspy and dry. "I have been riding two days straight. I need refreshments."

"I'll grab you a soda," I say.

"No soda," she says. "This thirst is fierce. Only pepperoni rolls can quench it. . . ."

Skaelka answers none of June's questions—
she just shoves another fistful of pepperoni
rolls into her mouth and washes them down
with a gulp of ranch dressing.

Finally, Skaelka leans back in the booth. I have a feeling that whatever she says next—it's gonna change everything. My foot is bouncing on the floor, going a mile a minute.

"Monsters are choosing sides," Skaelka begins. "Many have pledged their allegiance to Thrull."

"But Bardle told me that many were on the side of good," I say. "Like the Scrapken."

"Some, yes," Skaelka says. "But many are not. Which made acquiring information difficult." She gestures to her wounds, and June winces. I can tell she feels bad that Skaelka had to sacrifice to get this info. But then again, we're fighting evil, everyone's doing some sacrificing.

"The Outpost you seek is controlled by Rykk," Skaelka says. "He is a former Rifter—now involved in many bad businesses in many bad places."

"Rykk," Globlet growls. "So he's the one I talk to about my snow globe. . . ."

"If this guy runs the Outpost, he'll know where to find Thrull and his Tower," June says. She leans forward. Using her investigative-reporter-on-a-deadline voice, she asks, "So where is this . . . *Rykk*?"

Skaelka digs into her rucksack, then tosses a large gold coin onto the table. . . .

"Whoa," I say. "There's dried monster blood on this thing. But I wonder if . . ."

I begin scratching at the crusted gunk. Soon, I see words beneath the blood. I squint to read them—and I just about burst out laughing.

"This is a token! From Chaz and Slammers! The arcade metropolis!"

June takes the coin from me. "Lemme see."

"Chaz and Slammers is where Ryḳk resides," Skaelka says, knocking back another cup of ranch. "It is the Outpost where the Boss Rifter was going, before you defeated him. . . ."

"But there are, like, a *million* Chaz and Slammers locations," I say. "How are we supposed to know which one is Ryḳk's Outpost place?"

"Springtown!" June says happily. I glance over. She's using her binoculars as a magnifying glass. "It says it here on the token: Springtown!"

"What? That's halfway across the country," I say. "Maybe more!"

June looks at me sidelong, grinning. "Then I guess we're going halfway across the country."

"Ryḳk will not help you for free," Skaelka says. "But I may be able to assist you. Ryḳk is a collector. He appreciates hard-to-acquire objects and items. Items like this . . ."

She pulls out a knife, lifts her tail up onto the table, then begins cutting. I realize she's sawing off one of the small spikes that dot her tail. She flinches—just barely—as purple monster blood drips onto the table.

Skaelka starts to hand the severed spike to June. June's hesitant to take it.

"June," I whisper. "You can't refuse a gifted appendage. It's just rude."

Reluctantly, June takes it. I stifle a laugh as I watch June almost put it into her pocket, then decide that might be weird, so she instead wraps it in a napkin and just awkwardly holds it.

Skaelka leans forward. "I must warn you: this Outpost . . . it is a dangerous place. You will never find a more wretched hive of—"

"Fun?" I ask. "'Cause the commercials make Chaz and Slammers look *super* fun."

"No," Skaelka says. "It will contain—"

"As many skill-based games as you can play in a lifetime? 'Cause the commercials claim that Chaz and Slammers has—"

"No!" Skaelka snaps—and I decide, OK, I'll shut up for now. "There will be cruel, conniving creatures, beasts who would eagerly pluck out your organs and boil them as soup."

"Doesn't matter," June says before I can answer. "'Cause we're going. The Outpost may be dangerous, but no way it's worse than what Thrull and his Tower have in store for our dimension. If we don't act now, before they do, I worry those vine-skeleton warriors are gonna be the least of our problems. . . ."

chapter four

Suddenly, the front doors fly open and Quint
bursts into Joe's Pizza. "Jack! June! Come, quick!
It's finally finished!"

"Your *Downton Abbey* ancestral family tree?"
I ask.

"Your toothpick replica of the Death Star?"
June asks.

"Even better!" Quint says. "Come on! I just
need to stir the formula. . . ."

"OK—that sounds *foreboding*. . . ." June says.

"But also . . . rad?" I say.

Moments later, we're following Quint through
Joe's Pizza. I wave hi to a few buddies as we
walk through the kitchen and into the huge
cold storage room. Inside, I see three massive
tanks. Quint hurries up a stepladder and starts
stirring.

"It smells like hot dogs and sweat," June says.

"And I *love* it!" I say. "How long did it take you guys to build this??"

"Wasn't that big a project," Dirk says with a shrug. "I used to help my dad at his work sites, and they were bigger than this. The biggest!"

We all stare at Dirk for an awkward moment. "What?" Dirk says, "My dad was a master builder. Before I was born, he worked on, like, the space station, the old Yankee Stadium, lots of celebrities' houses."

We continue to stare at Dirk, and the awkward moment grows longer. Thankfully, Quint jumps in. "Now, the formula is nontoxic to humans—but extremely toxic to Thrull's vines."

"After the battle with Thrull and the Tendrill, I *knew* we'd need more goo-slime," Quint says. "A *lot*."

Dirk nods. "And this morning's skeleton battle proved the nerd was right. Luckily, while you've been off playing zombie hopscotch, we built this," he says, showcasing the factory like Vanna White. "Three full tanks of goo for the next time those skull-heads show up."

"Good timing," June says. "Because I also have big news! SKAELKA'S BACK! And she found out—"

"WHERE THE OUTPOST IS!" I exclaim triumphantly.

"OK, duder, thanks for stealing my thunder," June says. "But yeah—Skaelka found it. And that means, it's time for us to leave."

Quint thinks for a short moment, then nods. "OK, then. We knew this day would come."

Dirk taps the tank a few times. "Well, all right."

"Yes!" June says, totally amped up. "We're gonna find the Outpost! Then discover where Thrull is building his Tower! And then we'll go destroy it! And then we'll save this dimension and any other survivors who might be out there!"

I swallow.

I knew that *someday* we'd have to head out and hunt down Thrull's Tower. But until now, that always felt like some faraway distant errand. But now it's actually happening—and the reality of *leaving Wakefield* is sinking in. And I feel . . . well . . . I'm not sure . . . I'm trying to get my head around it, when June jumps in, all excited.

"Now that we *finally* know *where* we need to go," June says, "we can chart a course. And all good road trips have a pre-planned itinerary."

"We'll need a map," Quint says. "Preferably, a very old one with a thousand creases that you can never get folded back up correctly."

"I have a map," Dirk says, "and not just any map. It's the ULTIMATE road trip map."

"Um, *amazing*," June says. "Where is it?"

"At my house," Dirk says. "My, uh, old house."

Everyone's quiet for a moment.

None of us have ever been to Dirk's house. He never brought it up and we never asked. Part of me thought maybe he never actually had a house; just couldn't picture it. I half imagined that before all this he just lived off the land and stolen lunch money. . . .

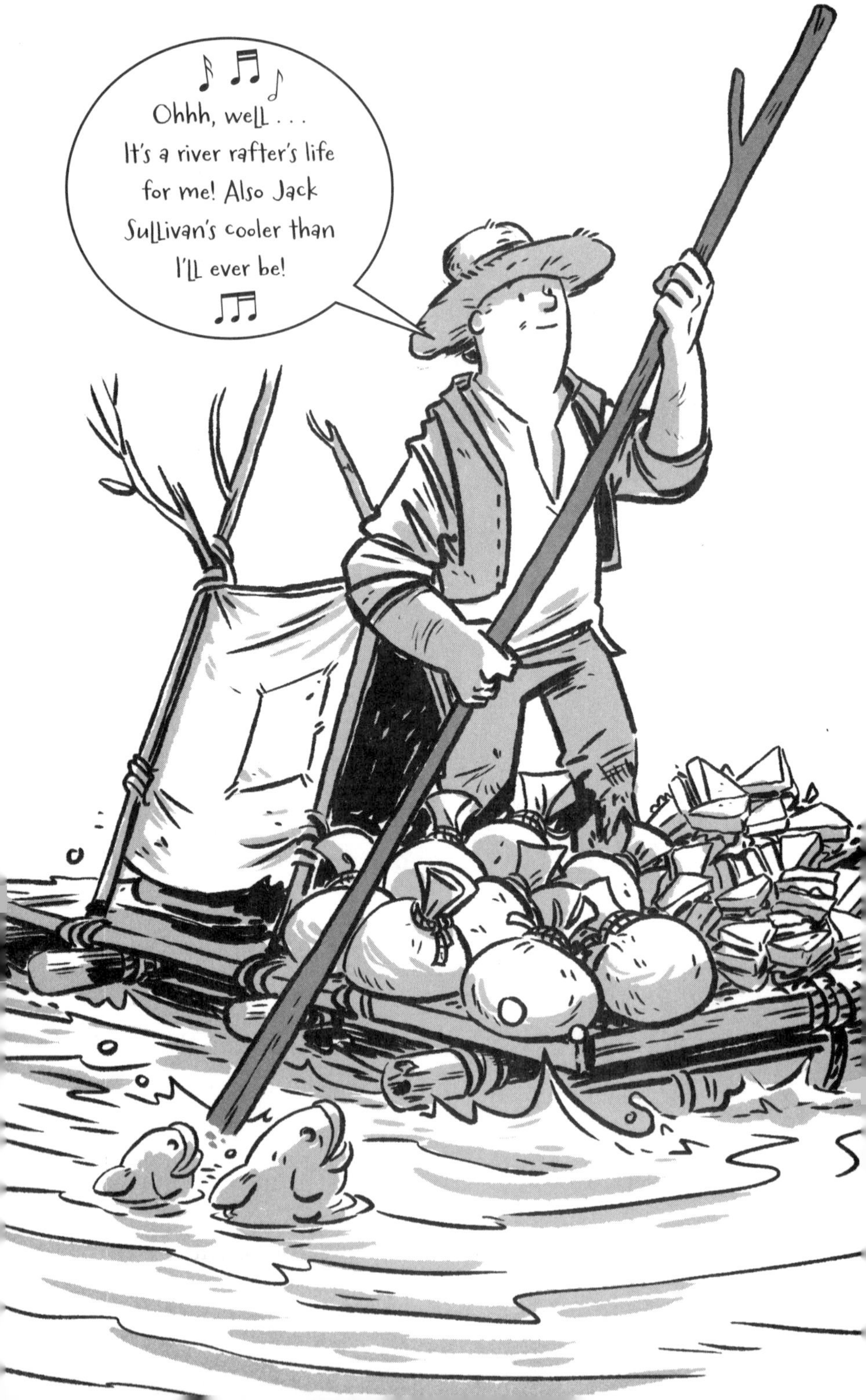
Ohhh, well . . .
It's a river rafter's life for me! Also Jack Sullivan's cooler than I'll ever be!

But I've gone to dozens of different schools. And if that taught me anything, it's that school bullies—and that's what Dirk was, 100 percent, before the Monster Apocalypse—can come from all sorts of backgrounds. You can't pin 'em.

"OK, then," June says. "Time for a mini practice road trip to Dirk's house before the real road trip, the big one, WHERE WE SAVE THE WORLD!"

Dirk's house ends up being just a regular house on a regular street in a regular neighborhood. We had passed it a million times before, but never knew it was where Dirk grew up.

"Oh wow," June says as we follow Dirk inside. She takes a deep breath. "INCREDIBLE. I forgot what it was like to be inside a house that doesn't smell like Reese's and melted Swedish Fish."

"Yeah, it was just me and my old man," he mumbles as we look around. "Kept it simple."

Quint, June, and I pace a few feet behind Dirk, watching him. It's gotta be weird for him, being back here after all this time. So much has changed; this feels like walking into a time capsule. There's even a stack of unopened mail on the mantel.

I think we all probably have a billion questions. But mainly, I just wanna know: Was Dirk ever, like, a *kid*?

"So, uh . . . let's see this map," June finally says.

"In here." Dirk sounds relieved to be on task.

He leads us into a small den behind the small kitchen. I see a couch, a well-worn recliner, a TV—and one *huge* map!

Across the top of the map, I read the words: "DIRK AND DAD'S ULTIMATE ROAD TRIP!"

The map is covered in pins. "Are the pins all places you've been?" I ask.

"The pins? Nah, they're places me and my dad were *gonna* stop," Dirk says somewhat proudly. "On our Ultimate Road Trip. Each pin is a different roadside attraction."

"That's super fun," June says, smiling.

"Yup. We were gonna go *everywhere*," Dirk says.

Quint asks, "What happened?"

Dirk looks away quickly and shrugs. "Uh. I mean, the, uh, Monster Apocalypse—it kinda messed up our plans. And my dad was busy working. He worked a lot."

"Of course," June says somberly.

I'm not digging the mood here—it does *not* feel like the start to an adventure-filled road trip.

"Hey, Dirk. This map is perfect," I say. "For real." I point at the little dot that says Springtown. "It's just what we need to navigate our way to the Outpost."

"And look!" June says, helping Dirk unpin it from the wall. "We'll pass, like, *dozens* of the places you were gonna go! Dirk, we're going to check off tons of stops on your road trip!"

For a split second, I'm worried Dirk is ticked off. Like we're trying to hijack his father-son road trip—replace his dad or something. . . .

For a long moment, Dirk stands there, staring at the map.

Then he turns around—and a huge smile is spreading across his face. "We're goin' road-trippin', guys. We're goin' road-trippin'."

chapter five

In the movies, everyone's like, "Road trip!" and the next scene is a big shot of a convertible cruising down the highway and there's a fun road trip song blasting.

But in real life, you gotta do stuff first: like pack. Packing is *awful*, so I decide I'll only bring a *few* of my favorite things. But then I realize, all my things are my favorite things. I wouldn't have them if they weren't my favorite.

I need the microwave, this toilet, that fancy fur hat . . .

and this pile of stale Snickers bars, the couch, the window from the western wall . . .

and this pocket lint I've been collecting, the stereo system, my books . . . eh, forget the books . . .

but I also need my key chain collection and . . .

C'mon, jerk.

Of course, I also have to bring my Zombie Squad—and I don't think they'll fit in the back seat.

But just as I'm realizing I have a problem— I learn that Quint has already solved that problem.

The tree house starts shaking and I hear the song from *The Goonies* blasting from some very serious speakers. I rush out onto the deck. My eyes can barely believe the vehicle I see rumbling to a stop down below.

Classic Mama (upgraded!).

BIG MAMA ROAD TRIP EDITION

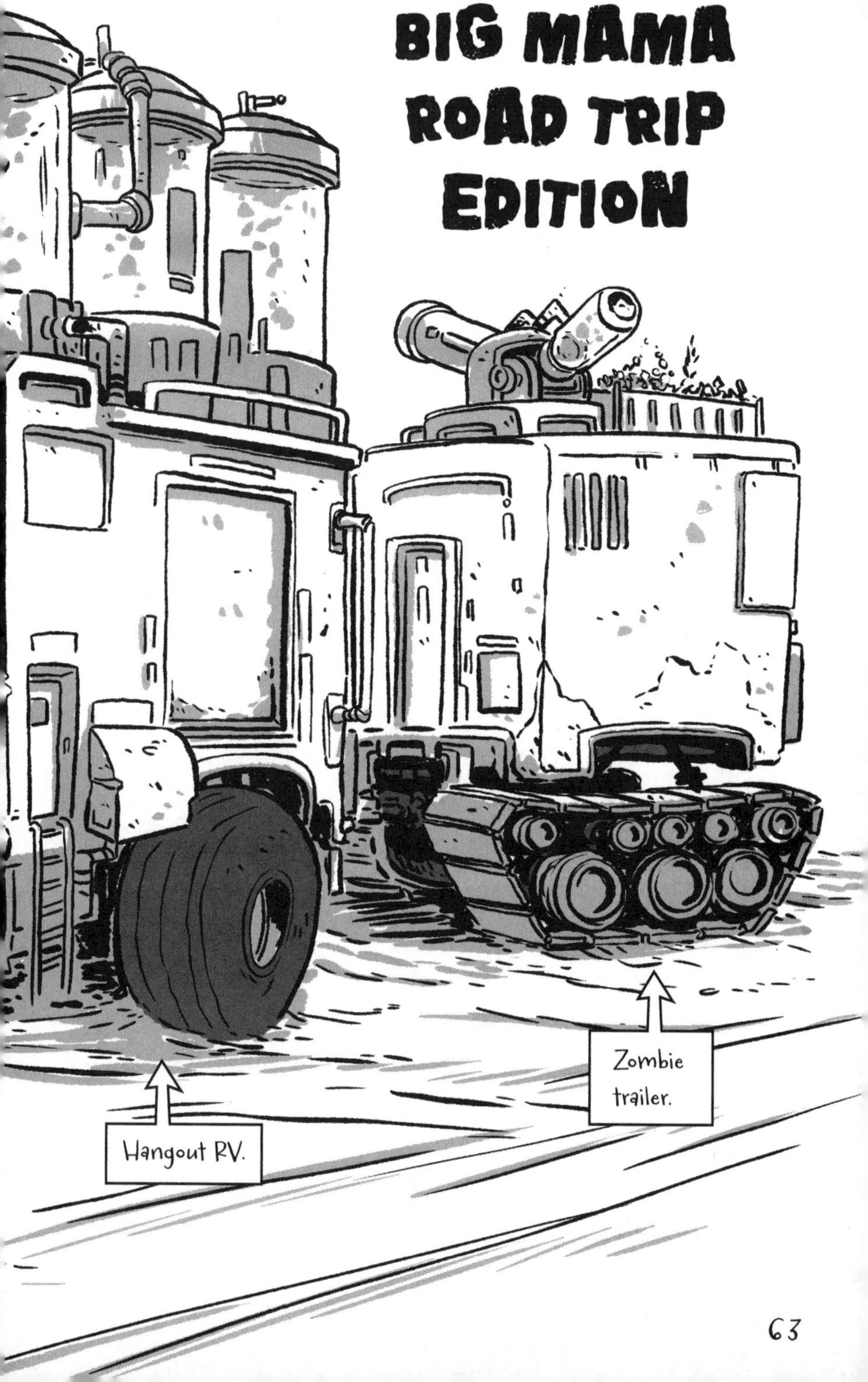
Zombie trailer.
Hangout RV.

In a flash, I'm downstairs, running my hand along the massive new version of Big Mama.

"Check this out!" Quint says. "The motorhome is connected to the back of Big Mama, so we can go to and fro without stopping."

"I'm all about going to and fro!"

"And back here," Quint says, pointing to a big horse-trailer type thing, "is where your zombies can stay."

Monsters are piling out of Joe's to see our new tricked-out ride. Seeing our monster friends together like this makes me realize, again, that

this is *actually happening*. We're saying good-bye—for I dunno how long—to the tree house *and* Wakefield *and* our monster friends. And that means there's no way we can leave town without having one final . . .

MEGA MONSTER GOOD-BYE CELEBRATION PIZZA BASH AT JOE'S!

Toward the end of the party, I find myself getting choked up as I watch June and Biggun dancing to an old '80s song about good-byes.

I walk outside. The tree house looms above me, more impressive than ever. The idea that this might be the last time I see my tree house, my home, under the moonlight, is too much.

"Jack, am I interrupting your tears of joy?"

Wiping at my eyes, I see Skaelka. "These aren't tears of joy, Skaelka. These are—nevermind, you wouldn't understand."

"I have a favor to ask, Jack. A great favor."

I sigh. "Yes, Skaelka. I already told you—if I don't return from this big quest, you can have my collection of wallets taken from zombies."

"Oh, not that. I already took those. This favor is much bigger. . . ."

I've never seen Skaelka so serious. Oh man—does she need a kidney? Am I her go-to kidney person? Because I feel like she and June are probably more buddy-buddy than me. And June's got a way better diet. And—

"Jack, do I have your attention? So that I may ask the favor?"

"Geez, Skaelka. Yeah. Go ahead. You're scaring me."

"What I saw out there, in the wilds—Thrull's power is growing. . . . There are things that I must do—and I must do them quickly. So I ask you . . ."

Skaelka taps her ax, thinking, then steps toward me. "I need a companion, Jack. One who is fast, brave, loyal. A monster who is *good*."

That's Rover, all right, I think.

A lump is growing in my throat. I suddenly feel like I'm in a post-apocalyptic reboot of *Lassie*.

"Hey, Rover?" I say softly. I kneel down, placing my hand beneath his jaw, gently raising his head until we're looking each other in the eye. "Do you know what Skaelka is asking?"

Rover's ears hang flat. After a moment, his eyes look to the ground. He understands—and he understands that he must go.

So finally, I stand. "Rover's my friend, Skaelka. I don't own him—so it's not really up to me. But it looks like he's ready to join you."

"Jack, I will guard Rover with my own life. I promise."

"Well, yeah, duh," I say. "You better."

Skaelka nods, business done, then returns to the party. I collapse to the ground and give Rover so, so many good-boy scratches.

"Hey, buddy," I say. "One last ride? The two of us?"

Rover smiles happily.

"Good. 'Cause there's one last thing I have to do. . . ."

chapter six

Rover runs. He runs like he did the first time I climbed into his saddle—wild but focused, untamed but agile.

And I ride like it's that first time, squeezing the saddle grip so hard I'm afraid it might snap.

He's hurtling through Wakefield, navigating the pitch-black roads and alleys and cut-throughs with some sixth sense.

After one particularly massive leap and perfect landing, I catch him glancing back at me, giving me a look like, *Did you see what I did? Did you think it was cool? Am I the best boy?*

Yes, he *is* the best boy. And leaving Rover is gonna hurt like nothing ever hurt before.

The only way to make sure it hurts less—is to make sure I'm back to see him again. And that he comes back the same way.

"You be safe out there, OK, Rover?" I say as we reach our destination. He purrs, and I pat his side and promise him I'll do the same.

So, Warg entombed Bardle in this strange rock structure. She said it's not *their* custom, the monsters', it's just hers. A way of remembering.

And I'm glad she did.

This way I feel like I can still talk to him sometimes.

Over the past few months, whenever I had a lousy day, I would come here and sit by the stone and just talk out loud. It helped. And, yeah, talking to a rock is super weird. But, I mean, there *are* weirder ways to grieve. . . .

71

I pick at the grass. Pulling out clumps, letting them slip through my fingers, watching the wind carry the green blades.

"Bardle," I finally say. "I have to do a thing. The craziest Mission: Operation yet. But I don't want to. Which is weird, because epic missions are my thing. I should be ALL ABOUT THIS."

Saying the words aloud makes me realize that my fear has zero to do with the dangers of the journey. Sure, the whole thing sounds impossible and there's a high likelihood it will lead to death, but that's not why I'm scared.

I'm scared because the ONLY WAY to go and do all of THAT is to leave behind all of THIS.

It's got me nervous. Anxious.

My wrist is itchy.

The Cosmic Hand.

"Bardle," I say. "This thing you left me with, the Cosmic Hand? It's itchy. And, buddy, that is a supremely messed-up thing to do—give someone a big important gift, right as you die— and not tell them that it's gonna be *really itchy.*"

I shake my head and laugh a little. "I mean, that's like if your great-grandaunt gave you one of those itchy wool sweaters for your birthday, made you promise to wear it every day—and then just croaked. . . ."

I've moved tons of times. Never cared. I *liked* moving. But now? Wakefield, the tree house—it's the first time I've ever had a *real home*.

That's why this is so hard. Because I want to go on an epic adventure. But I *also* want to stay here and have nothing change ever. I can't have both, though.

To do the epic quest, I have to leave. And leaving feels like tearing down everything we've built here. Ending it.

I'm just not ready.

Looking at the Bardle rock has me recalling the time he tried to do a BMX bike jump even though he'd probably never seen a bike before.

And then I'm howling with laughter, delirious, as I remember him sprawled out on the ground in a goofy heap, grumbling, "No more bike jumps."

"Are you laughing at my rock?"

I turn around. It's Warg.

"No. Not at all. I mean—I'm laughing near it."

"What is so funny?" Warg asks.

"I just remembered something. . . ."

"That you enjoy laughing at deceased Bardles?"

"Nope! I enjoy having fun," I say. " 'Cause I'm Jack Sullivan. And I massively ENJOY FUN!"

That's why I've thrived during this apocalypse. I get it now. I just needed to laugh with my old friend to shake that understanding loose.

To succeed, I must be . . .

JACK SULLIVAN! SUPER-FUN-TIME-DOING-TONS-OF-EXCITING-STUFF-AND-BEING-GOOFY-AND-HAVING-A-BLAST APOCALYPSE ROAD TRIP GUY!

"Warg," I say. "I want this quest. I need this epic Mission: Operation. Quint, June, Dirk, and I . . . we're going to find the Outpost. Find out where Thrull is building his Tower. And then we're gonna save the day like saving the day is a thing we were born to do. 'Cause it is."

Warg opens her mouth to reply, but I'm on a roll now. "And," I continue, "we're gonna have a blast along the way. Because if we're not at least *trying* to having fun every single day, then what's the point of *any of this*?"

"Yes, bu—" Warg says.

"Well, anyway." I pat her on the arm. "Thanks for the pep talk, Bardle! You too, Warg. I'll catch you on the flip-flop!"

chapter seven

The next morning, I'm launched out of my bed like it's spring-loaded.

Because it is.

See, Dirk got annoyed with me sleeping in and then complaining that his epic pancake buffet breakfasts were cold—so he and Quint supercharged my mattress springs. But this morning, when the spring-loaded launcher sends me out the window, I'm not even mad. . . .

SPROING-OING-OING!

Back inside, I do a sweep of everyone's bedrooms, banging on doors. "Rise and shine, sleepyheads! Up and at 'em! We were supposed to be on the road nineteen minutes ago!"

"READY AND RARIN'!" June says, practically exploding out of her bedroom. She looks like a camp counselor, whistle around her neck, action fanny pack clipped to her waist, lists in hand.

Quint appears, standing at attention like he's ready for roll call.

"OK, Dirk, get the rest of your stuff," June says, consulting her notebook list. "We gotta get this show on the road!"

"Garden's in the back," Dirk says. "Everything else I need is right here." He motions to a small plastic grocery bag, stuffed with a few crumpled shirts and pairs of underwear.

"That can't be all you're bringing!" Quint says. "What about clothes? Sunscreen? Change of shoes? Rain jacket? Winter jacket? Spring jacket? Autumn jacket?"

While they're discussing how many jackets are appropriate for a post-apocalyptic road trip, I sneak away to say good-bye to Rover. I did most of my good-byes last night—but I saved Rover for today.

I try to do it quickly, like ripping off a Band-Aid. But no matter how quickly you yank it off, it still stings. Also, sometimes there's sticky black gunk left stuck to your skin.

It's the worst. . . .

And then we're throwing our stuff into Big Mama, climbing in, laughing, joking, and setting off. . . .

Fifteen minutes later, Big Mama is rumbling through town. My friends goof around, all full of "this is the start of something epic" energy. But I sit quietly, watching the town roll by.

We pass my old house. There's a big hole in the ground where the tree house used to be, before the Wormungulous relocated it to the Joe's Pizza parking lot.

Suddenly, the hairs on the back of my neck stand up—like I'm being shocked with static electricity. There's something behind the house, through the trees. I don't know what, but I swear it moves.

I rub my eyes, which are—whatevs, I'll admit it—raw from saying good-bye to Rover.

When I look back up, whatever it was—it's gone. But I can't shake the feeling that someone or *something* was there . . . watching us. . . .

We're turning onto the highway when my eyes refocus, and I see a crowd clustered on the sides of the road.

Quint turns and grins.

Dirk slaps me on the back. "This part was a surprise. Figured you'd dig it."

It's all of our monster friends standing and waving. Bidding us farewell. . . .

We wave and we shout and Dirk blows kisses. But soon, the monsters are in our rearview mirror, and it's open road as far as the eye can see.

The Fun Land entrance slides by out my window as we pass the amusement park. It's not the same place it was a year ago: invading vines have ravaged the park, and the rides are crumbling beneath them.

Up until now, my entire world pretty much revolved around Wakefield. Is this the last time I will see the *only* town I have ever truly considered a home?

June must know what I'm thinking because she leans over and watches Fun Land—and Wakefield—fade behind us on the highway. "Don't worry," she says. "We're gonna be back someday. I promise."

"How can you promise something you don't know?"

June shrugs. "I'm just cool like that."

Big Mama rounds a curve, and I am officially the farthest from the tree house I've been since the Monster Apocalypse began.

My eyes pop: suddenly, it's like the whole

world beyond Wakefield is laid out in front of us. It's a new landscape—strange and altered.

I see a monster on the horizon, bigger than big: a cosmically colossal creature. It lumbers like a brontosaurus.

I see buildings with vines exploding through the centers. I glance at my friends, and I see the same look on each of their faces—it's like, *Yeah, this new world is scary, strange, and different.*

But, man, it's also kind of beautiful. . . .

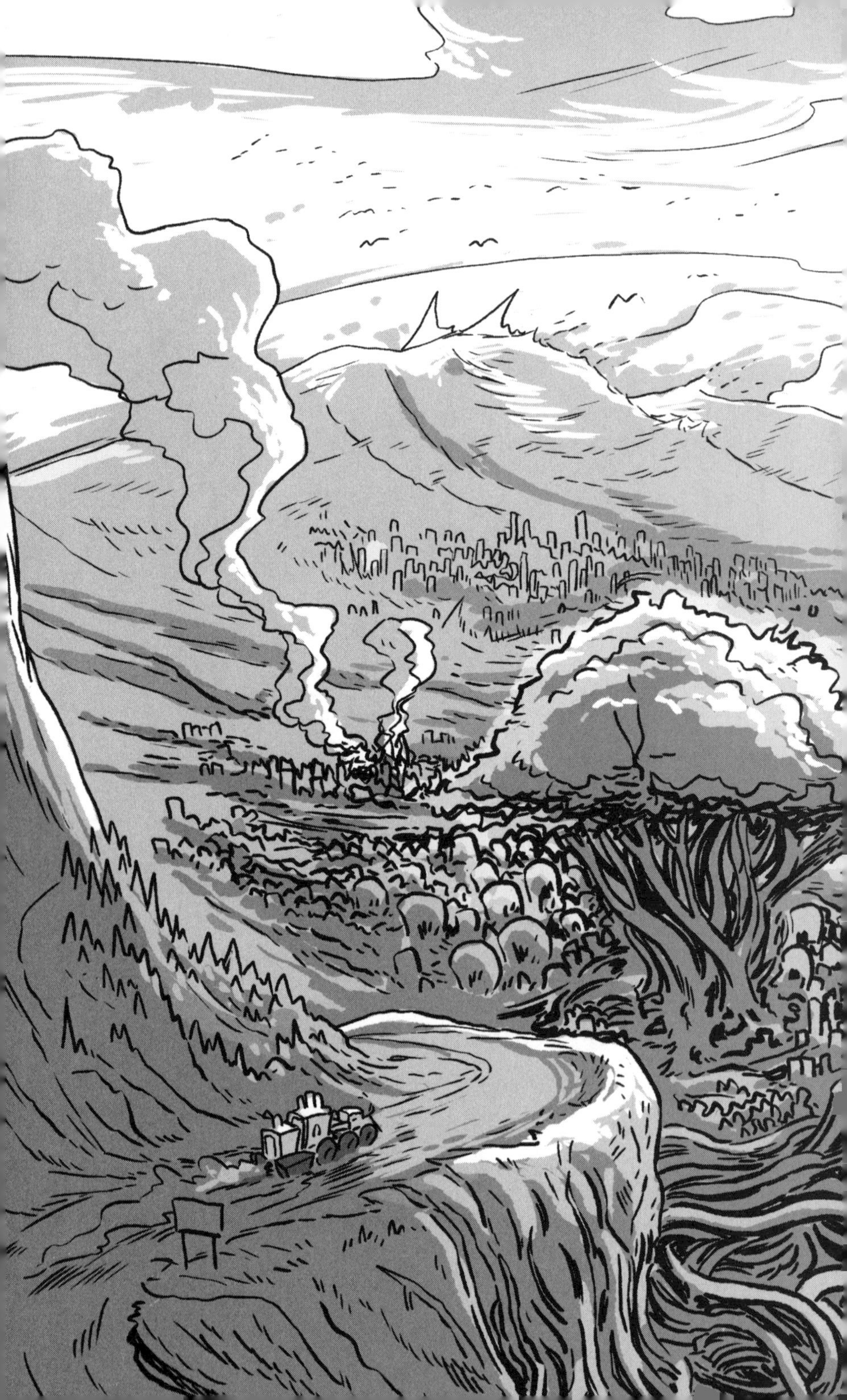

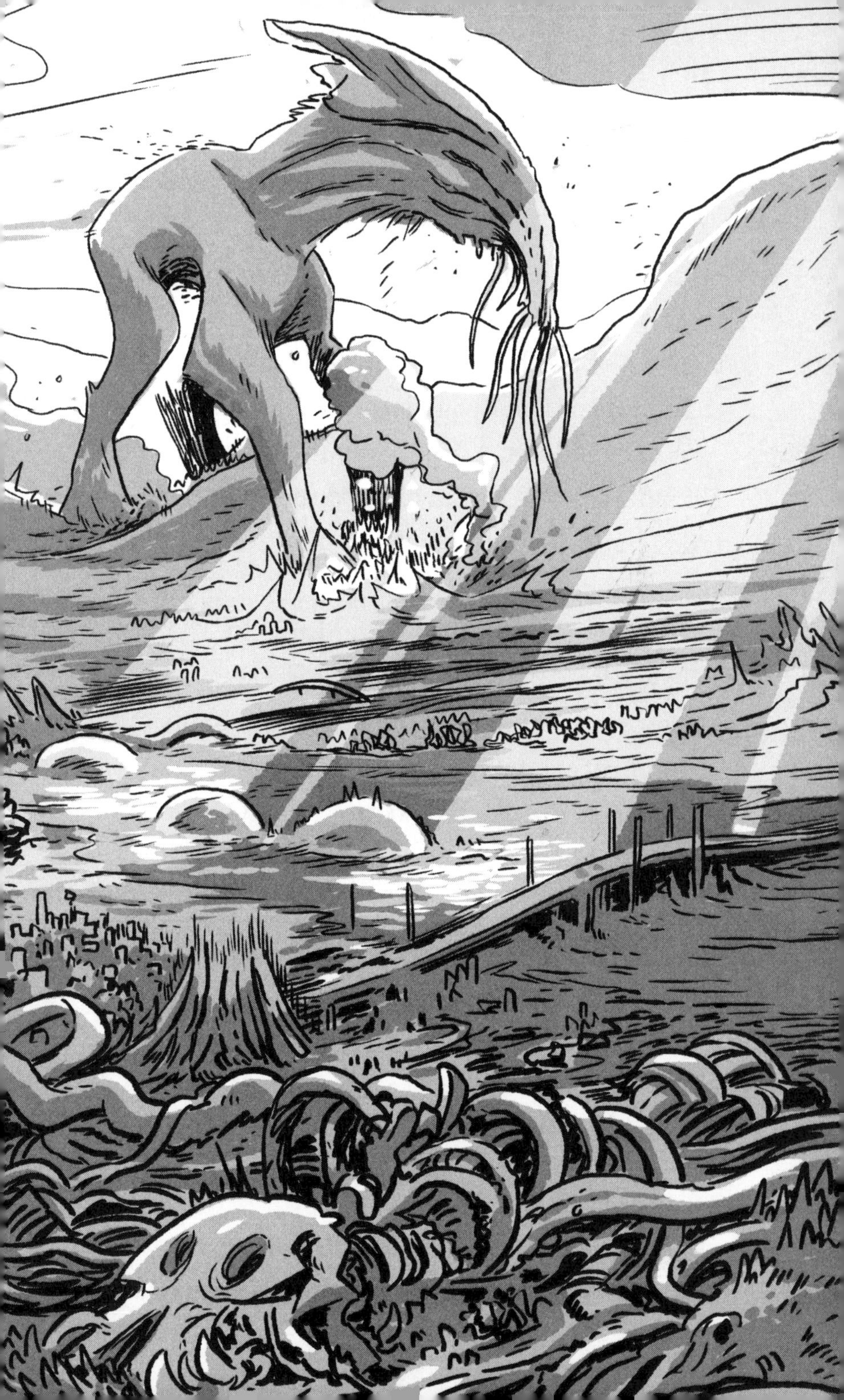

"I told you guys things were getting weird out here," June says as we gape at the landscape.

June has told us all about what she and Neon— the wingless baby Wretch she saved—saw on their adventure. Stuff like Wringed Wretch nests the size of football stadiums and entire cities turned into monster-filled swamps.

We crest down a windy mountain road, then Dirk points Big Mama toward the western wilderness. "Everything's so different," he remarks.

"It's Thrull," Quint says ominously.

I swallow. If Thrull's done this—then who knows what other threats this world holds. . . .

But I refuse to be a downer. Because yes— danger lies ahead, but so do EPIC ROAD TRIP SHENANIGANS!

chapter eight

"Nope. No corn dogs," Dirk says. "This isn't the tree house anymore. We've got my little veggie garden—but that'll only last so long. Out here, we're gonna have to learn how to survive."

"We're like the Lewis and Clark of the apocalypse!" Quint says.

"Totally!" I say. "We one hundred percent *are* Lois and Clark. From *The New Adventures of Superman*! I used to watch that on Nick at Nite."

"Not *Lois* and Clark," Quint says. "*Lewis* and Clark!"

"Right, sure. Them too," I say. "We're all four of them: Lewis, Lois, Clark, and Clark. OK—June, you be Lewis. Dirk, you be Lois! And then—hmm—Quint, who do you want to be?"

"Are you asking if I want to be Clark or if I would rather be Clark?"

"Yeah, if I wanna do, like, a nickname thing—which Clark should I call you?"

Dirk groans.

"It's too early for groaning," June says, looking at the map. "We still have a hundred and twenty-seven miles until Apocalyptic Road Trip Attraction Number One. The Wor—"

"World's Largest Collection of the World's Smallest Stuff!" Dirk cuts her off eagerly. "Featuring Some Bonus Actual Large Stuff! You don't have to tell me what it is—I *know*."

"One hundred and twenty-seven miles . . ." Quint says. "I estimate that will take us less than three hours!"

Seventeen hours later, we're pulling into the parking lot.

Dirk is like a dog that hears the word "walk"—he's practically scratching at the door. "I am *so* ready to see a ridiculously large collection of tiny stuff plus some actual large stuff!"

"Wait, and the large stuff—is that stuff that's normally large?" I ask.

"Nope!" Dirk says. "That's stuff that's normally tiny. Get it?!? It's kitschy!"

"It's what? Who are you right now, Dirk?" I ask. Quint and June are hurrying inside. "GUYS! WHAT VERSION OF DIRK IS THIS?!"

"This is Road Trip Dirk," he says. "Get used to it, pal."

———

A few minutes later we're standing in a round room that's jammed full of really tiny stuff. It's dusty and smells like mothballs and the walls are a pale cream color.

Dirk is quiet.

After a moment he takes a seat on a bench the size of a tissue box. I glance nervously at June and Quint. They shrug. We're all worried that Dirk is epically bummed by our first stop on his dad's road trip itinerary.

He looks down at the ground and sighs deeply. "It's just . . . it's just . . . just . . . that . . ."

Then he leaps to his feet, smiling so wide it looks like his cheeks might pop. "It's just that . . . it's so . . . little! I FREAKIN' LOVE IT!"

Dirk and June and Quint head off to explore the rest of the museum. But not me—I'm more of an "end of the museum" kinda guy. 'Cause at the end of every museum is perhaps the greatest concept ever birthed by the human brain: THE GIFT SHOP.

Ahh yes, the gift shop.

One time, my class went on a field trip to the planetarium, and I picked up a nifty little stress ball shaped like Saturn. I had no idea I wanted that—but then I saw it—and *I HAD TO HAVE IT, I NEEDED IT, I THIRSTED FOR IT LIKE A VAMPIRE THIRSTS FOR FRESH BLOOD.*

And I got it.

I forget what happened to it, probably left it on the bus.

But my point is: gift shops make lousy museums worth it. You suffer through a bunch of dull exhibits about photosynthesis or whatever, knowing that, at the very end, the gift shop awaits . . . a smorgasbord of *fantastic junk*! Stuff no one needs! And everyone knows the *best* stuff is stuff *you don't need*.

Most times, I got to the gift shop—but had zero dollars to actually purchase the indispensable knickknacks I craved.

But not today! Today, I'm *getting everything*. I'm gonna walk out of here looking like the official *mascot* for gift shops. . . .

I eye the shelves and spinning spindles. The cases and counters.

And I go absolutely *bonkers*!

My only mistake? Waiting until after my
shopping spree to hit the bathroom . . .

Luckily, I don't need to figure out the toilet
situation because a moment later . . .

I hear a tremendous ROARING followed
by my friends doing a tremendous amount of
SCREAMING.

I yank open the door—and I nearly get
exploded by a speeding Dirk. Quint and June are
right behind him, darting through the gift shop,
racing for the exit.

"Jack! Time to go!" Quint yells.

"I *can't* go! The toilet's too tiny! How is anyone supposed to—"

"NOT LIKE THAT!" June shouts. "*Go*—as in *leave.*"

The entire place begins to quake—and I decide not to ask questions. I put my head down and run, following my friends outside.

"We found the world's largest scorpion-looking monster!" Dirk shouts, filling me in.

"With the shortest temper!" June adds.

Behind us I hear the world's largest crashing and thundering. I race to Big Mama as the building explodes. . . .

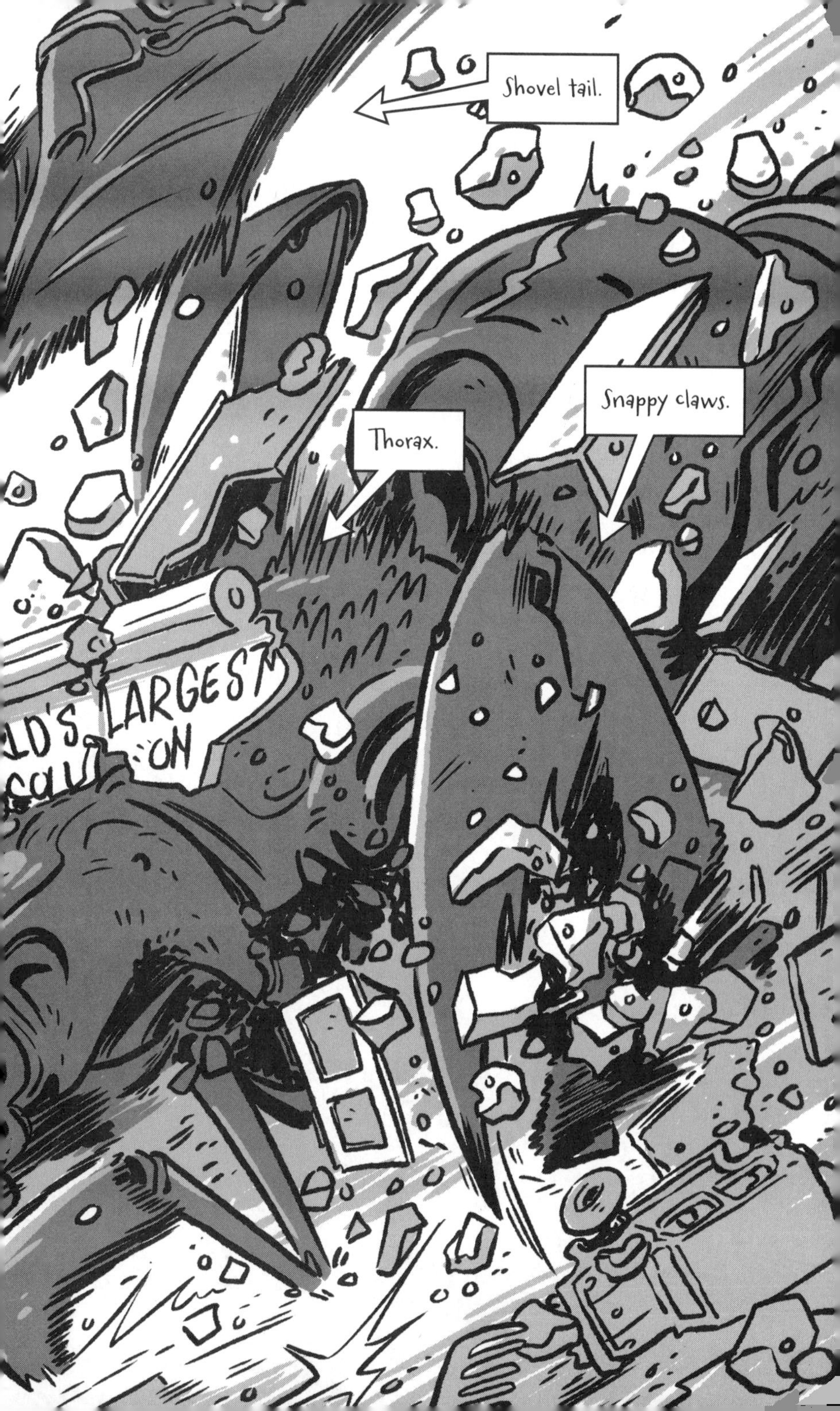
Shovel tail.
Thorax.
Snappy claws.
LD'S LARGEST
ON

"OK! I've seen enough!" Dirk says as he hustles into Big Mama after Quint. June and I run in behind them as Quint starts the engine.

"Aaaaaaand just need to buckle my safety belt, check the mirrors . . ." Quint says, making adjustments. "Safety is always—"

"QUINT! GO!" the three of us shout.

Quint's buckle clicks—then his foot stomps the pedal. The turbocharged engine growls, Big Mama's tires squeal on the broken asphalt, and then we're speeding out of the parking lot.

"It's chucking junk at us!" June calls with her head out the window. "REALLY TINY JUNK!"

I poke my head out the window and see—

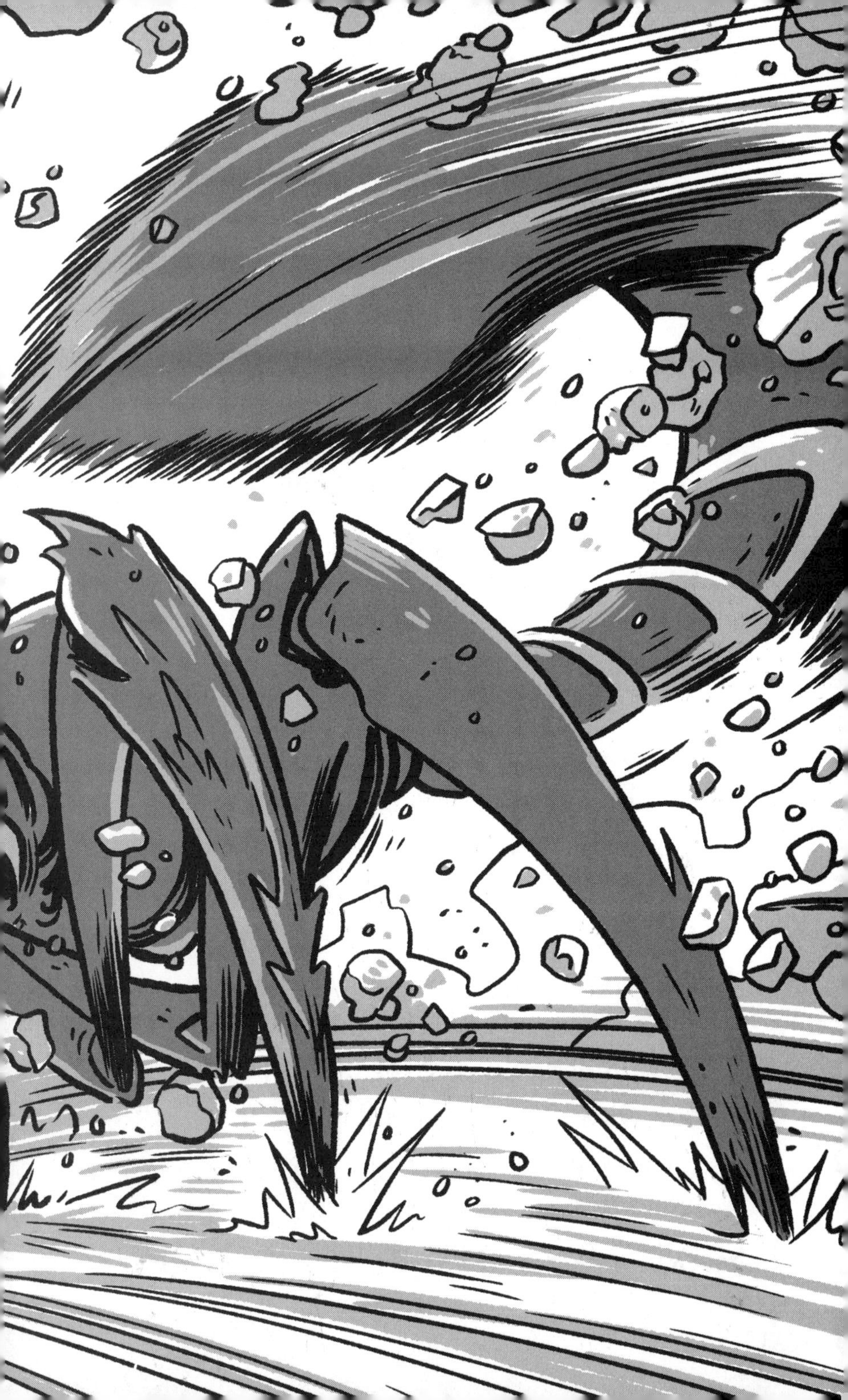

The monster is using its shovel tail to hurl stuff at us. *Really tiny stuff.* It pounds the side of Big Mama like hail. The world's smallest Easy-Bake Oven smashes against the bumper.

Then comes the big stuff. . . . A hot dog the size of a sleeper sofa slams into the side of Big Mama. A life-size Barbie bounces off the windshield. A life-size Ken slams into the zombie trailer and its super-handsome blond-haired head pops off.

"My zombies!" I cry. "I gotta check on 'em!"

I hurry to the trailer. Thankfully, they're OK.

But Dirk's vegetable garden is not—because an instant later, the world's largest pencil sharpener smashes through the rear wall. Carrots and string beans tumble out.

I cautiously peek through the busted hole in Big Mama's side. The monster is in the parking lot, watching us go. I stare into the inky-black nothingness of the monster's eyes.

I can't help but think—that scorpion thing felt like *more* than just some random angry monster.

It felt like something specifically out to stop us.

Something loyal to Thrull.

It's just the first of many strange new monsters we'll encounter, now that we're out of Wakefield.

But that monster . . . That monster felt like a

warning. Or an omen—a sign of horrific things
to come.

Before I can think too hard about it, my
friends' sudden SCREAMING snaps my attention
to the front of the truck.

I hurry through Big Mama, heart pounding—
only to find . . .

Through my giggling tears, I figure now is the best time to break the "bad news."

"Guys," I say. "I'm afraid the veggie garden is gone. Guess we'll have to stop for gas station snacks."

Dirk quits laughing for about two seconds—then starts up again.

"It was worth it," he pants as we all break out in more laughter.

chapter nine

The road trip is in full swing. Open road!
Adventure! Headed for the horizon!

Quint pulls out a book called *Road Trip Games for Families.*

"Where'd you get that?" I ask.

"I checked it out of the library before we left."

Of course Quint checked it out. He'll probably even pay the late fees.

"It says here, the best way to make a long trip fast and enjoyable is to keep your friends and family entertained and laughing. Now, there are some *very* exciting things in here. Best of all— it's fun for all ages! What should we play first?"

"Hmm," June says. "How about we play . . . SOME MUSIC. Crank it up to eleven!"

Quint grumbles—and plays Yahtzee alone for the next hour. Each time he yells "YAHTZEE!" I nearly wet myself.

We play a few rounds of Truth or Dare. I dare Quint to lose a game of Yahtzee . . . to himself.

Dirk chooses Truth, and June asks what got

him started on the whole gardening thing.

"It was my dad. He always said if you know how to grow your own food, you're set for life," Dirk says. "Although, he mostly just ate microwave burritos. . . ."

"Speaking of food and survival and such," I say, "is anyone getting hungry? Because that sign there says 'Super-sized Rest Stop: Next Exit.'"

"OK, OK," Dirk says, and I try to hide a smile. With Dirk's vegetable garden gone, we're gonna do *so much* gas station fine dining. . . .

On the way out, I grab up a little clip-on air freshener. Big Mama is quickly becoming a toxic-waste site.

I grabbed Waffle Sundae Syrup Blast. But believe it or not, *nobody* likes the smell!

"I didn't know it was possible," June says. "But Big Mama is starting to stink worse than the tree house *ever* did."

The stench is *so bad* that we agree to spend one night outside of Big Mama. We stop at a motel that advertises an "Olympic-sized swimming pool."

It's definitely not "Olympic-sized"—but that's the least of the pool's problems. . . .

So, at the next gas station, I pick up an air freshener that I'm sure we'll all agree on: Deep-Dish Pizza. But once again, nobody likes my choice in manufactured scents. My new air freshener has been hanging from the rearview mirror for less than *two minutes* when Dirk flings it out the window.

"Hey!" I cry. "I was still smelling that!"

I peek my head out and watch the air freshener flap sadly in the wind. It finally flutters to the ground, then a strange, evil-looking rhino monster trots out onto the road, sniffs the air freshener, and promptly keels over.

"Everyone's a critic," I mutter.

"Guys, important question," June says. "Where are all the cows?? We've been driving for *days* and we've seen *zero* cows! I wanna yell 'moo' at a cow. Is that so much to ask? Like, is it even a road trip if you don't get to yell 'moo' at a cow?"

Two days later, June is in luck. We spot a cow grazing in an old Box Factory parking lot.

June excitedly lowers the window, does a little "ahem" cough in preparation, then unleashes an impressively powerful "*MOOOOOOOO!*"

But unscheduled (and often horrifying) stops are half the fun of a road trip, right? Even if you almost die? I mean, that's what all the best road trip movies have taught me.

And that's exactly what I'm thinking when we stop to take pictures in front of giant hollow stucco dinosaurs. I slap some touristy gear on my zombies, then send them up to pose in the mouth of a pastel T-Rex.

It's a great photo, even if it's not exactly what I had in mind. . . .

It takes us half a day to get Lefty back. Leading her into the zombie trailer, I say, "I'm *super* sorry. That's the *last* dinosaur encounter we'll have on this trip. I SWEAR."

After that, we rapid-fire blast through tons of Dirk's Apocalyptic Road Trip Attractions.

At Mother Goose's Storybook Forest, Dirk prances through the trees, waving a stick, shouting spells. Dirk screaming, "EXPECTO PATRONUM!" at a cardboard cutout of Humpty Dumpty is maybe the highlight of my life.

We stop at about forty-one different Old-Fashioned Old-Timey Trading Posts until I realize that they're all just excuses to sell fireworks. They jam the front with rocking chairs and Davy Crockett hats, but the real attraction is clear: fireworks. Quint buys one pack of glow worms and proceeds to nearly burn down Big Mama.

"Dudes," June says. "Road trips rule."

"Indeed!" Quint says. "More middle-school kids should take epic road trips across monster-filled apocalyptic landscapes of doom."

After each Road Trip Attraction, Dirk crosses it off his map. And each time, he's got this dopey grin on his face.

After all the crud he's been through, the dude deserves it. . . .

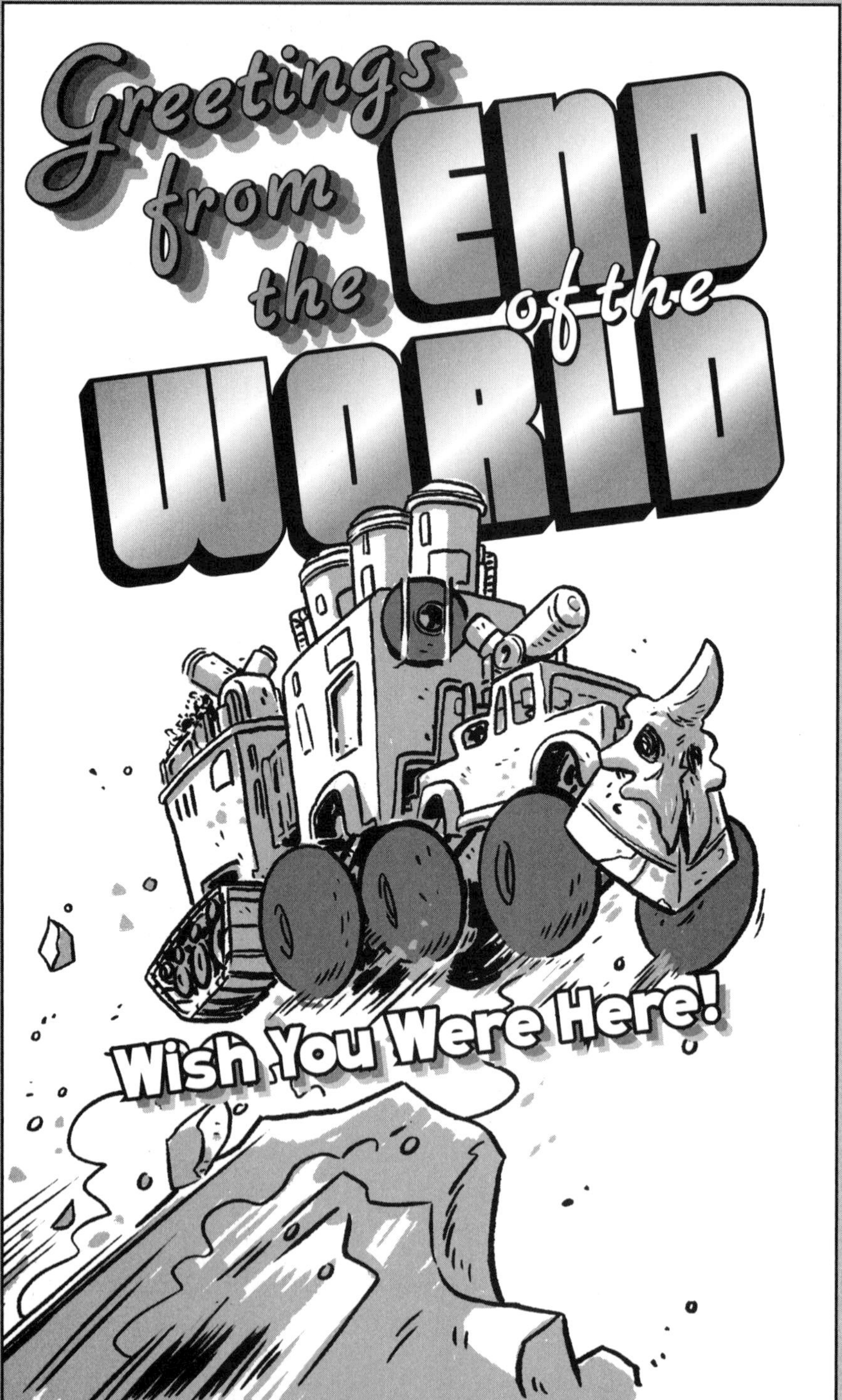
Greetings from the END of the WORLD
Wish You Were Here!

chapter ten

OK, we're starting to get a little moody.

The cause of the present moodiness isn't, like, June monopolizing the radio or Quint hogging all of Dirk's legroom.

It's a bathroom issue—the issue being, it's now nearly impossible to stop to go to the bathroom.

Thrull's influence is *everywhere*: vines slither, the air is foul, and sometimes we'll speed past a monster that emits that old distinct odor: *the stench of evil.*

All that makes every stop more dangerous than the last . . . and every bathroom break typhoon-level treacherous.

To help us brave on, I brought back my Feats of Apocalyptic Success—but updated! I call 'em—

⚡ Feats of Apocalyptic ⚡ (ROAD TRIP TOILET) Success

It makes going to the bathroom a game. And games make us brave, so pretty soon we're all completing Feats right and left.

FEAT: Daredevil

Go in total darkness.

FEAT: Never Bashful

Complete a bathroom break with a zombie in close proximity.

FEAT: Toilet Seat Sweeper

Lift ninety-nine rest stop toilet seats without finding anything awful.

I've only got, like, seven more toilet seats to lift when—

SKREEEE!!

But all the added danger means we're already on edge as we approach the next apocalyptic road trip attraction.

Dirk and his dad had a pamphlet for every attraction they planned to see. He reads them aloud, getting us all jazzed up on the way to each one.

"Supposedly, this place houses the corpse of a mythical monster that was found in a nearby mine," Dirk starts telling us, once we're a mile away. "It's got, like, huge oval eyes and fingers the size of bread sticks and is all encased in a glass tomb or something!"

The attraction sits on the side of an endless stretch of highway. There's no real town: just a single intersection, with a gas station, a diner, a general store, and our destination: the Entity on Interstate 8.

But as we approach, it's clear that something's not right. "I'm not sure we should stop . . ." Quint says, slowing Big Mama to a halt in the middle of the highway.

"Hate to say it," June says. "But I might agree."

"Bah, c'mon," Dirk says, stepping out of the truck. "We can handle it!"

But then we hear the noise: it's a spine-chilling slurping, gnawing, grinding.

"This all just feels . . . wrong," June says.

"It's like the vines are *eating* this tiny town," I say in horrified disbelief.

Dirk nods. He's coming around. "They're swallowing this whole place."

"Turning it inside out," Quint notes.

The town's only intersection is now a monstrous sinkhole—and that's the center of the monstrous vine infestation. Thousands of dripping tendrils snake out from its depths, writhing and wriggling. It reminds me of a biology class, where we learned about veins, and how they all carry blood to the heart.

That's what this is like. Vines like veins, devouring the town, carrying raw material into the sinkhole.

I hear a wet smacking sound: vines slowly swirling, searching for their next meal. Buildings are half-eaten, with long pieces of pipe jutting out haphazardly, like skewers. A car is grabbed. A porta potty is yanked. Soon, this place will simply cease to exist. This is the power of Thrull. . . .

"Think this roadside wonder is closed," June says. "Permanently."

Just then, a big, baggy souvenir T-shirt—no body, just shirt—waddles out of the attraction.

The shirt shuffles toward us.

Then the shirt topples over.

A monster, not much bigger than Globlet, emerges from the shirt, then stands. The monster has six eyes—and all six are blinking with a mix of confusion and fear.

The stunned monster stares at us like we're not real. Fair enough—we're staring at it like we don't *want* it to be real.

The monster's mouth opens. It makes a series of high-pitched SNAPPING sounds.

"I think it's scared," I say. "Or hurting. Those sounds seem, like, pained."

"It needs *help*," June says.

Then, suddenly, she rushes toward the monster. Toward the dying town. Toward the vines, which are swirling faster now.

"This place is being sucked under!" Quint yells. "All of it!"

Dirk's voice cracks, uneasy. "The vines are like quicksand."

Dirk's right. Everything is being pulled in quicker and quicker, like a black hole whirlpool.

"June!" I plead. "Get back here!"

"I'm not leaving it!" she cries.

Suddenly, vines burst through the ground beneath us. "Watch out!" I yell, leaping to the side while Dirk yanks Quint away.

More concrete shatters—and a dozen thick vines seize Big Mama. . . .

"Get off our truck!" Dirk barks.

KAAA-KRAAAK!

Quint spins toward me. "You go help June!" he
orders. "We'll free Big Mama!"

"And put a hurtin' on these vine-jerks in the
process," Dirk adds with a snarl.

In a flash, I'm racing after June.

She has reached the monster and is struggling to save it. But the vines already have hold of it, and it's being dragged into the vine-sinkhole.

"Hang on!" June cries, and squeezes the monster's hand tighter, pulling harder.

I dive onto my belly and grab the monster's other arm. Even as I'm trying to help pull it free, I say, "June, we have to go!"

"We almost have it!" she barks. "C'mon, little guy!"

But I realize, with sudden unease, that the monster has stopped struggling against the vines. It's no longer fighting the strange horror.

It's almost like it doesn't *want* to be helped.

THRULL . . . THRULL'S ARMY WAS . . .

And then the monster is yanked from our hands. Pulled under.

"No!" June shouts. She paws at the vines, but it's too late. The monster is gone. There's nothing left but the enveloping, pulsating vines.

Behind us, Big Mama's engine roars to life. Dirk's at the wheel, fighting to reverse out of the vines' grip.

I scramble to my feet and stagger back from the pit. "We gotta go, June. We gotta!"

June stares silently at the swirling pit, the horrible hole that pulled the creature under and stole its life.

Then we run.

When we reach Big Mama, the door flies open and Quint pulls us in. Dirk stomps the gas, but Big Mama doesn't move. "We got vines!" Dirk barks. "Grabbing the front tires!"

"On it!" Quint says. He scrambles over the dash and squeezes through the front window hatch. He crawls onto the hood, then drops two swollen goo-slime water balloons onto the vines.

There's a familiar sizzle—but the vines don't recoil and melt like usual. They turn gray and slow down—weakened, but not destroyed.

After one more burst of Big Mama's turbo-charged engine, the vines break and we're free.

As we peel away, I see the vines moving toward the attraction building. The Entity from Interstate 8 falls, and they begin devouring it.

"Dirk, I'm sorry we didn't get to see it," I say.

"I'm just bummed you couldn't save that little guy," Dirk says solemnly.

Then the entire attraction collapses: glass shattering, wood snapping and cracking. The vines twist and tighten until the roof splits and the Entity—the thing we came to see—pops up and out.

Then the vines consume that, too, and it's gone forever.

There's a moment of silence while we process everything that just happened. What we saw. What the monster said.

"The goo-slime barely worked," Quint says. "It still killed *some* of the vines, yes. But they were so strong, it just wasn't enough."

Which can't be a good sign. If the vines are getting stronger, or growing goo-slime resistant, then where does that leave us?

The sun is sinking behind the highway horizon. Fog rolls in, and the tension and unease in Big Mama is thick.

I'm thinking about the way the monster didn't even try to fight. Didn't attempt to escape the vine-quicksand. It's almost like our world is falling apart so quickly that the monster didn't want to stick around for what comes next. Like a movie so bad you don't even stay till the end.

I close my eyes—and I can see that final look in the monster's eyes again. It's like the little dude was *convinced* Thrull would win, that Ŗeżżőch would eventually arrive, and that our dimension is already finished.

Like it was certain that Thrull is truly unstoppable. . . .

chapter eleven

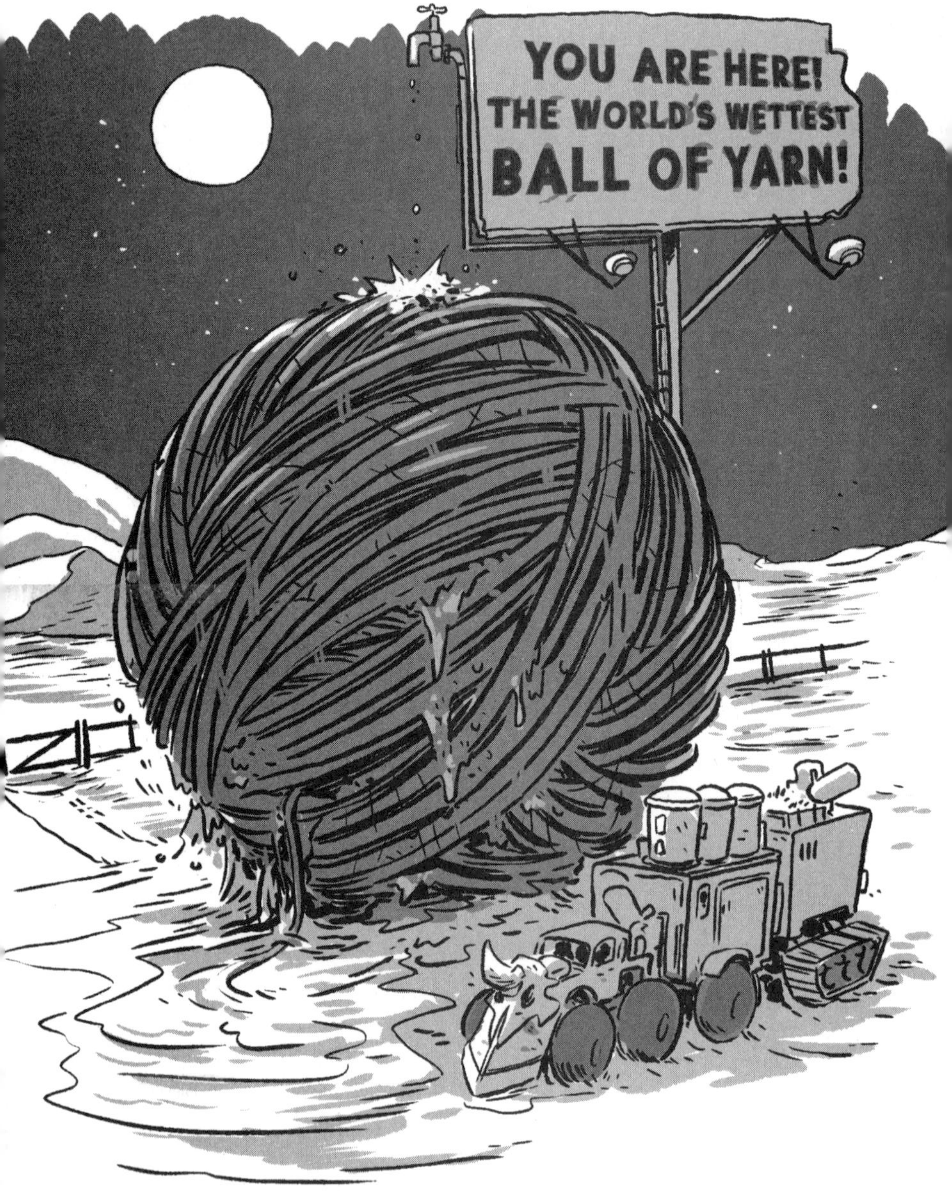
YOU ARE HERE!
THE WORLD'S WETTEST
BALL OF YARN!

That night, we're all still pretty shaken and freaked by what happened. I suggest we relax with a board game night. It's a good idea, but then Quint goes and picks Risk—the least relaxing game ever. Also, the slowest game ever. Playing a game of Risk is like adopting a turtle— you're in it for the long haul.

And the game's usual sluggish pace becomes downright glacial when zombies join in. . . .

Dirk makes popcorn balls coated with peanut butter and stuffed with M&M's and some leftover candied carrots he salvaged from his demolished garden. Sounds gross, but the carrots actually worked. After a few bites, I find myself staring at my Zombie Squad. "Hey, Quint," I finally say. "Do you think they need to, like—y'know. Like . . . *y'know*."

June looks up. "Go to the bathroom?"

"No, no. Like—*eat*."

Quint considers this for a moment. "I do not think so," he finally concludes. "I've noticed the zombies do not fall apart or decay. They are not like the zombies portrayed in comics, film, and television. It's been over a year—and the zombies don't look all that different now from when this all started. I believe they bite not due to hunger, but only to create *more zombies*."

It's an interesting theory. It would mean the zombies are only here as part of Ŗeżżőcħ's larger plan. And it's pretty smart, when you think about it—portals open up, Ŗeżżőcħ sends through this zombie plague: a plague that can turn almost every person in our dimension into one of his soldiers.

In fact, it's downright brilliant.

Why send your own army when, instead, you can unleash a plague that turns the existing population into endless legions of subservient zombie soldiers?

But, of course, Ŗeżżőcħ didn't expect his general, Ghazt—the one who was supposed to lead that army—to *lose his power*. To *me*.

"OK, I lost Kamchatka. That's enough Risk for me," June says with a yawn. She stands and heads for her bunk bed. "Let's hope those vines don't come knocking tonight."

"Ha. Let 'em come," I say. "I'll sic my Zombie Squad on 'em. Alfred can probably take down Thrull *alone*."

My friends laugh—but it's an uneasy laugh. Because we have no reason to be that confident. What we saw on Interstate 8 took us by surprise. We almost lost Big Mama, and we did lose that poor little monster.

I tell my friends good night, then take my zombies to their trailer. Lefty and Glurm quickly resume staring at the wall, per usual. But Alfred's got his head up—watching me as I try to leave.

I feel a tiny connection to the guy. After all,

we've seen stuff together. In Wakefield, he saw what Thrull was capable of. And he saw Ṛeżżŏċħ through the portal. Some part of Alfred might still remember that.

We need to stay ready, buddy. Ready for Thrull—and whatever he throws at us . . .

chapter twelve

My eyes snap open.

I'm awakened by an earthquake, or something like one. Could be a stampede of Mack Trucks. Possibly an elephant tap dance routine.

"WHAT'S HAPPENING?" Dirk shouts. I roll over and spot him on the floor, trying to squirm out of his sleeping bag.

"Shake loud . . . ?" Quint mutters, still half-asleep.

"C'mon!" June says, springing out of bed.

In moments, we're awake and dressed. During the Monster Apocalypse, you sorta get used to throwing on a pair of jeans at a second's notice. We're like modern-day minutemen, minus the muskets, wigs, and weird obsession with tea.

June shimmies open the door and we stagger outside. Greeting us is the single largest moving object any of us has ever seen. . . .

In the moonlight, all I can make out is a *massive* form rumbling toward us. No, "massive" is underselling it. This is leviathan-level large.

"Wait," Quint says, rubbing his eyes. "Is that . . . ?"

"It is!" I say. "It can't be, but it is. It's a mall!"

June says, "Not just a mall. THE Mall. That's the Millennium Super Mall, biggest mall in the hemisphere!"

CRUUUNSSHHHH-GRRRRRRRRRR

As the thing's crumbling path brings it into full view, Dirk says, "Biggest mall in the hemisphere is ridin' a centipede-looking monster. Great."

RRRRRMMM!

"*Colossal* centipede," I add. "Combined with a slug or a snail or something. . . ."

"Mollusks," Quint says. "Slugs and snails are both mollusks."

"So does that make this big thing a . . . MALLusk?" June asks.

"Oh, June, dude . . ." I say. "Nice. So nice."

Dirk is stomping back to Big Mama. "Yeah, well—your 'Mallusk' is about to mush us into a fine paste. Let's move!"

We rush back into Big Mama—and it's chaos. Outside, the ground is splitting as the creature approaches. Inside, the metal floor is twisting and windows are bursting from their frames!

"Hang on!" Dirk barks from up front. "We're gettin' out of here!"

I hear a door pop open. Outside, I spot—

"My zombies!" The vibrations must have popped open their trailer door—now they're staggering around outside.

I reach for my Slicer while Big Mama sputters forward unsteadily. "Wait, guys! Not yet!" I shout. "I have to get my squad! I ne-ee-ee-ee—"

Suddenly, the ground rolls, Big Mama lurches, and I'm flung out the door!

My stomach flips. I realize the ground has

been split into two. I'm separated from my friends, being carried off. It's like I'm on an iceberg that's drifting out to sea. In moments, Big Mama is hundreds of feet away. And the chasm is only growing wider.

Then I can no longer see Big Mama at all. I only see the massive Mallusk charging over and through the ground like a freight train that's jumped the tracks. . . .

CRUUUUNSSHHHH-GRRRRRRRRRMMM!

No way I can reach my buddies now—and I won't be able to until the mall passes. But I've got my Slicer, so I search, scanning for any sign of my squad. With the chasm behind us, there's really only one place they could have gone: forward.

So I go forward. And as I make my way down a cracked, torn-up street, I think, *It's way too early for this.*

Far behind me, the roar of the Mega Mallusk continues. It's foggy and I can barely see anything. But there's a strange glow up ahead, so I decide to follow that—thinking it might have attracted the zombies like moths.

After a few hundred feet, I cross a moss-covered interstate and discover an old roadside motel. A rusted sign reads: THE C'MON INN. The moon bathes it all in a strange blue glow. "Like this place wasn't creepy enough," I say under my breath. "Thanks a lot, moon."

Interdimensional foliage grows wild across the parking lot. Cars, skewered by some strange species of rigid and razor-sharp vine, are suspended in the air. A VW Bug rests, upside down, in the gnarled crook of a tree that radiates a fiery red.

I push forward.

My Cosmic Hand grips the Slicer as I reach the motel's front door and nudge it open. And there they are: my three zombies, huddled together behind the front desk.

"Alfred," I say with a sigh. "You should know better than to run off."

All three of them groan.

"All right, let's hit it, gang." They shuffle around the desk on my order and follow me outside. I'm relieved I didn't have to search that whole dilapidated joint. I direct the zombies toward where I last saw Big Mama.

I'm about to follow when something catches my eye: a wall of hanging vines, like a curtain. I turn. It hangs between the two wings of the motel. And—it takes me a minute to be sure, but yep—the vines are moving.

The zombies shuffle past me—headed for Big Mama.

Then—

"*Jaaaaaack*," a voice whispers, taunting.

It's a voice I recognize.

The hanging wall of vines is forming something. Or *someone*.

I gulp.

Because, as I step forward, I know what—or *who*—it is.

Thrull.

chapter thirteen

Except, it isn't Thrull.

The vines only *look* like Thrull for a quick, dream-like moment. Then the face vanishes as the vines split further, and I'm face-to-face with the most horrific monster I've ever encountered.

One that I thought I would not see again . . .

Never. Ever.

In a million years.

I mean, of course I didn't think I'd see this monster again—I already *slayed* this monster. . . .

No **way**.

It's Blarg. I see the hole in his skull. I *put* that hole there. I can still feel the way the bone cracked as I slammed the Slicer into the evil beast.

No doubt about it, this is Blarg—lifeless, skinless; he's returned as a skeletal soldier.

Suddenly, his massive jaw opens—and he howls. Cries of terror, pain, and anger all rolled into one anguished wail.

The howl stops.

And a voice comes from Blarg's horrible bleached-bone mouth.

Not just a voice: *words.*

It's Thrull.

Thrull's voice. Thrull's words.

"Stop while you can, Jack," the voice says, *"and I may let you and your friends live."*

I swallow. This is more than *just* Blarg and this is more than *just* another skeleton soldier. This is a servant of Ŗeżżőcħ, one who now speaks for Thrull—speaks *as* Thrull.

I take a slow step back—fully taking in this abomination.

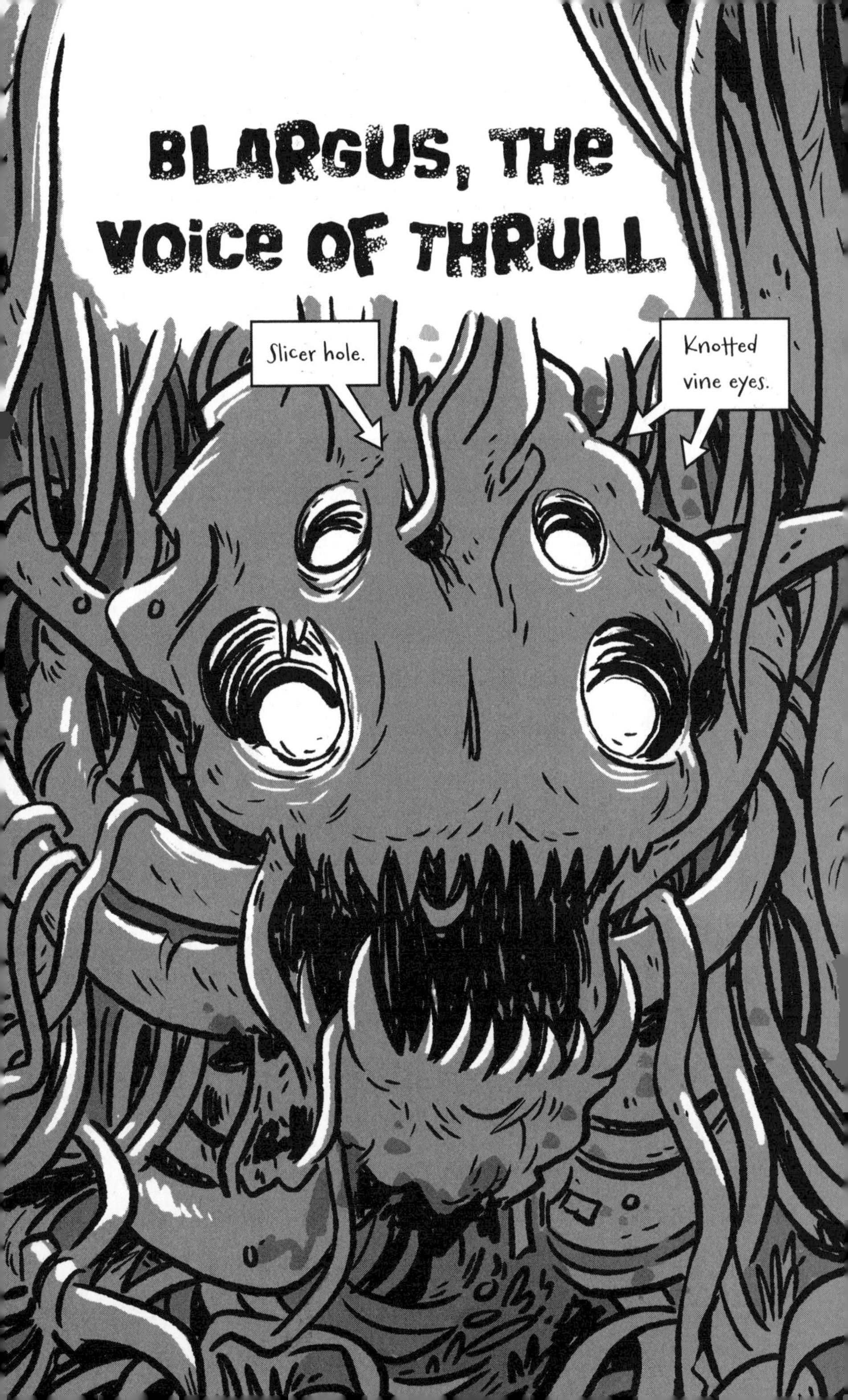
BLARGUS, THE VOICE OF THRULL
Slicer hole.
Knotted vine eyes.

"Go back to Wakefield, Jack . . ." the voice warns again. *"Play your little games. Live your little life. Do that, and I will not destroy you."*

"You know I won't," I say. "I'd rather die trying to stop you than do nothing. . . ."

"Even death would be a merciful end," the voice goes on. *"Continue with your journey, and I will do to each of you what I did to Bardle. Only much slower."*

I don't think Thrull is bluffing. I've seen quite a few things from Ṛeżżőch's dimension by now. They are almost all unimaginably horrible.

But at the same time, why is Thrull trying to convince me to quit? We must have him worried, at least a little bit—if not, he'd *want* us to press on. He'd *want* us to come for him— so he could deal with us easily.

But instead, he's trying to scare me off.

"What is it, Thrull? Mad about how things ended last time?"

This new, pale, bleached-bone Blarg carcass—Blargus—roars, and one huge hand swings toward me—

I raise the Slicer to block his next attack, but a
vine knocks the blade from my hand. In a flash,
vines are slithering around me. I reach for the
Slicer, but my Cosmic Hand instead finds a vine.

And then: I'm not there anymore.

I'm no longer standing outside the motel.

Instead, I'm whooshing through a tunnel
of earth and light and energy. And somehow,
I know I'm traveling *through* the vines—or, at
least, along their path. My brain and body feel

disconnected, like that horrible moment when the King Wretch showed me visions of a possible future. Except, here, what I'm seeing *is* real. And it's happening now.

I *see* the path that Thrull's army has forged to get here. I *see* the destruction Thrull's army has left in its wake.

Towns, cities—*anything Thrull can reach*—are being pulled toward the Tower. They are resources to be used in its continued construction.

The world rushes past like I'm in a low-flying jet, too fast to see everything clearly. It's hazy around the edges, and there's so much I can't quite make out.

And then I *see*, in front of me, an imposing structure. It rises up into a dark sky, pulsing with vines.

And I know.

It's the TOWER.

More massive than I could have imagined. More massive than anything ever built in this world. And surrounding it is his army: an infinitely vast number of skeletal servants.

They work—building, constructing,

shaping: helping the Tower to grow. Everything beyond the army is dim and the Tower is only a soaring, ill-defined shape, shrouded in shadows.

And then I'm zooming up the side of the Tower itself, through the vines that course through it. It must be a mile high. . . .

To the top. To the place where Thrull sits on a throne, like a king. He's *part* of it. Thrull, the vines, the Tower: all connected.

Thrull looks at me, seeing me—exactly as I'm seeing him. And he howls in rage and disbelief. . . .

The look of pure shock and confusion that crosses his face makes one thing clear: I'm *not* supposed to be seeing this. It's a mistake. His eyes are ablaze with red, glowing fury.

The rage practically radiates off him.

His fists slam onto his throne so violently that the entire world seems to recoil in pain. He stands, marching toward me, about to—

KA-KRAAAAAAK!!!!!!!

Suddenly, I'm back at the C'mon Inn.

"June? Wha-what just happened?" I ask, still a little dazed. Actually, *a lot* dazed.

"I saved you—that's what happened," June says. "I gotta say, you make a *great* damsel in distress."

Thrull's cries are still echoing in my brain as I kneel on the ground, disoriented and trying to make sense of everything I just saw.

"Come on, let's go! BoomKart's this way!" June says, grabbing my hand.

She pulls me along, and moments later I'm collapsing in the back of the BoomKart and she's gunning the engine. We zoom through the parking lot and over torn-up terrain.

"How far to Big Mama?" I shout.

"Not far," June says. "Your zombies just got there."

I glance back. I don't see Blargus. But he's coming. "Drive faster!" I tell June. "Trust me."

She hammers down on the throttle. The BoomKart whips around a corner, then we're speeding up what looks like a miniature mountain range. June punches the pedal, and as we crest the slope, I realize it's the edge of the crevasse that the Mega Mallusk carved into the earth.

I scream as we careen down the embankment, into the massive ravine. I spot Big Mama: our oversized road trip truck looks like a Matchbox car inside the huge canal left in the monster's wake.

chapter fourteen

Moments later, the BoomKart is sliding to a stop and June and I are leaping to the canal bed. We quickly begin hooking the BoomKart to the rear of Big Mama. My Zombie Squad shuffles back into their trailer.

"What happened?" Dirk shouts, poking his head out of Big Mama's cabin. The engine is running, ready to go.

"Where did you go?" Quint exclaims.

"I saw . . . something. . . . It's hard to . . ."

Quint's eyes go wide. He's looking past me, to the ridge. Dirk sees it, too. June spins. It takes them a moment to understand.

"That skeleton . . ." Quint says.

"It looks familiar . . ." Dirk says.

"Oh no," June gasps, realizing. "It can't be . . ."

"It is," I say. "Blarg. Actually, Blargus now. Y'know, like Blarg and carcass . . ."

"Just finish hooking the Kart up!" Dirk barks. "We gotta boogie."

Quint rushes to Big Mama's cabin. June throws a chain around Big Mama. And I look back just in time to see Blargus sliding down the canal wall. Jagged chunks of rock and soil rush downward, kicking up a storm of dirt.

RAAAAAAWWWR!!!!!

"You guys done or what?" Dirk shouts.

"Not yet!" I call as I push the BoomKart forward. "Wait until I say, *Punch it, Chewie!*"

But Dirk must have only heard that last part because next thing I know, Quint is roaring like a Wookiee in the passenger seat, and Big Mama is pulling away before June and I have secured the BoomKart!

"Just jump in!" I cry. June hops in and I scramble onto the back just as Big Mama peels away. The only thing connecting our BoomKart to Big Mama is a six-foot chain.

Big Mama speeds down the path carved by the Mega Mallusk, towing us like an inner tube behind a speedboat. And Blargus is right on our heels. . . .

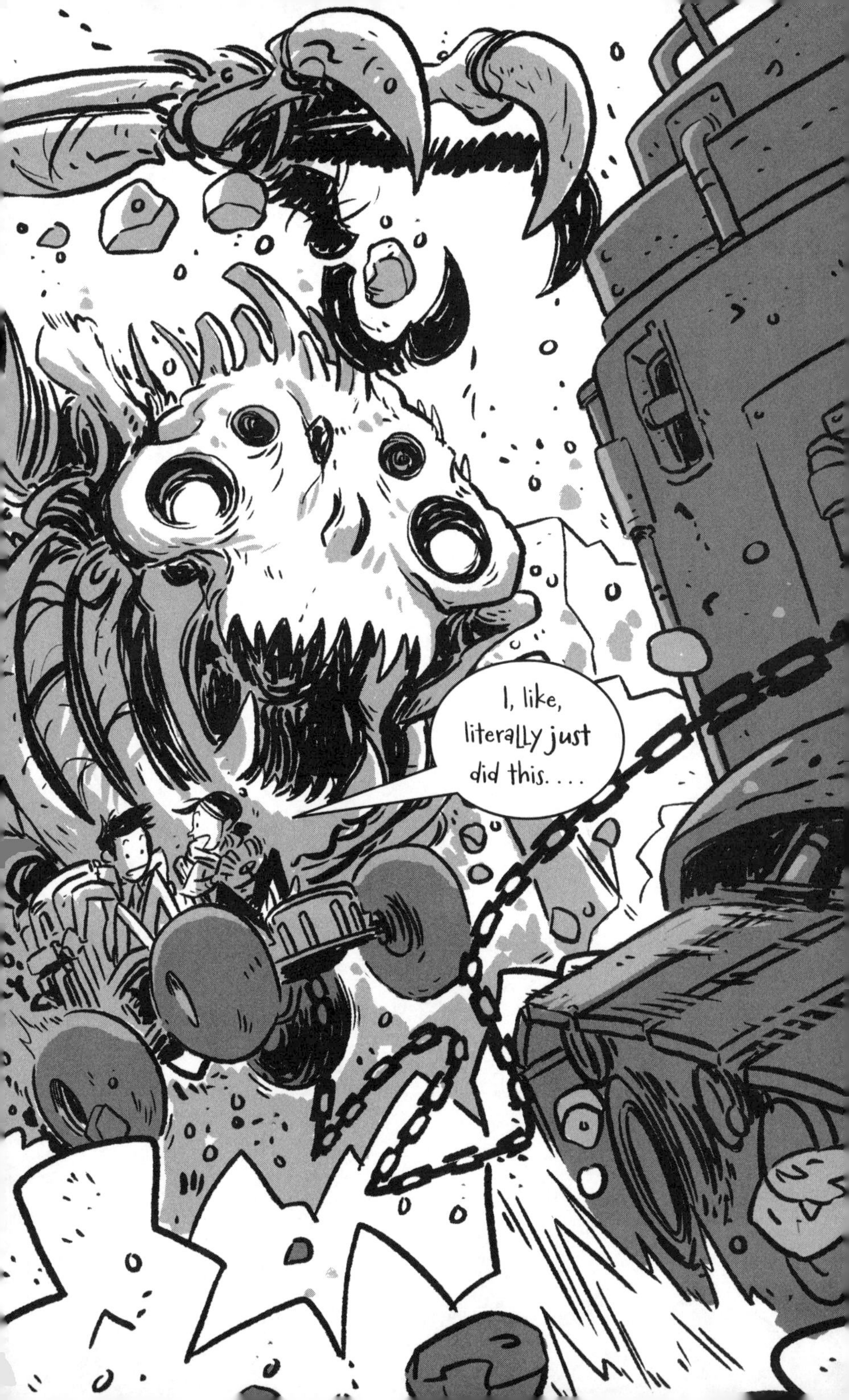
I, like, literaLLy just did this. . . .

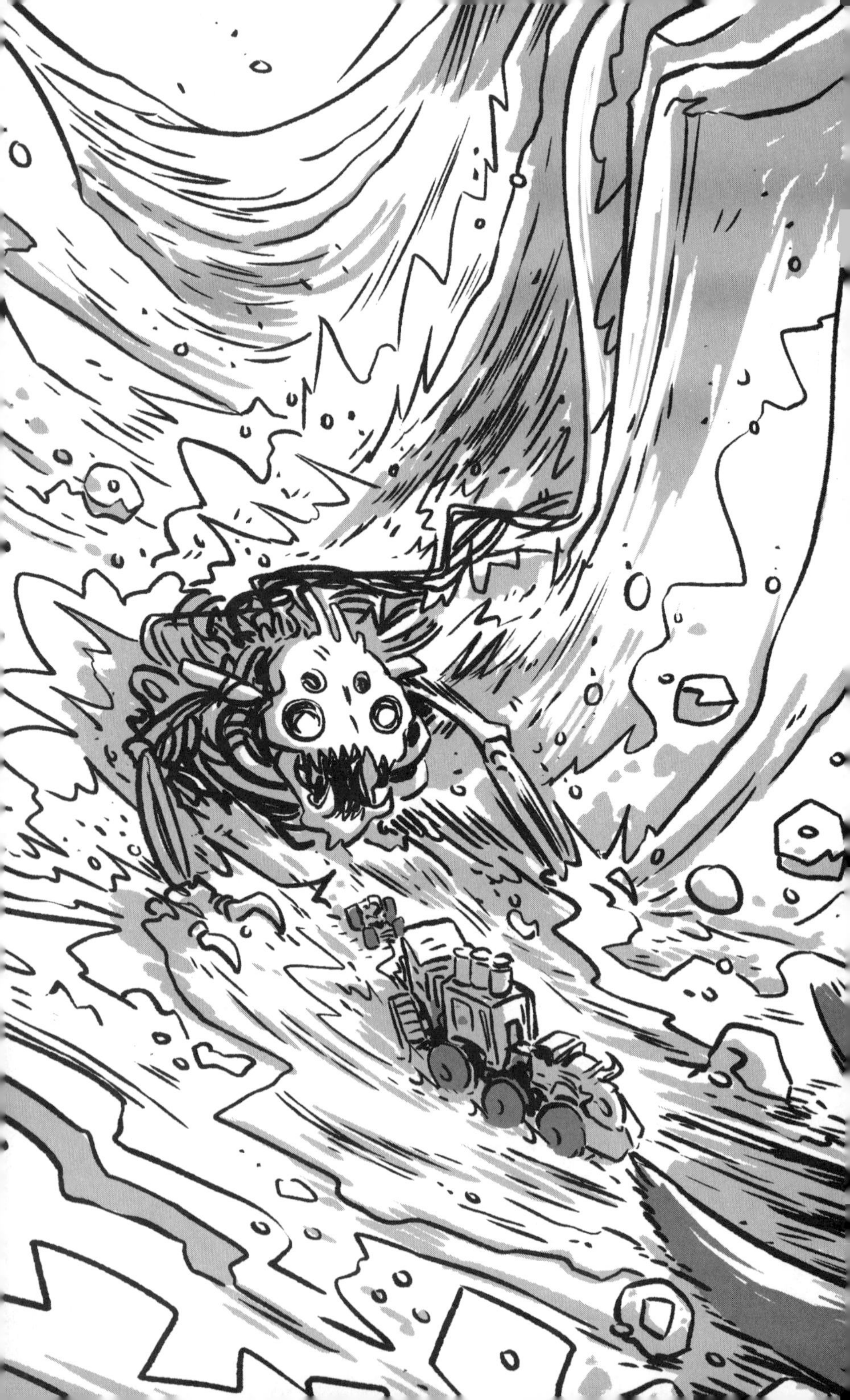

Blargus swipes at the BoomKart, but his bony paw slashes over our heads, taking off the zombie trailer's door. Metal slices through the air. Inside, I see Alfred blink twice, confused.

Quint suddenly appears in the trailer's open doorway. He cups his hands over his mouth and shouts, "More bad news! We're catching up to the Mallusk!"

On cue, the air turns thick with dirt. Stone zips through the air. The Mallusk is mincing the earth and throwing up debris in its wake.

"TELL DIRK TO GO AROUND IT!" I shout.

"NOT POSSIBLE!" Quint shouts back.

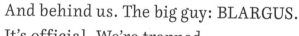

Just then, the BoomKart swings around, allowing us to see past Big Mama. The Mega Mallusk's legs are daggering into the ground. It's a mall monster meat grinder—too wide to pass.

"The side walls are too steep," June says, confirming my worst fear. "We can't drive up."

And behind us. The big guy: BLARGUS.

It's official. We're trapped.

Big Mama swerves and a splatter of goo-slime splashes us. June points to the roof. "More bad news! The goo-slime tanks! They're leaking!"

As I wipe the foul liquid from my face, I have an idea. . . .

With no time to lose, I swing the Slicer. Lefty, Glurm, and Alfred appear at the trailer door. "Squad! Get 'im!" I cry, and I swipe the Slicer sideways. All three zombies *leap* from the trailer, onto Blargus!

YAAAAAAIIIEEEEYYYY!

Our BoomKart drifts closer to Big Mama, and Dirk lets off the gas. "This is our chance!" June says. She seizes the moment and *leaps* from the BoomKart, landing hard in the back of the zombie trailer.

"Come on, Jack!" she shouts back.

I begin climbing over the BoomKart, but then—

KA-CHUNK! Big Mama goes over a massive bump, and I'm catapulted upward. I'm sailing toward the truck—but I'm nowhere close to making it. This is it. Death by BoomKart. Good-bye, cruel world!

Then—

Gotcha!

June pulls me up, and we crash down onto the floor just as—

SLAM!

Suddenly, Alfred is sailing past us. He smacks into the wall like a bird in a Windex commercial.

Blargus roars, trying to shake off Lefty and Glurm.

"The goo-slime cannons!" Quint says, running toward them.

"It won't work!" I say, stopping him, even as Blargus closes in. "Our goo-slime couldn't even destroy those vines back there. If there's any hope, we gotta douse him in goo-slime from head to toe."

"You're not suggesting what I think you're suggesting?" Quint asks.

"The tanks," I say. "We gotta dump 'em. Right at Blargus's feet."

"WE NEED THOSE!" June and Quint both shout.

I shout back, "It wouldn't be enough for the Tower anyway!"

"How do you know?" June asks.

But before I can answer, Blargus throws off the other two zombies, who land with a double thud in the truck.

"You'll just have to trust me for now!" I yell.

The three of us climb up onto the roof of Big Mama, and I enlist my Zombie Squad to help. The wind whips around us, and Big Mama jumps and shudders as it speeds along.

"Quick!" I bark. "Before we're tumbling off the roof!"

Together, the six of us take a running start and heave the three goo-slime tanks. I can feel them give way as they tumble off the back.

There's a tremendous *CRASH* as the tanks hit the ground, banging and clanging.

June and Quint stare at me—still unsure this was the right move.

"June," I say. "Fire when ready."

She raises her arm, takes aim with Blasty, and then—

FA-SHOOM!

Three bottle rockets scream through the air.

The timing is perfect. Her aim is perfect. The tanks go up in an epic eruption of goo-slime. . . .

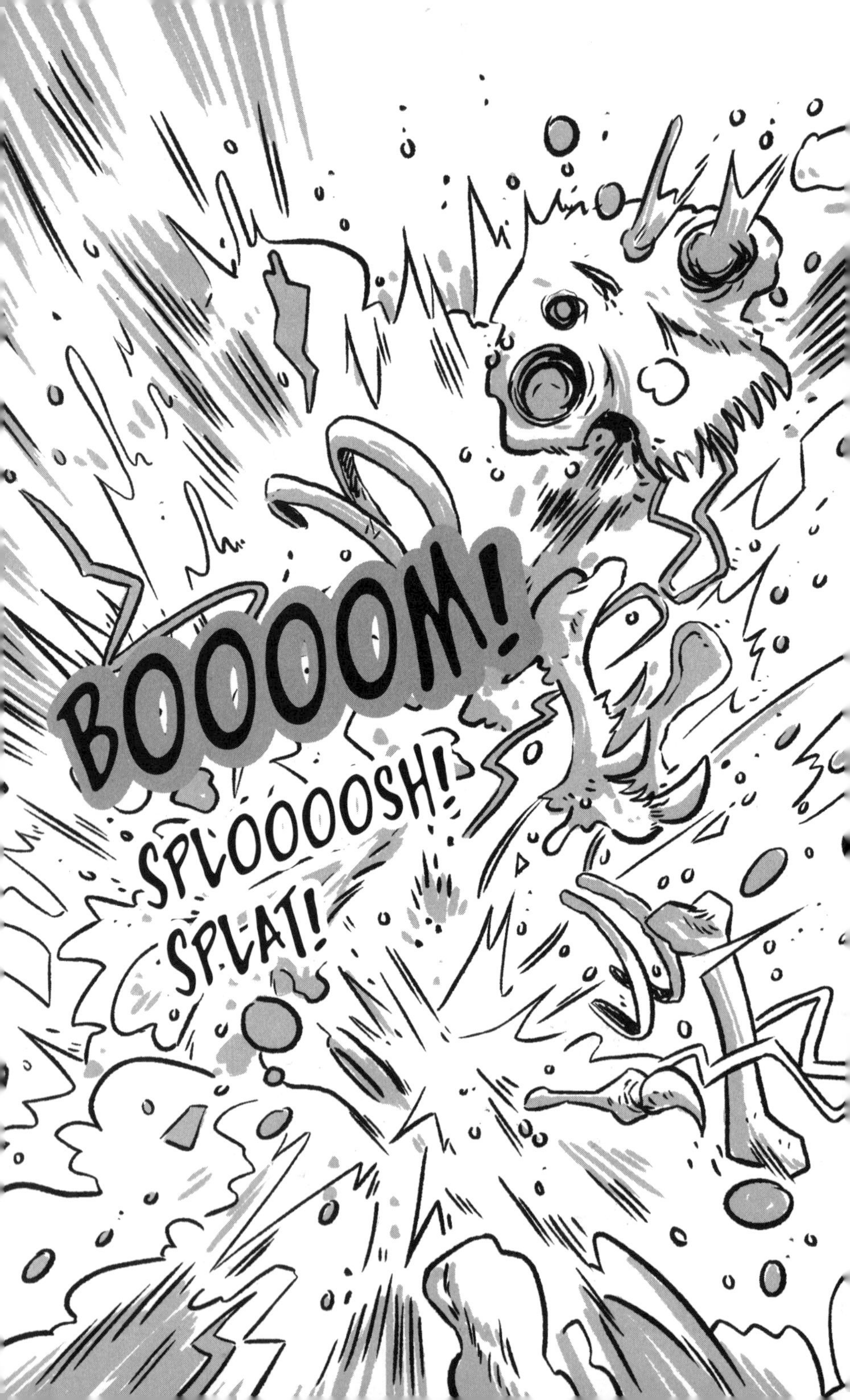
BOOOOOM!
SPLOOOOSH!
SPLAT!

Blargus explodes. His skull is launched straight up into the air, like a goo-streaked firework.

Chunks of bone and bits of vine litter the ground on the road behind us.

But as we scramble back inside, I wonder: Is he done for? For good? I hope. But the vines, their connection to the skeletons—I'm not certain we've seen the last of Blargus. . . .

"What happened back there?" Dirk shouts from the front.

What happened is—we just messed up the bad guy, big-time.

But when I feel Big Mama speeding up, I realize that's not what Dirk means. With the tanks gone, Big Mama is lighter, and suddenly, we're accelerating toward the Mega Mallusk.

"Slow down!" Quint yells back.

"Can't! Brakes are shot!" Dirk shouts.

We rush through the trailer in a panic. As we burst into Big Mama's cabin, I see we're zooming toward centipede butt.

"Help me turn this thing!" Dirk says.

All of us grab the wheel and yank hard. Big Mama tilts, nearly flipping, as we cut right and hurtle up the ravine at full speed.

We sail over the canyon edge before hitting
the ground with a hard—

KAAAA-SMASSSHHHH!

Big Mama's tires screech as we barrel ahead.
Dirk calls: "Everyone down!"

Quint throws on his seat belt. June and I
are hurled to the ground as Big Mama hooks,
swings, then veers us off the road. Dirk crashes
to the floor, crawling toward us army-style,
hands over his head, when—

SMASH!

Big Mama slams into a billboard! The cow
plow splits the huge metal pole! At once, we jolt
to a stop. There are sounds of metal scraping
and the smell of burnt tires in the air.

"Everyone OK?" Dirk manages.

June groans. "Better than Blargus."

"I am quite fine . . ." Quint says, but his voice
is muffled. I lean forward and see that his
airbag inflated, and he's now locked in some sort
of grappling contest with it—and losing. Finally,
he reaches his staff and slices the airbag open
with a POP.

I smile. OK. We're alive. And we wouldn't be if it weren't for my quick-thinking goo-slime sacrifice.

I catch my breath and eye my friends, ready to be treated like a hero—

Well, that did not go as planned.

"Hold on, hold on, guys," I say. "I saw something back there. When I touched Blargus and the vines. It was like I was transfixed—stuck in a trance."

"I saw it," June confirms. "Sorta creepy, too."

"Those three tanks of goo-slime weren't going to be nearly enough," I say. " I saw *the Tower. And the full skeleton army.* They're both bigger than anything we've ever imagined."

June and Quint drop their heads. "I'm gonna check the brakes," Dirk grumbles, getting out.

"So we got *this* close to finding out where Thrull and the Tower are," June says, "but now we have no way to fight them?" She sighs and angrily slams Blasty into Big Mama's already supremely dented dash.

"Guys," I say as reassuringly as I can. "Don't worry. Life finds a way."

"That doesn't apply here!" Quint shoots back.

I shrug. "Sorry. Alfred and I watched *Jurassic Park* a few days ago. I got Goldblum on the brain."

"Hey, dorks!" Dirk calls from outside. "Come see this!"

"Welp. At least we found the Outpost!" June says, undoing a tiny bit of her disappointment about Thrull, the Tower, and the goo-slime.

So we all pile out while Quint and Dirk fix the brakes. Luckily, it's just a simple patch to stop a leak—and then we're cruising again.

Dirk takes the exit, then follows the signs. Big Mama rumbles through a deserted city. Broken storefront windows look like jagged shark teeth.

Half-collapsed houses are encased in glowing purple foliage.

Up ahead in the distance, we see bright lights.

We're all silent as we continue on—I think we're all remembering Skaelka's warning about the Outpost. But someone inside knows the location of the Tower, someone named Ryḳk. And we can't destroy the Tower if we don't know where it is. This is our only chance.

A huge glowing sign looms into view moments later and confirms it.

We're here: *Chaz and Slammers*.

chapter fifteen

We park Big Mama, then ready ourselves for
what's to come. I wave the Slicer and my zombies
amble out of the trailer. "I might need you guys
to make an impression on this Rykk dude."

"And," Quint adds, "we may need the protection. . . ." He nods down the street. Two monsters are having a loud argument.

It ends quickly. . . .

Conflict resolution at the Outpost.

CHOMP!

SLURP!

Don't mind us. . . .

We shuffle across the parking lot toward Chaz and Slammers.

I try to keep my head down—don't want to draw attention to ourselves—but it's not easy. It's such an overload of monster activity that I *have* to look. I see one monster munching on a string of Christmas lights like it's a candy necklace.

Another is spitting a stream of blue liquid from its nose, writing its name on the wall.

"Fascinating," Quint remarks. "Gloriously fascinating."

"The story of a lifetime," June says.

All the activity leads to the main hub: Chaz and Slammers. Monsters stream in and out of the brightly lit four-story mega arcade.

"OK, guys," I say. "Put your gamer faces on."

Two hulking monsters guard the entrance. They're like hired goons from an old gangster movie, but with bigger horns.

THAT'S FAR ENOUGH, SKINBAG.

THOSE THREE DISGUSTING THINGS AREN'T WELCOME IN HERE.

Hey! These guys aren't disgusting! They're just my buds!

Goon #1 growls. "Talkin' about *them*." He points an ax at my Zombie Squad.

"You'll have to check 'em. We'll put 'em in the box," Goon #2 says. "Read the sign!"

This so-called sign is nothing but a bent bent street sign with a strange parrot creature perched on top.

NO ZOMBIES ALLOWED PAST THIS POINT!

WEAPONS ARE TOTALLY COOL, THOUGH! THE MORE WEAPONS, THE MERRIER!

"Um, OK," I say. I direct my zombies over to an empty batting cage. Alfred looks at me with the saddest eyes anyone ever saw on a zombie.

"Sorry, guys," I say. "I don't make the rules. And those dudes are scary."

"You'll get 'em back when you leave," Goon #2 says.

"*If* you leave," Goon #1 adds, laughing.

"Do I get, like, a claim ticket thingy?" I ask. "For my zombies?"

Both Goons just grunt. Guess that's a no.

Behind them, the doors to Chaz and Slammers slide open. I glance at June, Quint, and Dirk. We seem to all gulp at once. *Here we go. . . .*

Stepping inside is total sensory overload. After living for so long with minimal electricity, this is like Times Square. Lights flash. Electronic pings and dings explode around us like a Video Game Symphony Orchestra: John Williams Plays the Classics!

"So much electricity!" Quint whispers, impressed.

"How do they do it?" I ask.

Dirk nudges me and nods up. A few misshapen cages dangle from the ceiling—and inside, monsters sleep. Their tails hum with electricity.

"Little monster generators," Quint observes. "Their tails must power the entire place. Ingenious . . ."

And the place is BIG. Four floors of freaked-out fun.

It's a sprawl of monsters: all shapes and sizes and smells. Some slither, some stroll, some swing from the railings and wires. A large blob of pink jelly oozes past us, leaving a trail of bubbling sludge in its wake. It chats with another monster that reminds me of a basketball-sized housefly.

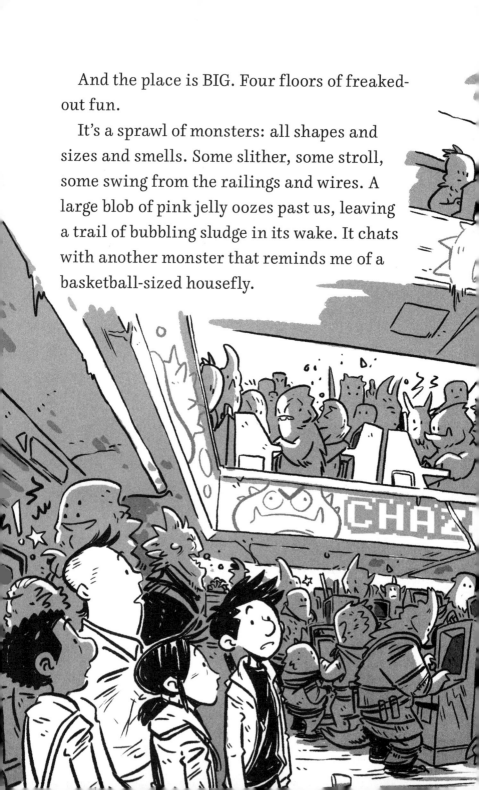

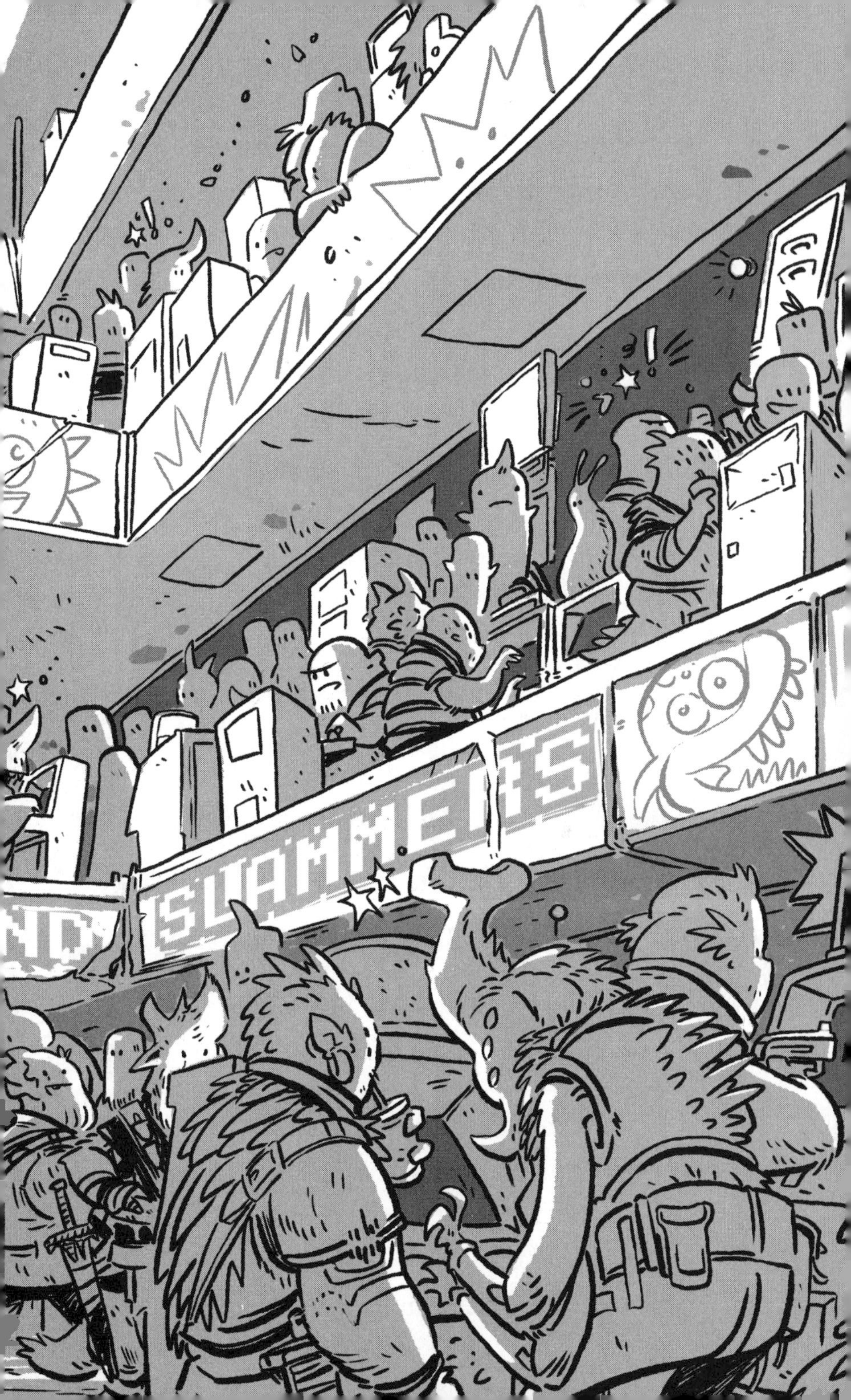
SLAMMERS

It'd be glorious if it weren't also terrifying.

Two monsters finish a game of Alley Brawl 8. The winning monster gloats, performing a swirling victory dance. The losing monster calmly takes out a metal wand, touches it to the winning monster, and—

"If I bite it in an arcade," Dirk says, "I will not be pleased."

"Let's just find Rykk so we can get out of here," June says. "And *quickly*."

"Literally any of these monsters could be Rykk,"

Quint says. "We have no clue what he looks like."

I spot a long serving counter in the center of the game floor. Monsters are seated around it, sipping bizarre beverages. One monster pours its drink down a hole near its knee.

"Let's try the dude behind the counter," Dirk says. "The dude behind the counter *always* has the answers."

The server is a gooey mass of a monster. Dozens of tentacle arms are serving various drinks and tonics. It has no *face*, but I still get the impression it's not friendly.

We find a few open stools and sit down. Before we even say a word, the server slides four fizzing drinks in skull mugs our way. "Do you think we have to pay if we don't drink them?" Quint asks.

"What do you mean don't drink them?"

We look over. Dirk's glass is empty, and he has a foamy orange mustache.

"Really, dude?" I say.

Dirk shrugs. "I was thirsty."

"Your little mustache is smoking," June notes.

Dirk says, "Yeah, it burns pretty bad. . . ."

Just then, the server blob oozes toward us. I quickly try to call to mind every movie I've ever seen where some tough guy has to get tough answers to tough questions. I'm about to put the squeeze on the server, or at least try, when—

Hey, big guy. Got a question for ya.

"Sorry, kid, can't help ya," the monster says. He slurs, even though no mouth is visible. "I only answer questions for monsters I know."

June uses her Blasty hand to reach for her drink. The movement looks casual, but it's anything but: a second later, she "mistakenly" fires a a zip-dart. It just misses the server blob monster, and slams into a mustard bottle, pinning it to the wall with a *THWACK!*

"Whoops," June says. "Silly thing. Just has a mind of its own. Could you pass me a napkin?" she asks the server blob, extending her hand— so that Blasty is now pointed directly at the monster's center.

The server takes a nervous ooze back.

"What's the question?" he slurs reluctantly.

"We're looking for an old friend of ours. You might have heard of him. His name is *Rykk*. . . ."

There's a collective gasp. A few monsters drop their drinks, and the sound of skull mugs cracking against the floor echoes in the silence that follows.

All eyes turn to us.

The server chuckles, disbelieving. "You fleshballs are friends of Rykk's, huh? And how do you know him?"

June stammers. "Oh, uh, from . . ."

"Soccer practice!" I exclaim. June glares. I shrug. Behind me, I hear Dirk mutter, "We are going to die. . . ."

The server monster laughs. At least I think it's a laugh. Might be a sneeze, I can't really tell.

"Oh, Ryḳk is gonna enjoy this," the server says. He gestures to the stairs. "Top floor. Have fun. . . ."

Suddenly, a bloodcurdling shriek comes from upstairs. The server blob glances up, laughs again, then slithers off to refill a drink.

None of us are eager to go up there, but June urges us forward. "We came here for answers," she says. "And we're not leaving without them."

We climb the stairs. Floors two and three are buzzing with action. A monster is body slammed into an air hockey table. Pinball machines are thrown like Frisbees.

But the top floor is different.

It's quieter. Most of the games have been rearranged to form a barricade, creating a private, hidden section in the back.

And a monster stands guard. She has curvy horns and a beak that's been sharpened into a blade, like a pain-dealing woodpecker. She's holding a sword that says: *I mean business*.

The guard glances at June. "No one sees Rykk without an invitation. Now remove yourself from this area or else I will be forced to make you become dead. And I really tire of making creatures become dead. It was fun at first, but after a while it grows mundane. . . ."

June pulls Skaelka's tail spike from her fanny pack. "Here's our invite."

The guard looks at Skaelka's spike. Her beak twitches.

And she lowers the huge sword.

"This way. . . ."

chapter sixteen

We follow the guard down a makeshift hallway
of arcade games.

Finally, we're face-to-face with a slimy hulk
of a monster. In front of him is a strange sort of
table, which vaguely resembles a pile of Jell-O.
There are shelves all over his lair, filled with all
sorts of bizarre odds and ends.

"Neat collection," Quint says.

This guy is definitely Ryk̜k.

He has an aura of danger and power and
violence about him. Partly because he's huge and
horrible looking—partly because of what he's
doing to the softball-sized rodent furball in his
hands.

The guard whispers something in Ryķk's ear.
He turns toward us with menacing eyes. "You
have brought me something?"

"Y-yes, Your, um . . . Most Shady One," June says. She plops Skaelka's tail spike down.

Ryķk examines it.

"It's for your, um, collection thing," June says. "We just need to speak with you. . . ."

He thinks it over for a second. Then he places the spike on a shelf behind him. "You have until I finish my meal."

Nobody speaks. All of us are too overwhelmed, then—

PLINK! Ryķk plucks a hair, then slurps it down. It's like watching a baby eat spaghetti. "Not many hairs left," Ryķk says. "I'd hurry, if I were you."

"We're trying to find Thrull's Tower," June says quickly.

Ryķk casually plucks and swallows another hair. "And why do you want this information?"

"None of your beeswax," I answer.

"IT IS MY BEESWAX!" he roars. His voice booms so loudly that we all flinch. "Any beeswax in this Outpost is Ryķk's beeswax! Look around you. Do you see beeswax? If you do, it is beeswax that belongs to me. Now answer—for what reason do you seek such information?"

"Because Thrull's using the Tower to bring Ṛeżżőcħ to this dimension," June says. I see her wipe sweat from her palms onto her jeans. "Ṛeżżőcħ is gonna destroy everything."

"So if you could just tell us where it is, it'd be great," I chime in. "If you have an address—or even a general *neighborhood*. Cross streets? Closest 7-Eleven. Then we'll be on our way—"

PLINK! PLINK! Two more hairs are plucked and slurped down. After a moment, Ryḳk says, "Your way . . . You will neither be on your way . . . nor will you get your way. Thrull is an ally. I will not divulge his location—certainly not to help humans."

"But Thrull's going to bring Ṛeżżőcħ here!" June says. "And Ṛeżżőcħ only wants to *destroy* this world—and rule over the ashes! If Thrull completes the Tower, you'll lose everything!"

I take a slow, heavy step forward. Very dramatically, I say perhaps the most ridiculous thing I've ever said. "The kingdom of Chaz and Slammers will fall. . . ."

For a moment, Ryḳk's monstrous smile wavers. "You make a compelling argument," he finally admits.

June breathes a small sigh of relief. We all do.

"But . . . you have given me nothing in return for this *information*," Ryḳk says. He squeezes the rodent furball, reaches down, gathers the rest of its hairs in his long fingers, and then—with one loud, aggressive tug—rips them out. He jams the fat, hairy handful into his mouth, then continues, not bothering to swallow. "And it looks like your time is up. The answer is no."

Ryḳk motions to the beaked guard behind us. "Feed the humans to the Grizkurl. Whole, or in pieces—I really don't care."

"Hey!" I yell. "This is bunk! We *did* give you something—that super-cool tail spike!"

Ryḳk laughs. A matted rodent hair dangles from his bottom lip, and it jumps as he speaks. "That was a gift for the privilege of speaking with me. Nothing more. Good-bye."

The guard lifts her huge sword.

"*WAIT!*" I shout.

Ryḳk's lair goes silent. Everyone is waiting to see what I've got. The problem is, I don't actually *got* anything. I quickly throw my arms around my buddies and turn.

"OK, huddle up," I whisper. "What's the plan?"

"We don't know!" Dirk barks. "You're the one who shouted 'wait' like you had an idea!"

"Right, right," I say. "OK, real quick, just blue skyin' here. Three ideas . . ."

My friends just frown.

Ryḳk slams the table. The guard readies her sword, about to swing. I lift the Slicer, ready to defend my friends to the death.

"Hold!" Ryḳk booms. The guard's sword stops. Ryḳk's looking at me. He leans forward.

The now bald rodent furball sees its opening, and quickly leaps to the floor and skitters behind an arcade machine. A moment later, it peeks its head out, like it wants to see what's gonna happen next.

Ryḳk sniffs the air. That's when I realize—he's not looking at me. He's looking at the Slicer.

"Ah!" he says. "Now *that* would make a nice addition to my collection!"

"You mean . . . the Slicer?" I ask.

Ryḳk nods.

I'm about to say, *Forget it. No way. It's my prized possession. Keep dreaming, you hair-eating weirdo.* But then—

I glance down at the blade. Like I called it before, when it was stolen: "*my lightsaber.*" It's been my constant companion during the apocalypse. Bardle *died* to keep its zombie-controlling power out of Thrull's hands.

And when I think about that—especially that last part—it's obvious what I must do. . . .

"Jack . . ." Quint gasps.

But he doesn't try to talk me out of it. Because he knows what I know—we have to do *whatever* it takes to get the information we need.

"But not yet, Rykk," I say. "First, I need it to defeat Thrull. You only get it *after* my quest is complete."

I feel a hand on my shoulder. I glance back.
It's Dirk. He gives me a gentle-but-firm "nice job,
bro" shoulder squeeze.

"And now for my end of the bargain," Ryķk
says. "The location of the Tower . . ."

There's a long silence, and then—

Ryķk's Jell-O table begins to jiggle. The cubes roll forward—and I quickly jump back as they tumble across the floor. They begin to expand, morphing and shifting, taking shape.

I've seen the Tower—but only as a vague, dreamy, shadowy thing. The Jell-O stuff is forming something specific. Then, with sudden horror, we all realize what he's creating.

"The Statue of Liberty?" June gasps.

I suddenly feel like I'm gonna puke. Thrull's Tower *can't* be at the Statue of Liberty. There are human survivors there.

Which means, if it really is there, then . . .

"What's happened to all the survivors?" June whispers softly.

chapter seventeen

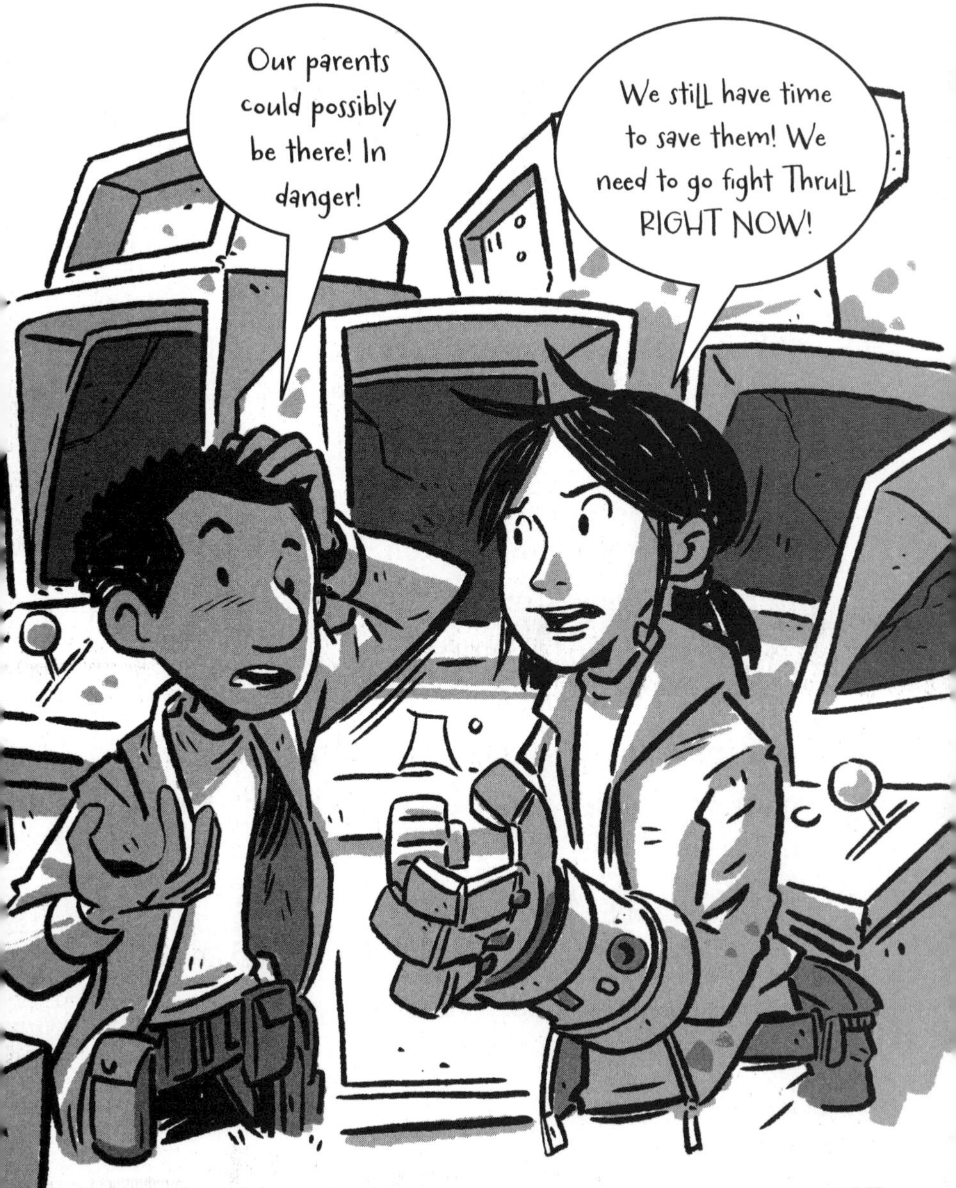
Our parents could possibly be there! In danger!
We still have time to save them! We need to go fight Thrull RIGHT NOW!

"Uh, can I talk to you guys in private?" I whisper, throwing Ryķk a winning smile, then dragging my friends away.

"Dude," Dirk says, "what are you—"

"We can't go to the Tower yet."

June and Quint look at me like I have a monster octopus tentacle for a hand.

"Ex*cuse* me?" June says. "Every second we waste is another second my parents might be in danger!"

"You know just as well as I do," I say, "that the goo-slime isn't strong enough. Not for the Tower. Not even close."

June scowls—I think she's about to launch into her next argument when, luckily, Ryķk interrupts. "Goo-slime?"

"Of my creation!" Quint says, turning. He's so proud that he hurries over to Ryķk. Zero fear. He explains what it is, what it does to Thrull's vines, and how he made it. He even produces a small vial to show him.

Ryķk reaches into a snack bucket, fishes around for another rodent furball, finds one, then hurls it at a nearby monster playing Pac-Man. "Werbert!"

Werbert looks up from the machine, realizes his boss is waiting on him, and quickly slithers over. He smells even worse than he looks.

"You!" Ryḳk barks, pointing at Quint. "Show Werbert your so-called goo-slime."

Werbert extends a long, snake-like arm. Quint pours some into Werbert's palm, and the monster shivers from the cold substance.

"Oooh!" Werbert croons, running a wormy finger across the goo-slime. "Fascinating."

Then, suddenly, Werbert begins retching. It's the loudest barf I've ever heard. He hacks and wheezes until he coughs up, from somewhere deep inside his body, a small jar.

"Gnarly," Dirk whispers.

Inside the jar is a severed vine. Werbert pours some of Quint's goo-slime into the jar. The vine writhes and sizzles but remains intact.

In the past, my goo-slime completely destroyed the vines.

But recently, it has not been nearly as effective. . . .

THAT IS BECAUSE THE VINES GROW STRONGER! EVERY DAY! YOUR "GOO-SLIME" IS NO LONGER POTENT ENOUGH.

"But, behold . . ." Werbert says.

We stand back as the worm monster retches once more, this time coughing up a glob of slime. It resembles goo-slime, only it's thicker and brighter; in fact, it glows with such neon brightness that it's hard to look directly at it.

"I call it Ğhṛužǧhŭt Spit," Werbert says. "In your tongue, it is something like 'ULTRA-POTENT, ALL-NATURAL, ORGANIC GOO.'"

"It's like *Ultra-Slime*," Quint says softly, eyeing the stuff with awe.

"Oooh, organic? I bet they charge double for that," I say.

Werbert pours a single drop into the jar. The vine instantly bubbles, sizzles, then melts. All that's left is brown paste and ash.

It destroyed it! Instantly!

Wow. A superweapon.

"Can I get a small taste?" Dirk asks.

We all gape at him, and his cheeks turn pink.

"Y'know, just to compare with the old stuff . . ." he says. "I got an iron belly. Comes from my dad. He was a poison tester for the army. Called him 'Steel Stomach Savage.'"

"Before he was a Universal Warrior?" I ask.

Dirk shrugs. "Was never clear on the timeline."

"Focus, boys," June says. She turns to Werbert. "Tell us—where can we get, like, a lot of this Ultra-Slime stuff?"

Werbert cackles. "You would die trying."

"That's the only way I know *how* to try," I say, because I say cool non-cool things like that.

Werbert ignores me and slithers toward June. "The creature who secretes this . . . *Ultra-Slime*, as you call it, lives in the Great Wet Village. But you must approach with extreme caution, for it—"

"Great Wet Village?" I interrupt.

"It is just beyond the Big Round Sweet Treat," Werbert blurts, splattering my shoes with drool.

"The what now?" June asks.

"Wait! I think I know what he's talking about!" Dirk says, and excitedly pulls out our map.

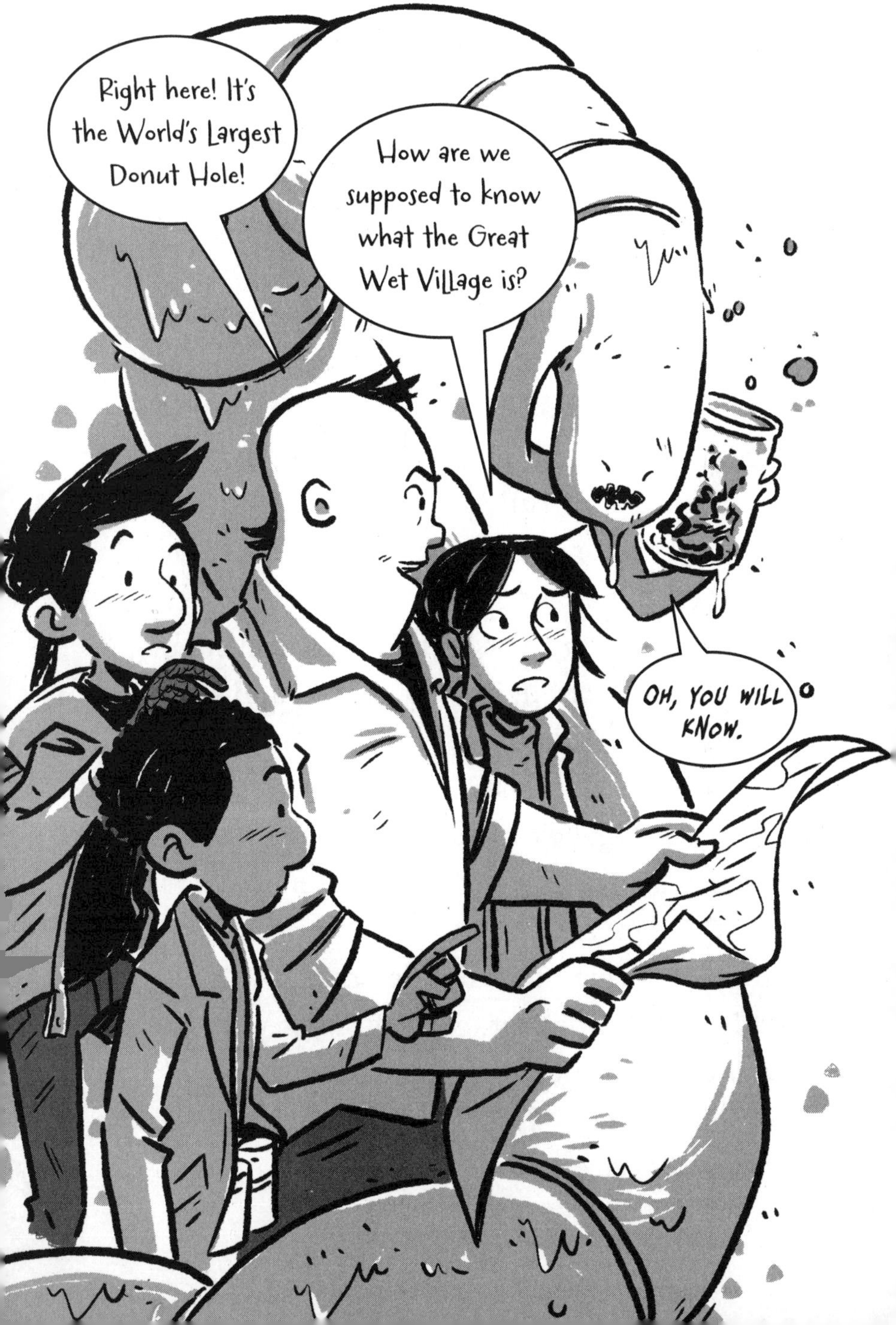
Right here! It's the World's Largest Donut Hole!
How are we supposed to know what the Great Wet Village is?
OH, YOU WILL KNOW.

June smirks and takes a step toward Ryķk.

"Since we're already promising you the most powerful weapon around," June says to him, "we also want your Ultra-Slime. It's only fair. . . ."

"Sounds quite fair!" Quint chimes in.

Ryķk makes a guttural noise of shock and surprise. "How DARE you speak to me this way!" he booms, suddenly rising. We all flinch. His voice cracks so hard—with such *energy*—that a few arcade machines rumble to life. Coins pour from one. "I run the show here—not YOU!"

"Hey, respectfully, dude, if you really want this thing," I say, tapping the Slicer, "it's in your interest to help us out."

There's a long pause while Ryķk considers this. "Werbert," he finally says, "hand over your remaining Ultra-Slime."

I look away. No need to see more retching. But I hear wet, goopy sounds and an excited squeal from Quint as Werbert produces more vials.

"Don't forget," Ryķk says, looming ominously over me. "Once Thrull is defeated, the blade is *mine*. Fail to deliver, and I promise you—you'll *wish* you had perished fighting Thrull. . . ."

"Yeah, yeah," I say. "Good doing business with ya. We'll see ourselves out."

Minutes later, we're back in the parking lot—and I'm wondering why every little thing has to be *so darn hard.*

As soon as I've got my zombies, we all walk swiftly back toward Big Mama.

"I can't *believe* we can't go right to the Tower," June says, kicking a rock across the pavement.

"But at least we know where it is. And we know what tool we need to fight Thrull," Quint says. "But yes, it is frustrating."

"It's *so much* farther out of our way," June says angrily. "It will take *weeks* to get to Thrull's Tower! And if our parents are there, they probably don't have that much time. . . ."

I catch her eye.

She frowns—then half-shrugs.

I get it. She wants to take on Thrull right away. If it was up to her, she'd be punching him in the nose at this very second. But she knows if we go there now, *we will lose*. And if we lose—then all is lost. . . .

"Looks like this is *just the beginning* of our journey," I say.

"When we *do* get that Ultra-Slime," June says, "I'm gonna melt Thrull into a fresh jam. Monsters will spread it on their morning toast."

"Right," Dirk says. Then, pointing dramatically: "Now, onward to the Donut Hole!"

And in spite of how crummy things feel, I crack a smile as we pile back into Big Mama.

chapter eighteen

There's a ticking clock now.

We have to hurry.

We all know that.

But at the same time, everything that just happened was *really heavy*. And it's already weighing on us. Everyone is on edge. Every tiny thing is about to make us *explode*.

Like, seven minutes ago? This was the scene inside Big Mama. . . .

Like I said, we're on edge. Stuff is heavy.

But it's only gonna get *more heavy*. So we *must* stick with what's been working: enjoying good old-fashioned road trip fun. If we don't, we'll all fall apart.

And we can't stop Thrull if we fall apart.

That's what I'm thinking when June says, "Jack, could you *not* suck chocolate fudge sauce off your fingers while you read from our shared collection of mystery novels starring heroic heroines?"

I lower our copy of *Murder She Wrote: Season 3 Episode 2: the Novelization.* "Sorry. I'm just naturally good at doing two things at once."

June rolls her eyes. "Oh really?" she says. "Like when you tried to show us how you could walk and chew gum at the same time and instead you tripped and choked at the same time?"

"Hey, hey, hey," I say. "Still did it at the same time, didn't I?"

And that's when it hits me. A plan . . .

"SPEED TOURING!" I say.

My friends, together: "Huh?"

"See it *all*! See it *quick*! Take photos with *instant film*!"

Again, my friends, together: "Huh?"

"Look—we're in a rush to get where we're going because of the whole—y'know—Thrull bringing Ŗeżżőch here to harvest our homes and maybe bite on us."

Quint nods. "Correct."

"But, same time," I continue, "we've still got Dirk's road trip! And we've got our brains to take care of. We gotta *enjoy* ourselves! So . . ."

"Speed touring . . ." June says, nodding. "I get it. We see stuff *really quick*. And we do it all the way until we get to the Great Wet Village."

"Right! We drive straight there, direct route—but whenever we've *gotta* stop for something, we make the best out of it! And we never spend a second longer than we need to anywhere. That way, we're productive, enjoying ourselves—but not wasting precious time! You in??"

Everyone smiles. They're in. . . .

———

Using the Slicer, I'm able to have the zombies pump gas. Glurm seems to be the best at that.

So, every time we need gas, we stop someplace nice—and we all get to enjoy the scenery.

And man, that scenery is *weird*. . . .

The closer we get to our destination—the weirder the world becomes. And that—

SCREEEECH!

I'm thrown forward! Big Mama slides to a halt! I smell burning rubber. "SORRY!" Dirk says. "My fault, my fault. Didn't see that 'deer crossing' sign."

But these aren't deer. Though they are slow—

Yep, things are definitely getting weirder now. And that means we need to reach the Great Wet Village as soon as possible.

And we will.

We're getting close.

We're speed touring our way there.

And outside Garfield City, we pass beneath two towering stone statues, carved to look like old Wild West legends. It feels like they're welcoming us.

And maybe they are.

Because two highways later, Quint suddenly
calls out from the driver's seat, "Uh, guys!
You'd better come see this!"

We rush up front and stare out the window
in shock.

Big Mama rolls to a dead stop.

Dirk opens the door and steps out. We all
follow. Our path, where we need to go—it looks
slightly hazardous. . . .

chapter nineteen

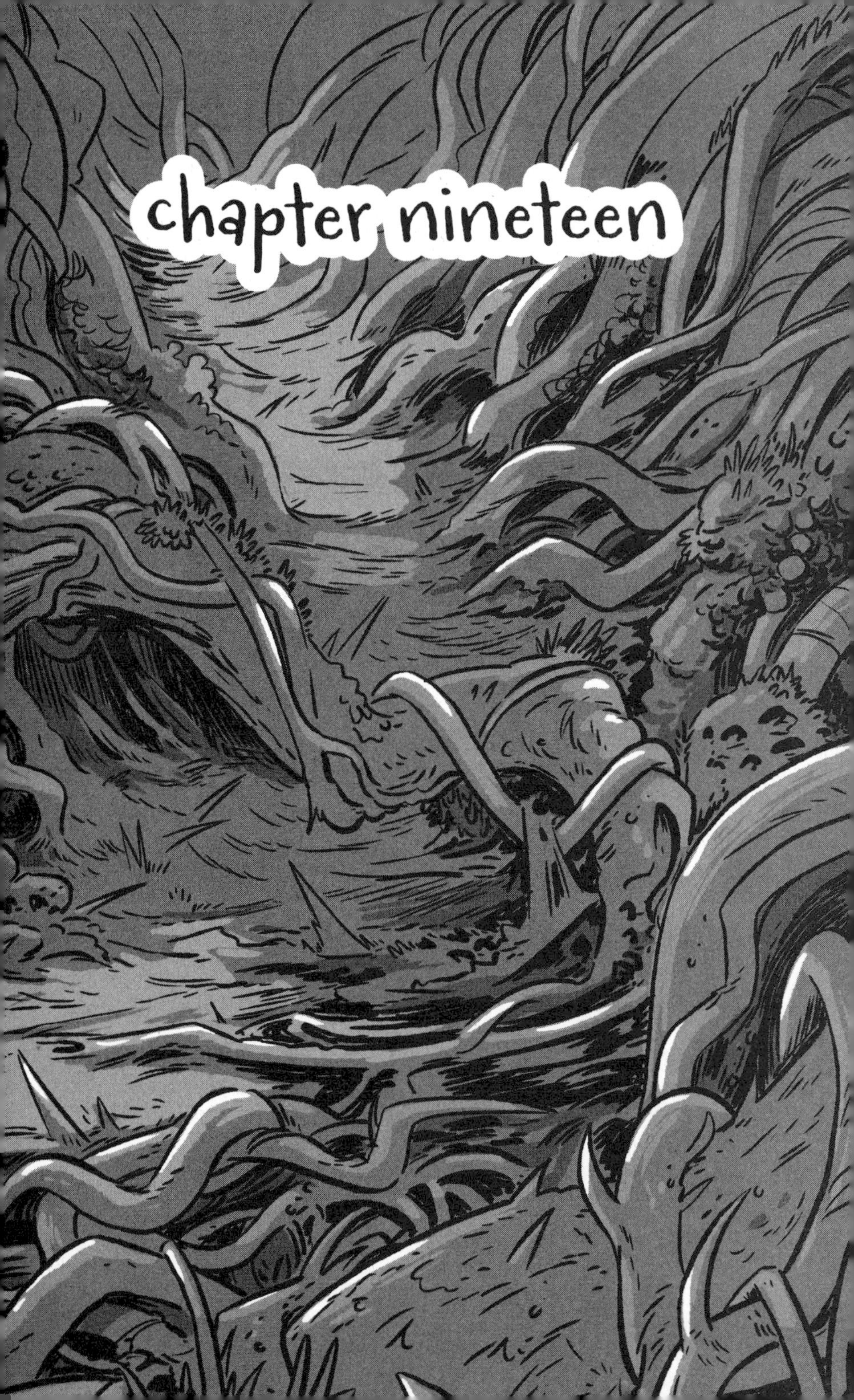

"June's right, friend," says Quint. "We may not have a choice. This is the only path through without losing days, maybe weeks."

But I'm still not sure about this. It can't be a coincidence that, like, the entire *world* has been carved and arranged to lead us straight here.

"We could turn back. Find back roads that lead around," I say. "Or maybe, like, *underroads*?"

"Tunnels," June says. "Those are called tunnels."

Softly, Quint says, "Jack, if you *really* think it's the wrong idea, we can turn back."

I know the importance of what awaits, but that doesn't mean I wanna go. I can't let fear guide this decision, though.

I swallow. "It's OK. I'm in. Dirk, drive."

He hits the gas, and Big Mama jerks forward. We rumble down the long, strange path. Soon, we can see a building up ahead: dark and ominous.

"Wait! I know this place!" Dirk shouts. "It's the Museum of Histories and Ancient Antiquities! This was on my dad's road trip list. Which is weird—he was *not* a museum guy."

"He was more of a gift shop guy, right?" I ask.

"Huh?" Dirk says.

"Sorry, nevermind, carry on," I murmur.

"I just can't think of a reason why he'd want to come here," Dirk says quietly.

I snort. "You don't say. . . ."

Big Mama rumbles forward. The vines crowd around the museum on both sides, and the path stops at the entrance. The closer we get, the more uneasy I feel—until a sense of dread nearly consumes me.

Big Mama thuds up the massive steps toward the main entrance, flanked by huge columns. My stomach is in ropes.

Dirk shifts gears and steers us forward. The truck nudges open the huge doors. And just like that, we're pushing through, into the museum.

Inside, the place is enormous, with high ceilings and marble floors. We pass a ticket booth by the entrance, and I can just make out a coat check behind the far wall.

Dirk eases us forward slowly, but then . . .

KA-SLAM!

Something explodes behind us. I thrust my head out the window, just in time to see a huge sculpture of a pale dude toppling over. It smashes—and blocks the front entrance.

"Well, I guess there's no turning back now," Dirk says with a sigh.

"Only way out," June says, "is through. . . ."

"If this didn't feel like a trap before . . ." I mutter.

This is usually the moment where Quint would get all excited about having an entire museum to himself—but still wouldn't let me touch the stuff that says *no touching*.

But Quint is quiet. We all are.

Big Mama rumbles forward. We're passing the gift shop—it looks like a good gift shop, but I don't even *consider* going in. Though I do lean down to grab a Space Ice Cream display, using the Cosmic Hand's sticky suckers to easily snag it, Wet Bandit style. I lift it into Big Mama and packs spill across the floor.

We all tear open wrappers as Dirk turns a corner. The food seems to calm us some. . . .

It isn't nearly as good as real ice cream. But in a world where real ice cream is basically extinct, it tastes like the best triple-fudge brownie sundae you ever had.

Y'know, I think it's **better**. . . .

Better than real ice cream? Don't be absurd.

I prefer Dippin' Dots.

That calmness fizzles out as we come to a large hallway. Darkness stretches in both directions.

"There's something about this place that doesn't feel right," Quint says softly.

"Something, buddy?" I say. "How about *everything*."

"No," he responds. "I mean something that I've overlooked. . . ."

Dirk goes left.

"We need a directory," June says. "To find the quickest way through the museum. Quickest way to the exit."

Leaving the entrance hall, I suddenly think I hear something behind us. But it's hard to tell over the sound of my own chewing. It's like eating popcorn at the movies—you wanna hear what's going on, but your brain just keeps hearing your own dumb chomping teeth.

I stop chewing, mouth open—listening. And the sound is gone. Or maybe it was never there. . . .

So, I continue again.

Then stop again.

And that time, for sure, I hear it.

"Drive faster, Dirk," I say. "Please."

"Can't go any faster," Dirk says. "We're driving *through a building*. And most of these, uh, whaddya call 'em . . . rooms?"

"Galleries," June says.

"Most of these artsy-fartsy *rooms* don't fit Big Mama."

"I just can't get over this feeling that I'm missing something so very obviously *bad* here . . ." Quint mumbles. "It's on the tip of my brain."

"There. Ahead," June says. "A museum directory."

Dirk eases us forward until Big Mama's headlights are shining directly onto it.

We all lean forward, searching the map for an exit. "Oooh, there's a *Lost Mammoths of the Tundra* exhibit!" Dirk says. "That'd be cool. Hey, maybe that's what my old man wanted to—"

"Shh!" June says suddenly, quieting Dirk. "Do you guys hear that?"

I'm simultaneously relieved and terrified that I'm not the only one hearing things.

"Yes," Quint says, his voice a whisper. "I do."

It sounds like it's coming from all around us. But it's too dark to see much of anything except for what's directly in front of us.

June flips a switch on Blasty, and a flashlight shines. She flashes it over the dark, shadowy corner of the hall that Big Mama's headlights don't reach. The beam passes a huge banner pointing to the largest wing in the whole place. Clearly, this is the museum's claim to fame.

Museum of Histories World-Famous Extinct Species Exhibit!
Like Taking a Stroll Through History!

"'See the third-largest collection of complete fossils in North America,'" I read from the sign.

"THAT'S IT!" Quint cries out, so loud that we all jump. And then I realize, too. . . .

Fossils! This is a history museum—it's full of fossils!

I look up, following June's flashlight beam. Vines crawl along the ceiling.

"We need to *leave* now," June says. "Before whatever *dead things* are in this museum realize we're here."

The words are barely out of June's mouth when the museum *quakes.*

"Think it's too late," I say.

From the distant reaches of the museum comes a tremendous noise: a sharp crack that causes the entire place to rattle. The sound echoes down the halls—and up my spine.

Quint glances around. We are in the center of a maze of halls, rooms, and galleries. "The trap is sprung . . ." he whispers.

"Lefty!" I shout, waving the Slicer. "Grab a map!"

Lefty explodes out of the zombie trailer. She grabs a pamphlet from the directory, then hurries back inside as Dirk stomps the pedal.

Big Mama roars to life, bursting *through* the museum directory and speeding down the main hall.

The sound seems to come from all around. Thudding, cracking—the entire museum shaking.

thud-thud . . .

thud-THUD . . .

thud-THUD . . .

Dirk drives faster, but the sound continues to amplify.

THUD-THUD . . .

THUD-THUD . . .

THUD-THUD . . .

June pokes her head out the window and shines

the Blasty flashlight behind us. The beam jumps around as we barrel ahead.

The light flashes on a true-to-life replica of a woolly mammoth.

Then a saber-toothed tiger.

Then a couple of water fountains that remind me that I'm dehydrated.

Big Mama spins out onto one ridiculously long hall that seems to stretch on forever. Glancing back, we finally see what it is that's chasing us.

You know how people say, "Seeing is believing"?

Well, I'll tell ya—that phrase does not apply to post-apocalyptic road trip monster enemies. Because I see what's chasing us—but I don't believe it. . . .

But Quint's scream. June's shriek. Dirk's thick gasp.

Those I believe. . . .

chapter twenty

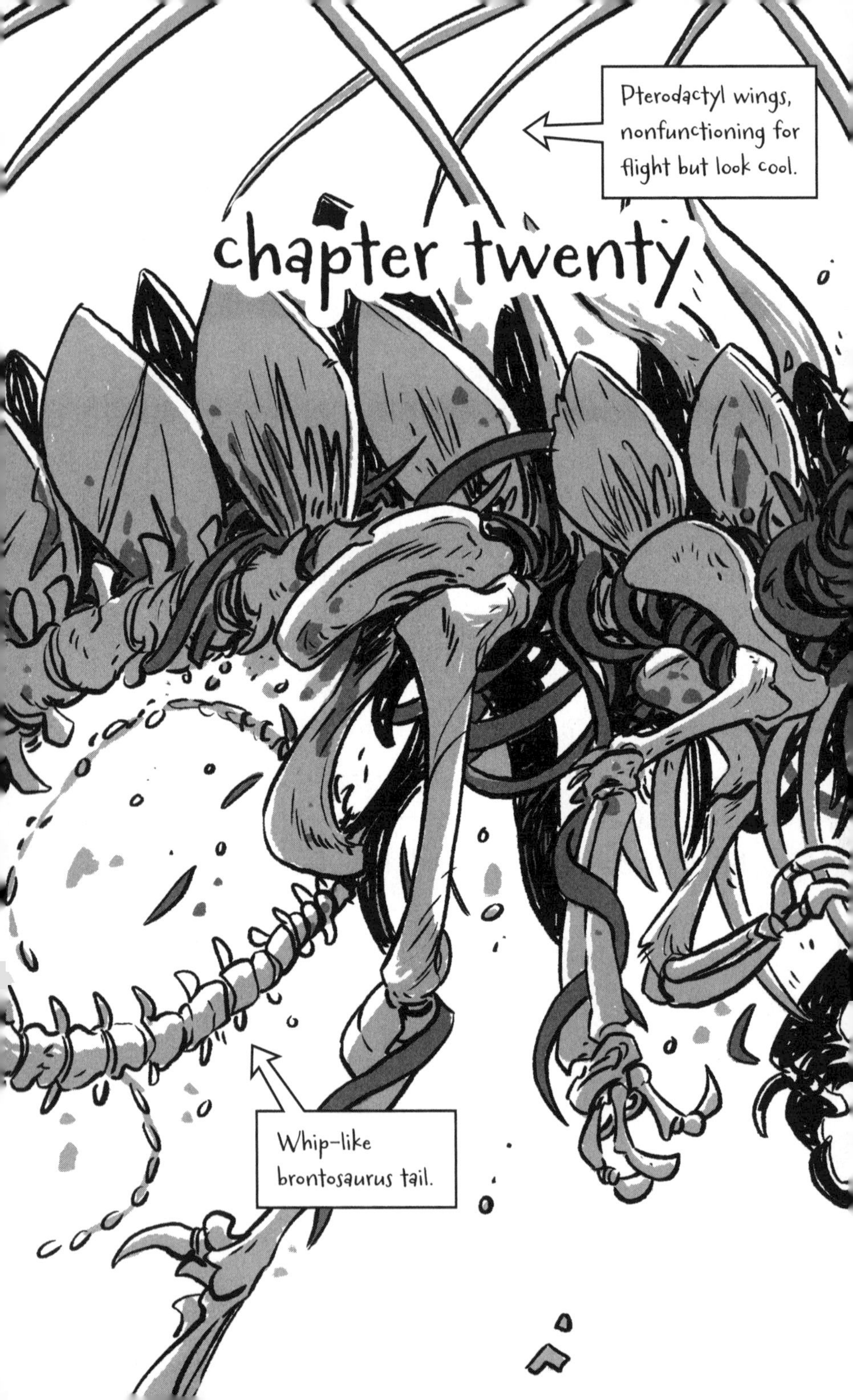

Pterodactyl wings, nonfunctioning for flight but look cool.
Whip-like brontosaurus tail.

DEATH FOSSIL!

Megalodon AND T-Rex jaws!

This freakish monstrosity keeps changing shape. It's like the bones are nanobots, shifting the creature from one horrible form to another.

Tires squeal on the marble floor as Big Mama roars past a huge hanging model of the solar system. An instant later—

SLAM!

The Death Fossil crashes through it, sending planets flying. Earth tumbles past us, then slams into a pillar and shatters.

"Nice symbolism," Quint remarks as we whip around a corner.

Dirk drives faster—but still, the Death Fossil gains on us. "Jack, we got a wall ahead of us," he says. "Which way am I going?"

"ARGH!" Dirk roars. He whips the wheel. Big Mama nearly flips as Dirk forces the vehicle into a last-second turn down another dark hall.

The unintentional fake-out tricks the Death Fossil and we hear bone skid against marble as it tries to slow down. Glancing back, I see—

KA-KRAMM!

The monster slams, headlong, into a wall of solid concrete. Bones explode. But we all know that will only slow the beast—not stop it.

Big Mama's wheels crash back to the floor, and the screeching tires echo like screams.

A long corridor stretches out in front of us. It's as dark as the rest of the museum, but my eyes are adjusting now. "Guys," I whisper. "I think there's something up ahead."

"STOP!" Quint cries, suddenly thrusting his arm past me, yanking the emergency brake. We are instantly flung forward—the seat belt against my chest feels like someone is smashing a two-by-four. The foul smell of burnt rubber fills the air as Dirk flips on the high beams.

"Oh yay," I grumble as the lights flash across hundreds of skinless faces. "More dead stuff . . ."

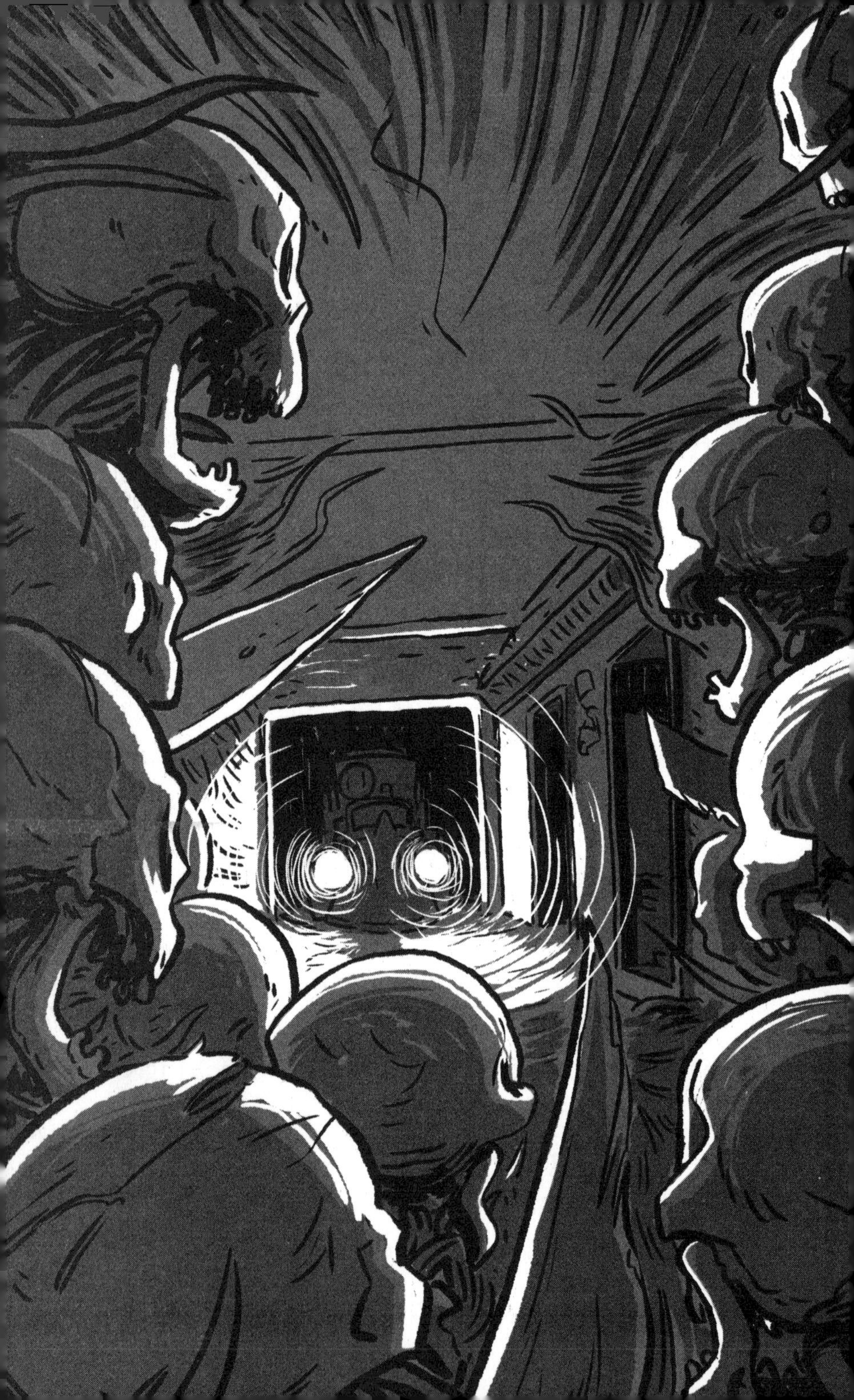

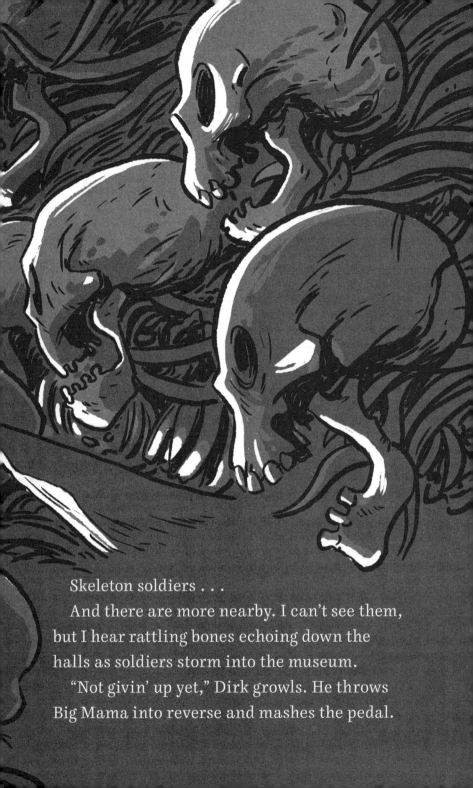

Skeleton soldiers . . .

And there are more nearby. I can't see them,
but I hear rattling bones echoing down the
halls as soldiers storm into the museum.

"Not givin' up yet," Dirk growls. He throws
Big Mama into reverse and mashes the pedal.

"Seat belts, gang!" June orders.
And just in time.
The Death Fossil has reassembled,
and its tail is smashing into us like a
wrecking ball.

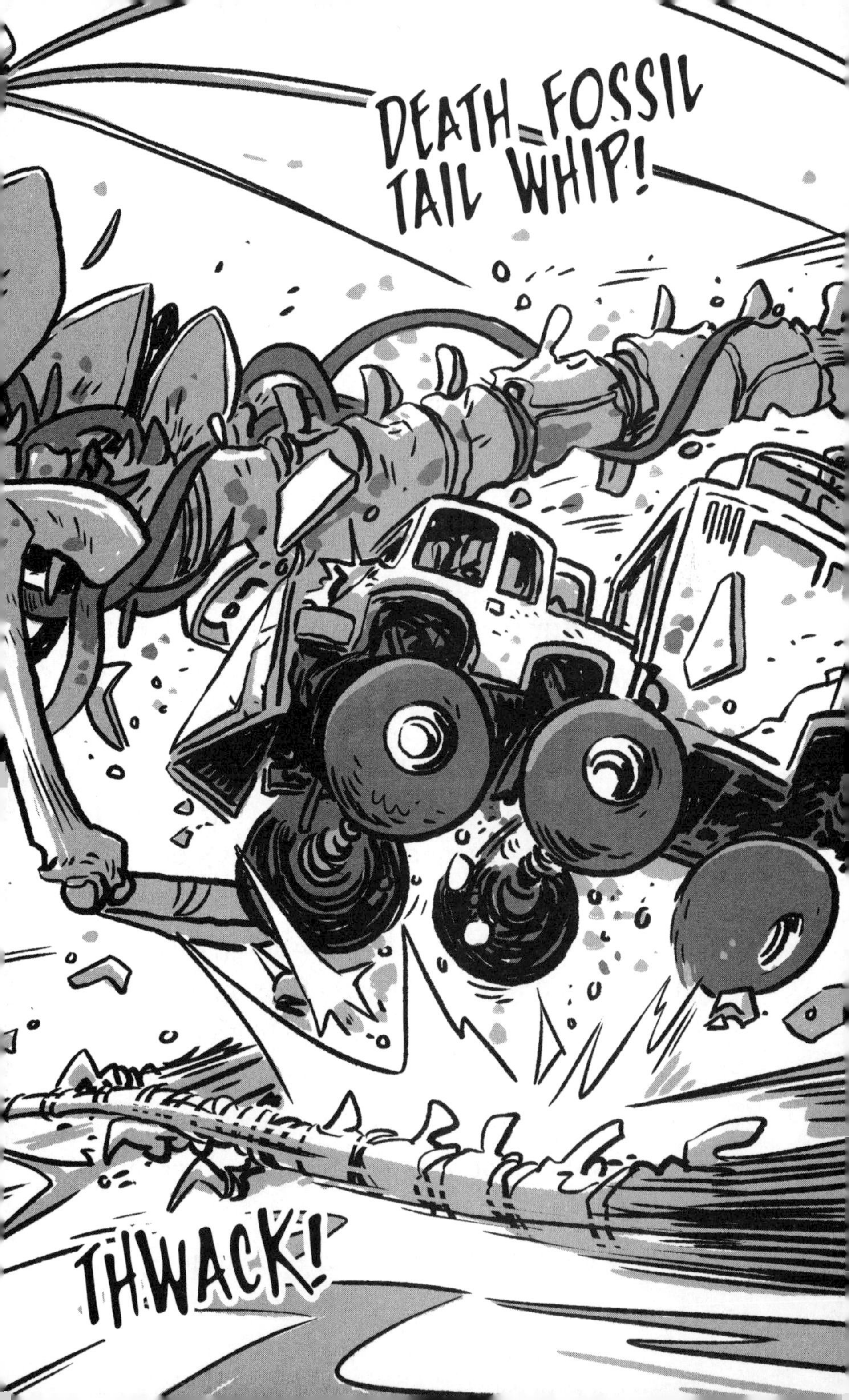
DEATH FOSSIL TAIL WHIP!
THWACK!

Big Mama pinwheels through the air, then crashes, wheels-down, with a horrible *KRUNCH*. Metal groans as we slide across the floor.

Inside Big Mama, it looks like we've gone zero gravity. I can barely tell which side is up. But when I glance out the window, I see it—

A set of double doors ahead, with an unilluminated EXIT sign above.

My heart speeds up but then quickly deflates.

Because there is zero chance Big Mama will be able to squeeze through them.

I catch a glimpse of the Death Fossil in our rearview, lumbering behind us. We seemed destined to fail.

The reality begins to set in, when—

"EVERYONE DOWN!" Dirk cries.

The Death Fossil's massive paw swings out, CRACKING Big Mama, sending us tumbling and then exploding through a huge hanging tarp.

An UNDER CONSTRUCTION sign flies up and ricochets off the windshield as we barrel through an archway. Part of the surrounding wall shatters. Stone pounds the ground as we skid across the floor of some new, dark, nearly empty wing of the museum.

There is a moment of strange, eerie quiet—

everyone is holding their breath. Then, through Big Mama's side mirrors, we watch the cracks in the walls splinter and grow until—

SMASH!!!

The archway collapses fully, sealing us inside.

Slowly, we pull ourselves from the wreckage. "Friends? Are we still alive?" Quint asks.

"Yep," June says. "Appears we are."

"But Big Mama's not," Dirk says. "She's down for the count."

Smoke drifts up from Big Mama's hood. I'm not, like, a mechanic or anything, but I'm pretty sure that's a bad sign.

I hear my zombies in their trailer, groaning. I pry open the twisted metal door and let 'em out to roam. "You're OK, guys. Stretch your legs."

This huge hall is tinted in a soft blue. It's moonlight—looking up, I see the ceiling is actually a large glass dome. Through it, we can see the night sky and a flicker of stars. Not the worst view I've ever seen.

The hall is mostly bare: just some scaffolding, construction tools, and paint-splattered tarps.

Quint pats Big Mama solemnly. "This was a mistake from the start," he says, coughing from the dust and debris. "We should not have come."

He's not wrong, but this is clearly not the time to say *I told you so*.

"I saw the exit," I say. "And there's no way Big Mama would have been able to fit. Even if she wasn't a busted, smoking wreck—we wouldn't have made it."

No one responds.

We're too busy listening to the gathering skeleton army at the caved-in wall. They're trying to get in—pounding and clawing.

Now and then, the smaller thuds are punctuated by massive THUMPS from the Death Fossil. Each strike causes the hall to shake; bits of marble and plaster pound the floor like hail.

"How long until they make it in here, ya think?" June asks.

"A few hours, I'd guess," Quint says. "And when they do—all we have is this. . . ." He opens his palm, revealing a handful of Werbert's Ultra-Slime vials.

No one says anything.

It's not enough. We all know that.

I open my mouth to launch into some heroic speech—but I stop myself. Because I have nothing good to say.

And right now, I don't even have the heart to fake it. . . .

chapter twenty-one

Big Mama is dead.

And for some dumb reason, my brain can't stop imagining us holding a Big Mama funeral. I'd say some pretty moving stuff, for sure—have everyone reaching for their handkerchiefs. . . .

I laugh softly to myself—thinking about a funeral for a truck. But then I'm thinking about Bardle. And realizing the loss of Big Mama is our second loss in *way too short* a time.

As the skeletons and Death Fossil continue to pound away at the walls, Quint and June make their way toward the hanging tarps.

I hop up on Big Mama's hood and lie back. Hands behind my head, I look up at the night sky through the glass dome. Dirk joins me.

"It's a pretty moon tonight," I say. Then, solemnly: "You think we'll live to see it again?"

Dirk's silent. Until suddenly, he sits up. "Wait a sec . . ." he starts. "That's no moon."

"Huh?" I ask.

Dirk doesn't respond—he's busy scrambling up onto Big Mama's roof. "Hey, don't go being all *Tomb Raider*-y without me!" I say, following him. Behind us, I hear Quint say something like, "Hey, June—have a look at this. . . ."

I don't look back to see what they're doing—I'm way too curious about Dirk's "that's no moon" comment. The little bit of extra height makes all the difference: I squint, and—wow. Dirk's right.

It's not the moon. It's something else entirely. It's something *good*.

Something *right*.

Something that feels like *hope*, like a *chance*.

"It's the World's Largest Donut Hole!" I exclaim. "What Werbert called 'The Big Round Sweet Treat'!"

"You bet it is!" Dirk says. "And it's close! So much closer than I thought!"

Suddenly, Dirk is laughing. He's hysterical. Laughing so hard he has to sit down.

"You finally losing it, buddy?" I ask. "What's so funny?"

"The Donut Hole," he says. "It's SO dumb. A plastic ball on a stick. But . . . I never would have gotten to see it without you guys. . . ."

"That's not true," I say. "You and your dad would have gone. Eventually."

Dirk shakes his head. The look on his face gives me déjà vu; it reminds me of when I found him in the tree house, after he was bitten by Evie's zombie.

"What is it, dude?" I ask.

"We wouldn't have gone," he says finally. "He was never going to take me. It was just another lie. Empty promise. Like all the others. Y'know?"

I don't respond. Because I don't "know"—not really. And what Dirk's saying is too big and too heavy for me to just agree. So I stay silent.

Dirk continues. "He didn't test poison for the army. He wasn't the Big Dagger on *Universal Warriors*—not *really*. He was a *reserve*; got on TV one time. He wasn't on the Pittsburgh Steelers practice squad. He didn't catch a great white shark with a speargun two different times. All lies. And I *always knew* they were lies."

"I don't understand," I say. "If you knew—"

"'Cause I *wanted* to believe them—because if he wasn't lying about *that*, then maybe he wasn't lying about a million other things. Like, well, doing our road trip someday."

I nod. Even though I never had a real dad, I get what Dirk's saying. And all this talk of dads and donut holes has me remembering Bardle. I think Dirk can tell.

"I wish your dad could have seen it," I say.

Dirk lightly kicks my sneaker. "Bardle, too."

"*Ah-ahem!*" June fake coughs. Poorly.

Dirk and I look up. June's next to Quint, who's peeking out from under a tarp that covers the entrance to another hall.

"Uh, did you hear all of that?" Dirk asks.

"Indeed," Quint says.

"And we love you, ya big lug head," June adds.

Dirk smiles. It's sweet but awkward—like eating a Charleston Chew in the dentist's chair.

Quint, being Quint, ends the silence. "Anyone want to see a few hundred ancient swords?"

"Um, yes, please," I say, leaping down from
Big Mama.
And moments later . . .

"I remember why my dad had this museum on the map!" he says. "Now, where is it . . . ?"

Dirk runs off, searching the glass cases. I just stare, mouth open, at hundreds of axes, maces, shields, lances, and more.

"Found it!" Dirk exclaims as he bursts in from the next room. He's swinging a sword.

"Whatcha got there, bud?" I ask.

The World's Biggest Dagger! It was supposedly used by the famed knight Sir Odrick the Orange to behead—

"Question," June says, holding up a finger. "Isn't a big dagger just, like, a small sword?"

"No! Well. I mean, yeah, I guess. But 'World's Smallest Sword' sounds lame. 'World's Biggest Dagger' sounds rad. That's why we were gonna come here—to see this, since my dad was the Big Dagger on *Universal Warriors*! Yeah, he was a backup—but that's still pretty cool."

Dirk turns the gleaming sword over in his hands, eyeing it with wonder. He looks up. "Remember when I said I needed a special weapon like you guys have?" Dirk asks. "I was thinking chain saw—but this is way better than a chain saw! I'm gonna call it . . . the Dagger. For my dad."

"Good name," Quint says. "Not particularly creative, but a good name."

As someone who's had their own trusty blade through the apocalypse, I feel nothing but pure joy for Dirk; I'm glad he finally found his.

But our warm, fuzzy moment is interrupted—

THUMP-THUMP-KA-KRASH!!!!

The Death Fossil pounding at the entrance to this wing. And the skeletons clawing and pulling at the rubble. From the sound of it, they're making progress.

"Big Mama," I say. "We'll use Big Mama. I know she's shot, but it won't matter. Not for what I'm thinking . . ."

"What do you have in mind?" Quint asks.

"Well, when Bardle died, Warg took his body," I explain. "I never got to say a proper good-bye. Never got to see him for real, one last time. But now, since we all know Big Mama isn't making it out of this museum, I want to send her off how *we* want her to go."

"I like that very much," Quint says. Everyone else nods their agreement. So I set the plan in motion.

"June, Dirk," I say, "wheel that giant crossbow into the main room. Quint, grab as many swords, axes, and spears as you can. My zombies and I will handle the rest."

With a swing of the Slicer, my Zombie Squad steps to attention. I concentrate—inside my head, telling them what they need to do—then I swing the blade again. They get to work. . . .

The once-muffled sound of bones scratching and clicking is now becoming crisper and clearer as the skeletons force their way through the barricade of rubble.

And that's OK.
'Cause we're ready for 'em—

This is our Hail Mary. Our three-pointer at the buzzer. And some other reference I'd make right now if I knew anything about sports.

We wait as the debris and chunks of wall break apart, revealing a small opening in the entryway.

Here they come.

First, it's just one skeleton ripping toward us.

Then more. And more.

Soon, the others follow, bursting through the rubble in a cluster of bone and vines.

It's go time.

"NOW!" I shout, waving my Slicer.

Right on command, Lefty, Glurm, and Alfred release the huge siege crossbow, and there is the loudest *FLING* sound anyone ever heard.

Big Mama hurtles forward at top speed. Equipped with an unreasonable number of Ultra-Slime-dipped jousting poles, she plows through every skeleton soldier in her path, until colliding head-on with the Death Fossil in a wicked *CRASH*.

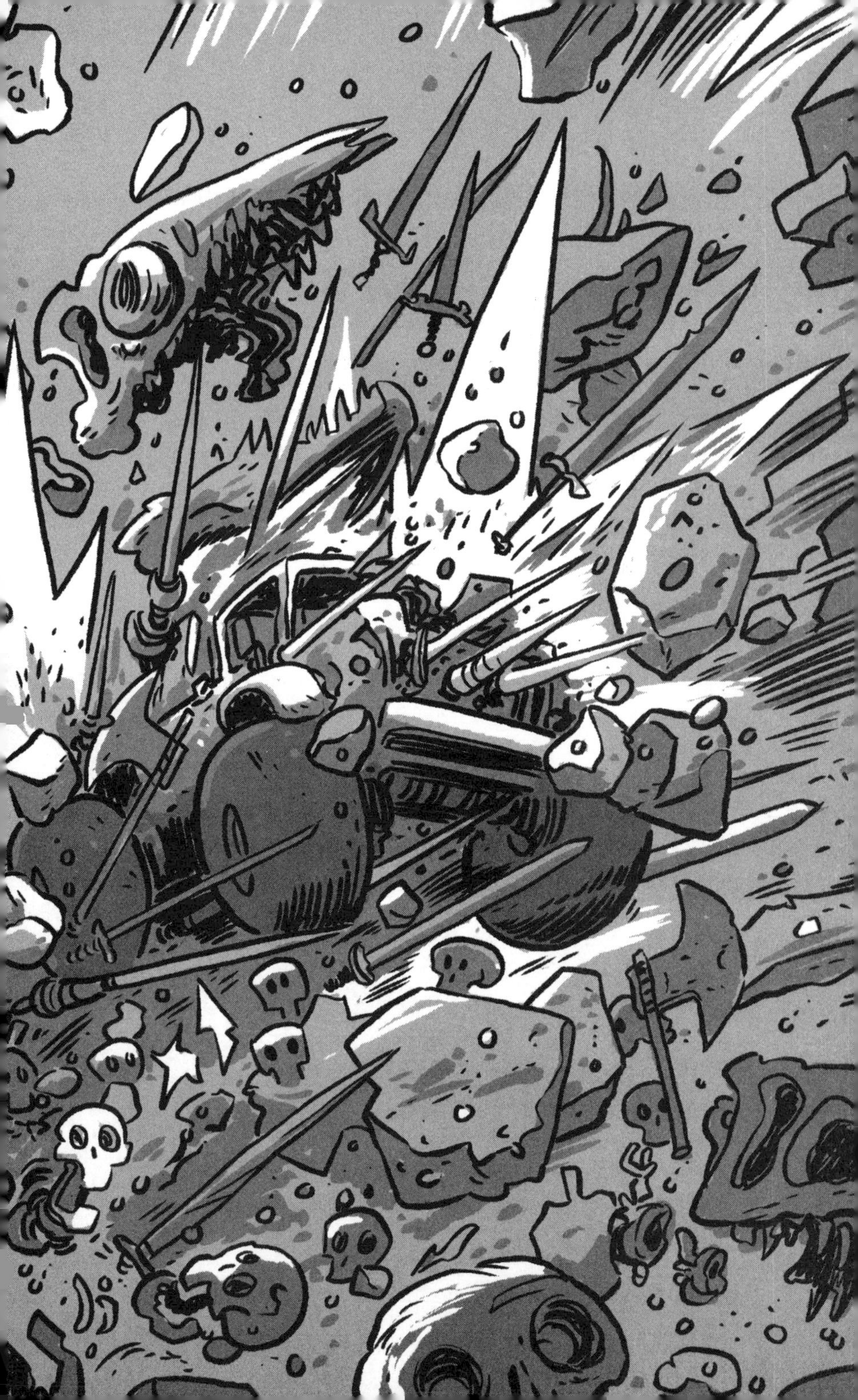

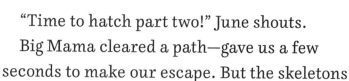

"Time to hatch part two!" June shouts.

Big Mama cleared a path—gave us a few seconds to make our escape. But the skeletons are quickly reassembling. We gotta move.

We hustle into our newly modified BoomKarts. Glurm rides with Quint, and Lefty with June, while Dirk rides solo—unless you count the Dagger at his side. Alfred drives me, because what's the point of having a zombie butler if you're not gonna get driven around like a B-list celebrity?

Seconds later—

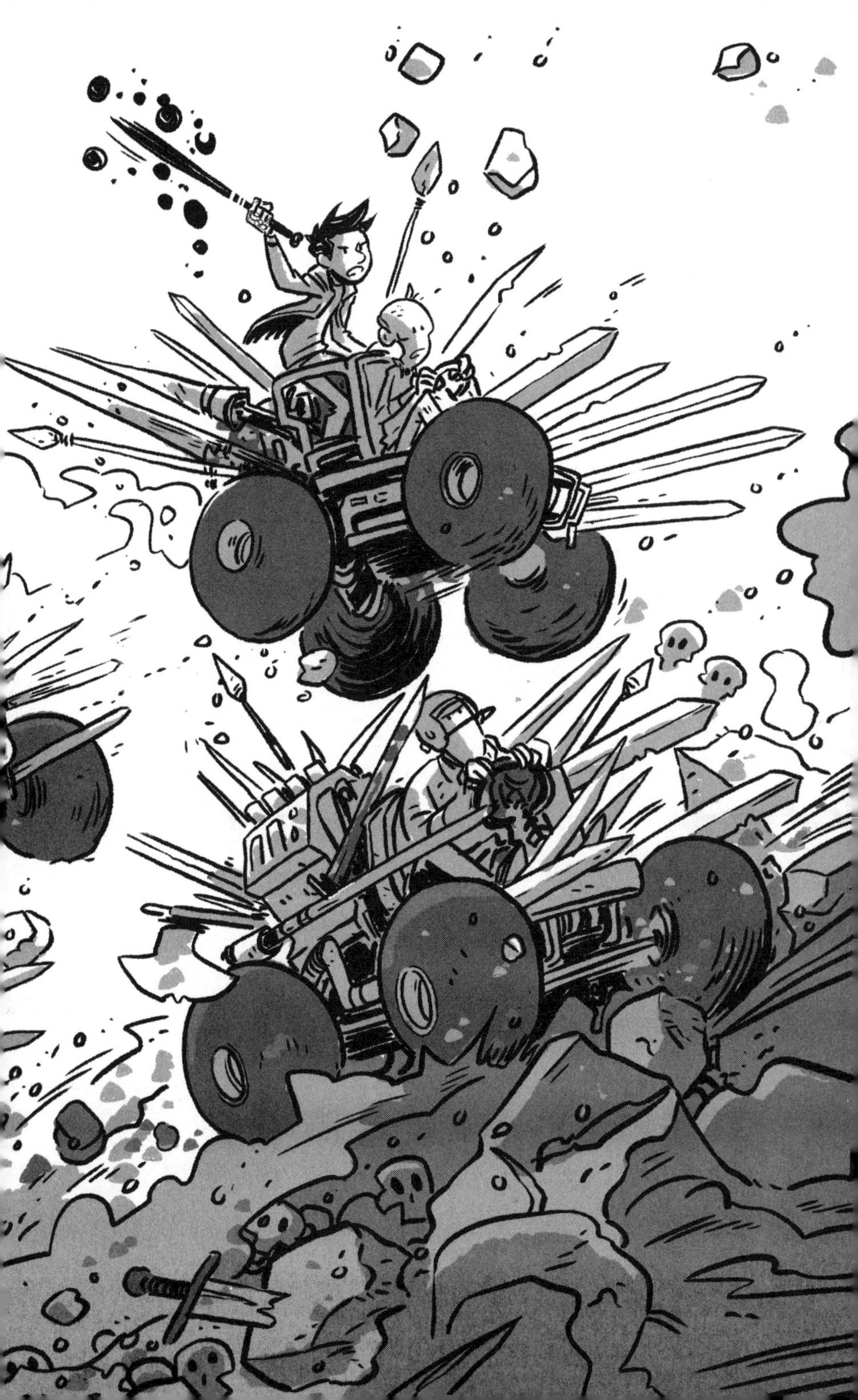

We burst out of the Arms and Armor wing, never slowing down—speeding through the museum while the skeletons swarm Big Mama. The pointy, slime-covered tips of our many weapons make this daredevil plan feel much safer than it is.

"Nice driving, Alfred!" I shout, straining to be heard over the roar of the engines and the rattling and clanging of centuries-old weaponry.

I hear the screech of metal twisting. Wood cracks. Glass shatters. I glance back: skeletons are ripping apart the wreckage.

Our new and improved BoomKarts are pretty rad, but it hurts to leave Big Mama behind. It hurts to watch Thrull's army rip her apart.

And I feel like I'm being ripped apart from the inside right along with her. But that was a pretty cool send-off for her—way better than a regular funeral. . . .

The exit doors—the ones Big Mama couldn't fit through—loom ahead. We make it outside into the museum parking lot, where a small platoon of skeleton soldiers awaits us.

But we were prepared for this. That's why we have a four-step plan. What are we, amateurs?

Our modified BoomKarts, covered in Ultra-Slime-soaked medieval weapons, explode through the lines of Thrull's skeleton army.

We swing left toward the World's Largest Donut Hole, whipping through a few straggling skeleton soldiers.

The soldiers are quick, but not BoomKart-quick. So even when I look back and see Thrull's army pouring out of the museum after us, I know we can outrun them to whatever lies beyond the Donut Hole.

Up close, the World's Largest Donut Hole looks even dumber than it did from afar. Kinda like most of the apocalyptic road trip attractions, I guess.

Perched on the back of the BoomKart, I have the best view of what's in pursuit: the entire skeleton army.

"That's it!" June yells as we speed past the Donut Hole. "The Great Wet Village!"

"Has to be!" Dirk cries.

I spin around to see what's up ahead.

It's a sign for Aqua City. The water park.

And it hits me. Water park. Great Wet Village. This is the place where we will either find the Ultra-Slime we need to stop Thrull *or* meet our untimely demise at the hands of a whole lotta skeletons.

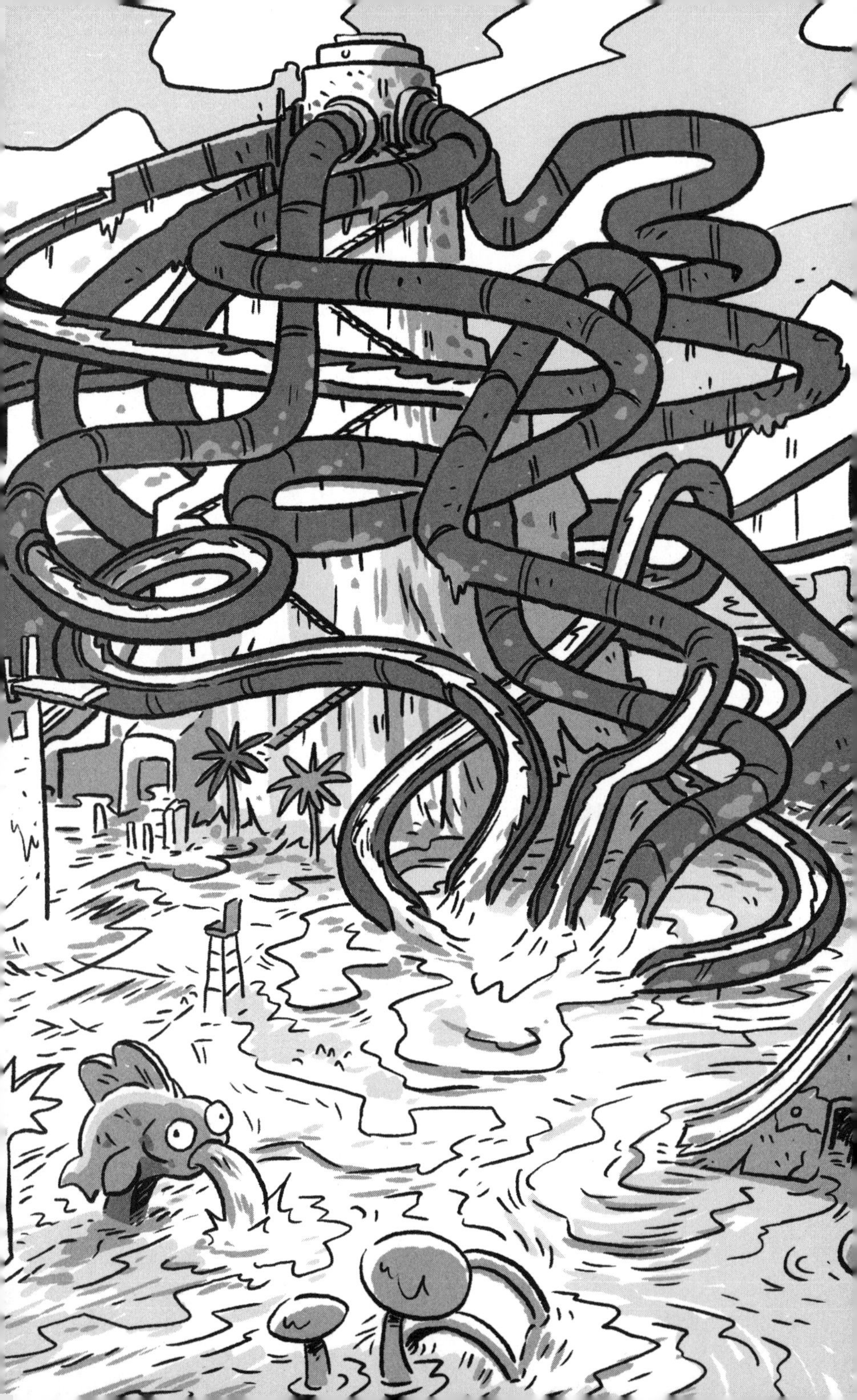

chapter
twenty-two

Aqua City is *massive*.

It's, like, truly a *city*: a city of wave pools, waterslides, log flumes, and lazy rivers.

As we enter the park, we discover the slides are glowing green. The whole place is *covered* in the all-natural vine-killing substance we now refer to as Ultra-Slime. Not just covered— the place is half-sunk. In some spots, I bet it's deeper than ol' Blargus.

The green goo is flowing down the slides, running through the wading pools, spilling across walkways, dripping from the snack shacks—it's EVERYWHERE.

"Werbert wasn't kidding," I say. "There's *a lot* of Ultra-Slime here."

"That's good news!" June chirps. "The skeleton army can't follow us. They touch that slime, and . . ." June makes a *sizzle* sound.

"But bad news, too," Dirk adds. "The

BoomKarts. We'll have to leave 'em here."

"Perhaps not . . ." Quint says. He's stepping out of his BoomKart and eyeing our surroundings. He scoops up a handful of slime—and, after watching it slowly drip through his fingers, announces: "I have a solution!"

Then, looking back in the direction of the skeleton soldiers: "But we will need to work quickly."

And we do.

We finish just as the skeletons are streaming into the park. Dozens of mindless bone-baddies climb over turnstiles, scramble across awnings, and squeeze through rusted fences.

"Gotta hurry, gang," I say.

"Ready!" Quint calls out.

I grin, impressed. Our BoomKarts are now rafts—each one mounted atop one of the inflatable donut floaties used for the lazy river. My zombies retrieve four shovels from a nearby supply shed, to be used like paddles.

"Push 'em!" Dirk says, and we each shove our rafts down into the slime. We leap on, just seconds before the army reaches us. Thousands of skeletons come to a sudden sliding, skidding halt—so sharp and fast that I can almost hear their bones screeching against the asphalt. The point where the Ultra-Slime washes up on the walkway is like the shore of a beach—and they can't go in.

The skeletons in the rear don't get the message right away, and they slam into the mass, sending the front line of skeletons tumbling into the slime. Even as they sink and sizzle, the slime-soaked skeletons are reaching for us, bone-fingers clawing.

But they've lost—for the moment. . . .

See ya!

Soon, we're floating down a lazy river of Ultra-Slime, deeper into Aqua City.

"So how do we find this slime-secreting creature thing, anyway?" Dirk asks.

"Good question," June says. "Like, *where* is all this slime coming from?"

Just then, we turn the corner—and we see it: the Double Trouble Dynamo waterslide—the biggest waterslide in the world. Slime pours down it.

"It's coming from there," I say. "No question. Now kick up your feet, and let the lazy river take us there. . . ."

After all, this makeshift lazy river is our best mode of transport, and at the moment, it's only going one way. Besides, with the skeleton army unable to follow, we've got time—*for once.*

Our rafts drift slowly through Aqua City's main drag. The place is less like a water park and more like a full-blown metropolis—a metropolis that was abandoned and left to rot. Every single day, this place was filled with thousands of families, slipping and sliding and soaking up sun.

Now it looks like a neon-green nightmare.

We pass entrances to cracked, dented slides. Snack shops filled with melted ice pops and rotten hot dogs. Gift shops with broken windows and caved-in roofs. Plush sharks—Aqua City's goofy mascot—float upside down in the slime.

As we float downriver, I notice that one of the snack shacks has been ripped from the ground and now lies on its side. There are jagged holes in the shack's roof, each the size of a manhole cover.

Even though the rest of the place is in shambles, *that* is different. Like it was done intentionally. Trying to lighten the mood, I say, "Hey, um. Question. Is it true that some pools have a special chemical in them that'll turn the water around you a bright red color if you pee in them?"

Dirk says, "One hundred percent true," at the exact same moment June says, "Absolutely not."

Quint just chuckles. "That urban legend is older than Ṛeżżőch. . . ."

Suddenly, the river curves, and we pick up speed. Behind me, I hear Alfred groan. I wonder if zombies get that stomach-flip feeling when they go down a steep dip or if that's just us living folks.

"Hang on!" Dirk shouts as the slime river drops,

carrying us around a collapsed waterslide. Our
BoomKart rafts are spit out
onto a concrete walkway.

And we're there. At the base of the biggest
waterslide in the world: Double Trouble
Dynamo. We're all stunned into silence as
we stare up at the towering behemoth.

"It, uh . . . it looks bigger up close," Dirk says. He has to shout, because the sound of Ultra-Slime rushing out of the slide is as loud as a thunderstorm. It gushes out onto the cement, splashing rusted beach chairs and tattered towels.

"Welp," I say, "who's ready for a climb?"

"We got this!" June says, bounding up the first landing two steps at a time.

"Dirk's gonna carry me!" Quint says hopefully. "Knapsack style."

"No," Dirk replies as he begins the climb. "No, I'm not."

Quint grumbles with disappointment as he follows.

I turn to my squad. Alfred is staring at me. Glurm's trying to smack a fly that's landed on his nose. Lefty is very slowly sliding backward on the slippery goo.

"You guys are gonna stay down here. You can just, um, well . . ." I trail off as I look around at the post-apocalyptic neon-green wasteland. "Tidy up or something."

Then I begin the climb.

Approximately 257,983 stairs later, I'm about to keel over. Or barf. Or both.

"HEY! Keep it moving!" June barks.

I manage to summon enough energy to lift my head. June's one flight ahead of us, staring down like a disappointed drill sergeant. "Stairs won't stop Ŗeżżőch or Thrull," she says. "So we can't let them stop us, either."

Point taken.

I continue the climb.

———

The sun is high when we finally reach the thirty-ninth level: just one level shy of the top.

We all sag weakly against the railing. This high up, the only sound is our heavy breathing and the steady dripping of Ultra-Slime. It sloshes over the sides above us, splashing down in thick streams.

We eye the final corner uneasily, because it leads to the final flight of stairs—and the final flight of stairs leads to the deck. Whatever strange monster is up there is producing this stuff—putting out gallon upon gallon upon gallon of Ultra-Slime.

Will it be some sort of monstrous insect

with a bug-butt as big as a tanker truck?? Or a mammoth bear-beast that hordes slime like honey??

"So what's the plan?" Dirk finally asks.

No one responds.

Dirk's face is twisting up. "Are you telling me I just hiked up a freakin' mountain—with no plan for what we're gonna do when we got to the top?!"

"Maybe we should walk back down and talk it over," I say. "Then come back."

June elbows me. Hard. "Whatever's up there is making all this goo—so we're taking it with us. *That's* the plan. Real simple. Now c'mon. . . ."

June might sound confident, but she turns the corner slowly and climbs the final flight cautiously. I raise the Slicer and follow. Slime drips on Dirk's dagger, which he holds at his side. Quint's staff is in an "I'll poke you, man!" position.

We go up the stairs, onto the deck, ready for anything. And—

"There's nothin' here!" Dirk exclaims.

"Sure there is," Quint replies. "Slime. Plenty of it."

That's for sure. The deck is *huge*—big enough to launch a NASA rocket. And the slime is ankle-deep—and it remains that way, even as it continues to pour down all five slides.

Then, suddenly—June's hand shoots out. She grabs my arm, squeezing hard. "Look . . ." she whispers. She sounds like she just spotted a rare bird and doesn't want to scare it away. "I think it's coming from there. The chair . . ."

At the far end of the platform is a lifeguard chair. Ultra-Slime streams down its legs. I slowly wade through the slime until I have a view of the front. And June's right—in that chair sits a strange, *strange* little creature—*so* strange-looking that I can't help but—

"EEK!" I cry out.

Yep, I said "eek." Not proud of it. But not embarrassed, either. We all eek now and then; I've heard some people eek their way through their entire lives.

But my sudden "eek" surprises Quint, which so startles Dirk that he shrieks, causing June to shout, "IS IT AN AMBUSH?!" and spin around wildly, aiming Blasty.

Moments later, we've all scared each other so severely that we're hiding in the corner, cowering behind a pile of moldy floats. Causing Dirk to ask, "Why are we taking cover behind a pile of moldy floats?"

I wait for my heart rate to get somewhere close to normal before I answer: "Uh, sorry," I say. "That thingy there, in the chair—it gave me the heebie-jeebies. I dunno why. Like—"

"Why is it just sitting up here, all alone, looking tiny and weird?!" Quint asks.

"YES!" I say, relieved that Quint gets it. "EXACTLY YES!"

June peeks over the top. "You two and your heebie-jeebies aside—it *does* look like that thing is what's creating the slime."

Dirk peers around the side. "Whoa. It's, like, *melting* off its body. Like goo-sweat!"

"The term 'goo-sweat' is not helping my heebie-jeebies," I say. "I don't ever wanna hear the term 'goo-sweat' again, ya got that?"

The science of that, though—this tiny thing producing so much, pushes Quint past his fear. He looks. "It's true," he says after a moment. "It drips slime, steadily—yet it loses no mass. Fascinating . . ."

I glance at my friends. "Fascinating—and odd-looking."

"DON'T SAY THAT!" Dirk says, clapping his hands over my ears. "He might hear you."

"How is *you* putting *your* hands over *my* ears gonna make *him* not hear?"

"Listen up!" June says, sounding *very much* like she's ready to get on with this. "Here's what we do: we grab it, toss it in a BoomKart, speed off to find some Big Mama–style storage tanks, then start filling them up. Whaddya think?"

"Fine," I say.

"Sounds logical," Quint replies.

We all look to Dirk. No response. That's because he's busy making googly eyes at the thing. "He's so dang adorable!" Dirk squeals. "I just wanna squeeze him! And poke him! And tickle him! And bite him!"

"Hey, Captain Cute Aggression!" June barks. "Did you hear what I said?"

"Huh? Oh. Yeah, but . . . I dunno. We can't just *take him*. We gotta ask first."

"Ask??" June says incredulously. "Did you look at that thing? It's got, like, two brain cells."

"Hey!" I say, spinning around. "I just said he was odd-looking. I didn't insult his intelligence."

June groans. "I feel like I'm in an episode of *Twilight City*. . . . We need that thing TO SAVE OUR DIMENSION. OUR FAMILIES!"

"Here's the deal," Dirk says, standing and sheathing the Dagger. "I'm gonna go talk to him. And *invite* him along. *Invite*."

June grumbles. "Fine, but hurry!"

Slowly, trying not to startle it, Dirk approaches. Each slow step through the slime makes a slurping, goopy sound. "Uh, hey, little buddy," Dirk says. "Whatcha doin'?"

The little thing turns to look at Dirk.

A second lifeguard chair lies toppled over, in the slime. It's weather-beaten and damaged.

Dirk slowly picks it up, then sets it down across from the little goo-dude.

June rolls her eyes. "What is this, an interview? That's the same setup I had on the morning news update at school!"

It reminds me of something else: the sort of "Hey there, sport" thing I would get from foster dads over the years—the better ones. Grown-ups love getting all dramatic when they've gotta tell you something important—like they think they're auditioning for a TV show. Pulling up a chair, sitting on it just right. Or they'll sit on the end of the bed and say stuff like, "How ya feelin', captain?"

But Dirk looks half-natural as he settles into the worn chair—until it breaks, and his butt plunges through. Now he just looks absurd.

June makes a sound like maybe, just maybe, she will throw me down the nearest slide.

She sighs. "We don't have time for this."

"So . . ." Dirk says. He coughs. "Must get, ah—lonely up here. You want to come with us, lil' Drooler? We're saving the dimension."

Drooler responds with a burp.

"That's it," June says, standing. She's about to march over there when—

RRRRRUMBLE!

The sudden rumble is followed by a creaking that radiates through the entire slide structure—everything shudders and sways.

I gulp.

Then a series of THUNK noises—each one louder than the last. And with each THUNK, the entire structure jolts.

"The skeletons!" June says. "They've made it, somehow!"

"No," Quint says. "It's not them." Quint's been quiet—and I see it's because he's been watching the skeletons the entire time. "They're way down there, where we left them. Though they do seem to be up to something. . . ."

"Then what *was* that?" June asks.

I think about the huge holes I saw poked in spots throughout the park, and I grip the railing as—

THUNK!

THUNK! THUNK!

THUNK! THUNK! THUNK!

The deck shakes and trembles. Suddenly, a shadow passes overhead, blanketing us all. Something HUGE is descending onto the deck, surging up, blocking out the sun . . .

-GARGANTULAX!-

"Now *that*," I say. "*That* is more the size I was expecting."

The Gargantulax leans forward so its many eyes are fixed on Dirk. Dirk shifts back in his seat but holds his ground.

"We mean him no harm!" Dirk says. "We're the good guys! We just need his help. He's the key to defeating all evil!"

But the Gargantulax doesn't understand. It just hisses at him menacingly.

"Come on, Dirk, come on . . ." June says, growling through gritted teeth. Her fingers are digging into the old rafts so hard they're starting to tear. "Just grab the thing and let's scram."

"SKELETON UPDATE!" Quint calls. "They appear to be concocting a plan. Much movement."

I peer back toward the water park entrance. The size of the skeleton army, even at this distance, is overwhelming. "From this height," I say, "they look like ants."

"*Worker* ants," Quint corrects. "They are moving with a purpose."

But we can't worry about that now because—

HISSSS!

I turn back as the Gargantulax snarls and leans in, closer to Dirk.

"Jack, look!" Quint says. "Despite its size, its legs don't sink into the slime. It's just like—"

"Legolas!" I say. "Walking on the snow!"

Quint grins—then adds, "Also, quite similar to a water strider."

From the look of it, the thing is mere seconds from chomping Dirk's head off. "Dirk, come on!" June shouts. "Just grab it and run!"

"SKELETON UPDATE NUMBER TWO!"
Quint announces. "They appear to be building
something. But they *themselves* are the building
blocks. It's happening very quickly now."

This is feeling like one of Quint and Dirk's
super-serious Ping-Pong games, where they
make me referee—and I watch the ball go
back, forth, back, forth. But here I'm watching
skeletons, monster, skeletons, monster.

Noise at Aqua City's entrance now—so loud
we can hear it all the way up here. It's the
skeletons clambering on top of one another,
like one of those cheerleading pyramids. But
this one's made up of *thousands* of skeletons.

The Gargantulax hisses and its head swings in
our direction. It's watching us.

More than that—it's watching us *watch the
skeletons*. Like it's deciding who to destroy first.

The strange skeleton figure is now complete.
My eyes bulge, and cold terror washes over me
as understanding sets in. Together, the army has
formed one single massive skeleton assemblage.

"This is bad. . . ." Quint says softly.

"No," I say. "It's *worse* than bad. WAY worse."

Squinting, I see the final piece of the skeleton
figure: Blargus. . . .

Like the candle on the cake, the hideous
cherry on top, Blargus is the peak of this
mountain-sized monster. . . .

"Guys," I say. " Look who's back. AGAIN."

My friends see for themselves. The entire park
seems to shudder as the towering mass takes its
first colossal stride forward. . . .

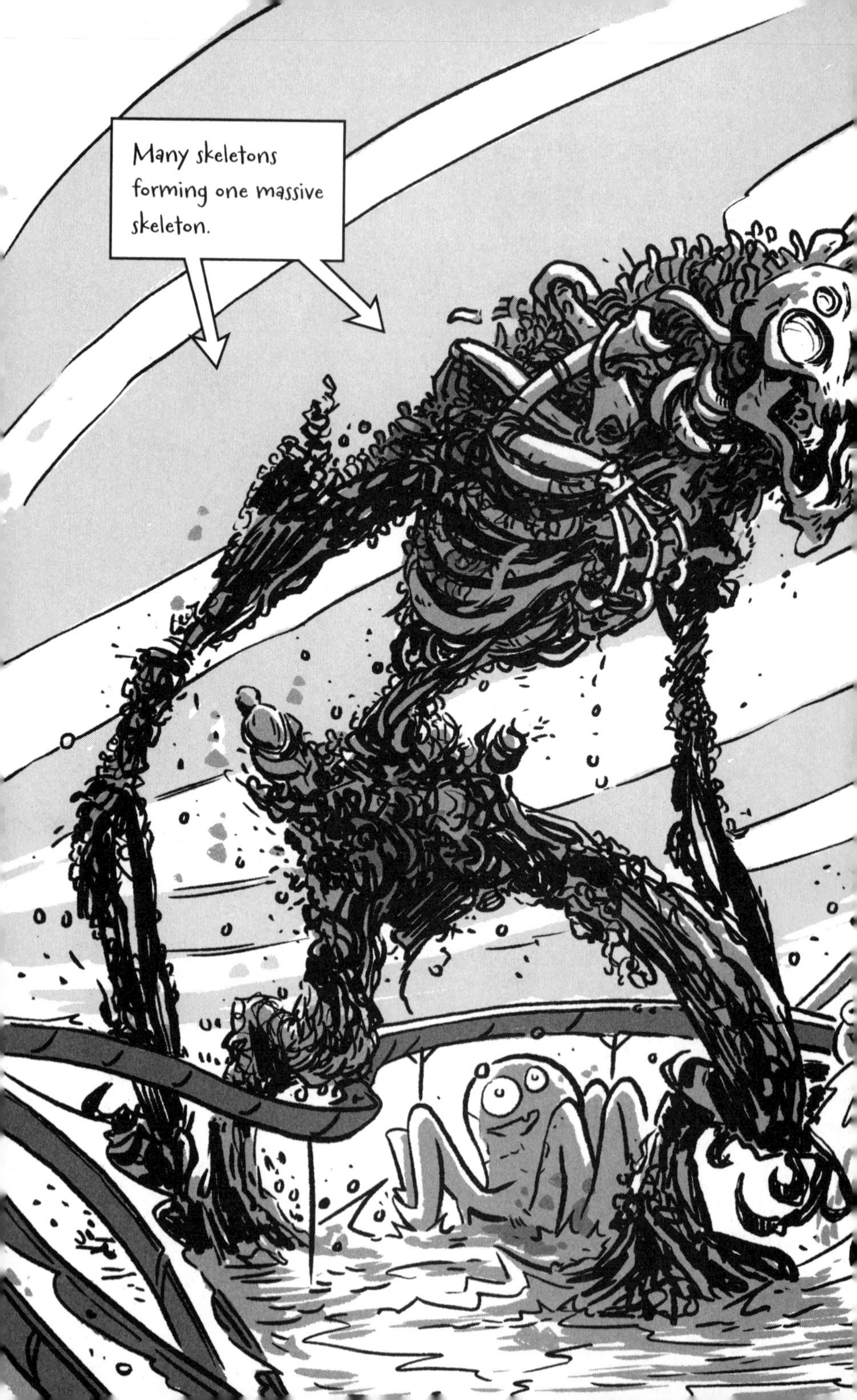
Many skeletons forming one massive skeleton.

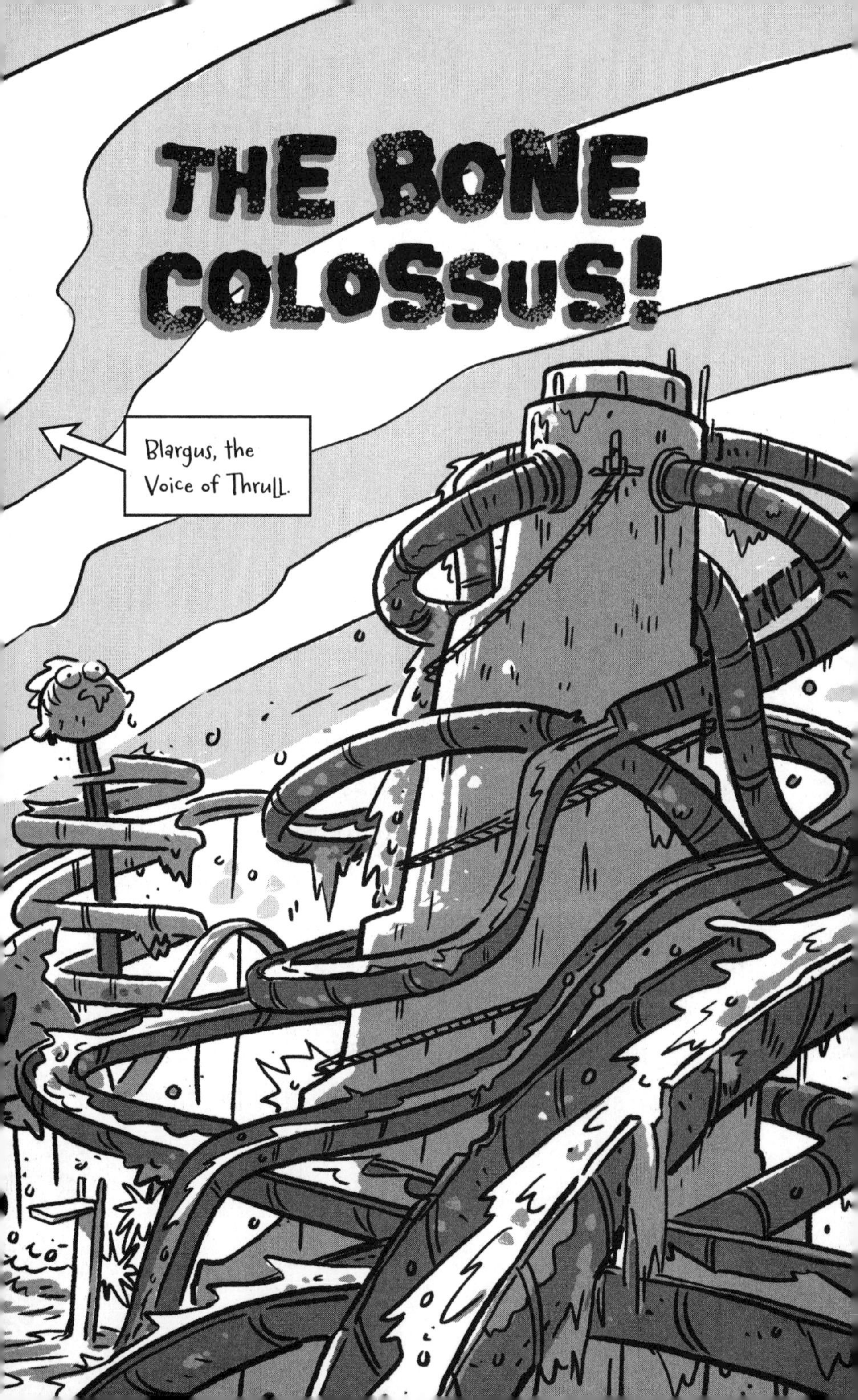
THE BONE COLOSSUS!
Blargus, the Voice of Thrull.

With each step, Ultra-Slime splashes, and part of the Colossus melts away. The Ultra-Slime dissolves the vines, destroying the skeletons who formed the bottom of the great monster's foot.

With the next step, the Bone Colossus's ankles begin liquefying. The sizzling sound echoes throughout the park.

But it only needs to make it to us—and each step carries it the length of a basketball court.

"Will it reach us, Quint?!" I ask. "Can it make it here and *still* be tall enough that the skeletons can reach us?"

Quint's eyeing everything, calculating the angles and dimensions in his head. "It's going to be close," he says. "It's going to be very close."

"I'm not waiting around to see what side of 'close' we're on!" June says. "I'm *saving* my parents one way or another!"

I see no fear on her face—just determination as she bursts out from behind the rafts.

In one swift motion, she lunges for Drooler. But Dirk slides out of the chair, blocking Drooler from June's grasp. "No!"

The Gargantulax roars.

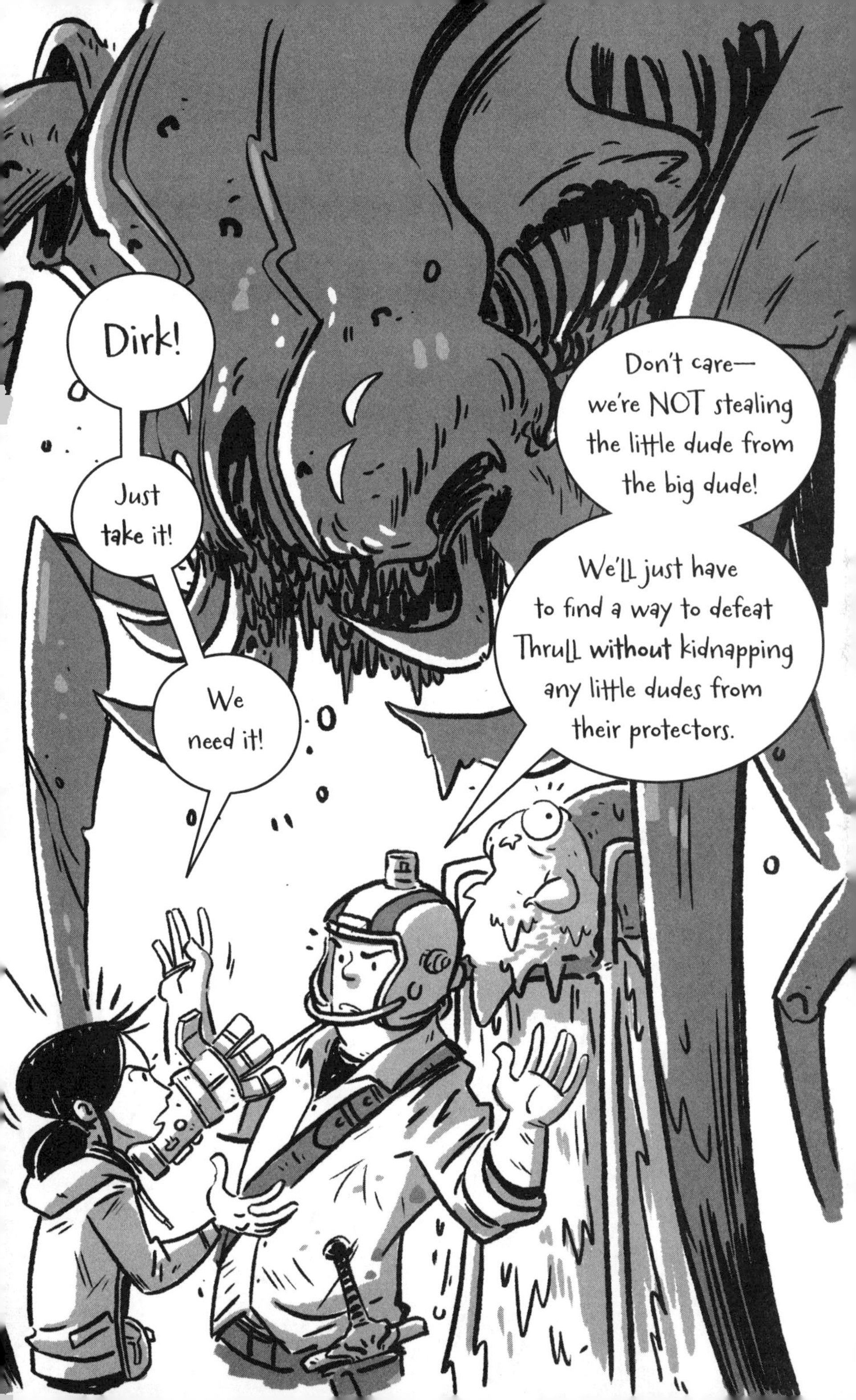
Dirk!
Just take it!
We need it!
Don't care—we're NOT stealing the little dude from the big dude!
We'LL just have to find a way to defeat ThruLL without kidnapping any little dudes from their protectors.

The Gargantulax looks at June and Dirk, then its massive head swings over to observe the Bone Colossus, then back toward June and Dirk. *It's connecting the dots*, I realize. *And unfortunately for us, it's connecting them all wrong.*

RAWRRR!

The monster's furious, wet howl knocks them back. Its mouth remains open. A single bite from its massive jaws could swallow Dirk and June whole.

"NO! We're not with the skeletons! We *hate* the skeletons!" Dirk cries out as he realizes. "We're on the home team!"

But the monster's mouth opens even wider. Dirk grabs Drooler, holding him out, trying to explain. But it's too late. . . .

chapter twenty-three

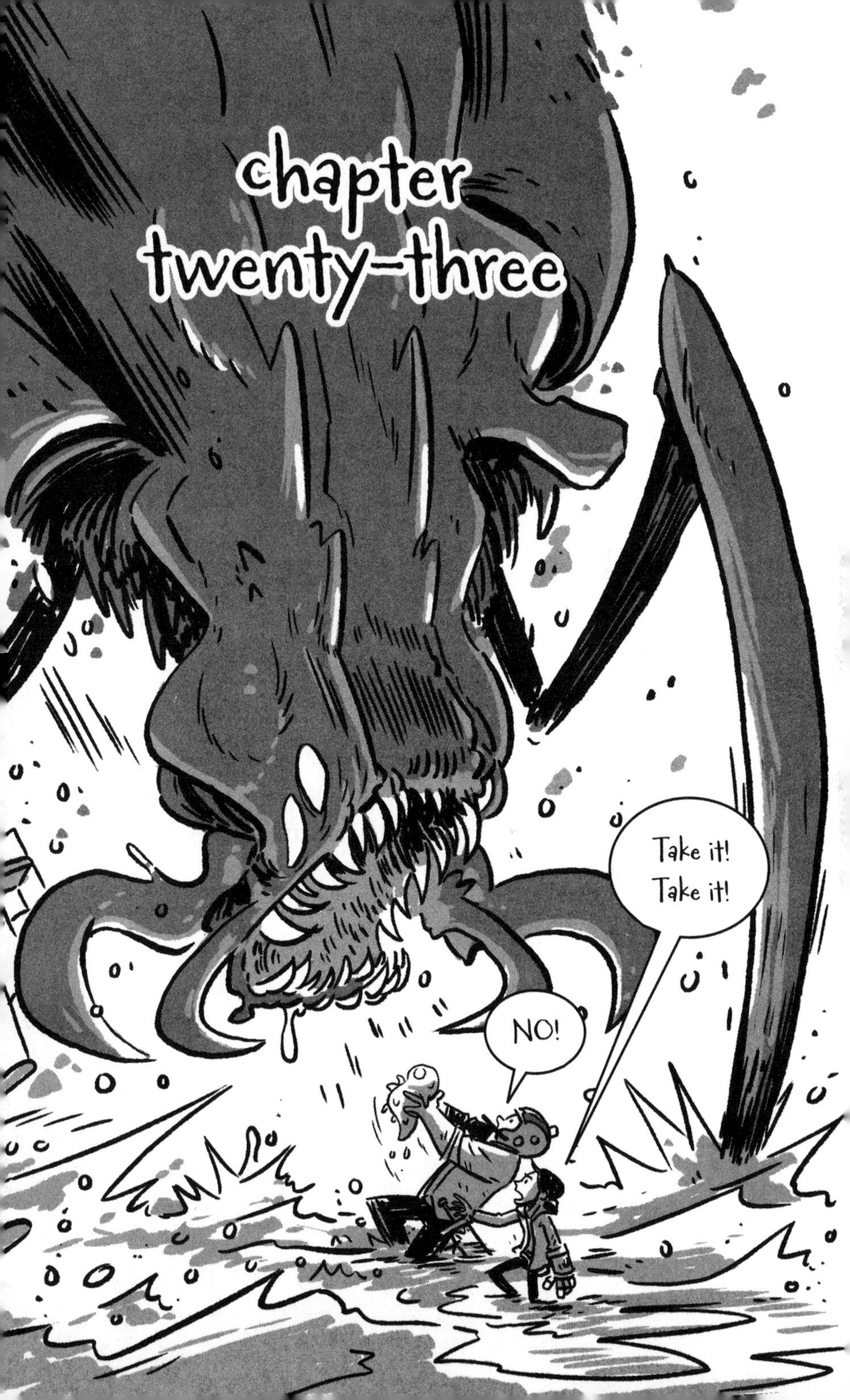
Take it!
Take it!
NO!

Dirk inches backward, still cradling Drooler. June has her non-Blasty arm on Dirk's wrist, stopping him from handing the creature to the looming Gargantulax.

"Guys!" I shout. "Behind you!"

They spin around, expecting danger.

"Sorry! I meant 'behind you' in a good way!"

"WHAT?" Dirk barks. But June sees what I see. The mouth of Double Trouble Dynamo: the slide is their only possible escape route.

I grip the Slicer tight, about to rush forward and slam it into the Gargantulax. It should be distraction enough to allow for a daring Dirk and June getaway.

But then there is an unmistakable roar, so loud that it rattles my bones. A screech so awful that it twists my insides: *Thrull*.

I whirl around. Thrull's roar comes from the mouth of Blargus, atop the Bone Colossus— and they are nearly upon us. . . .

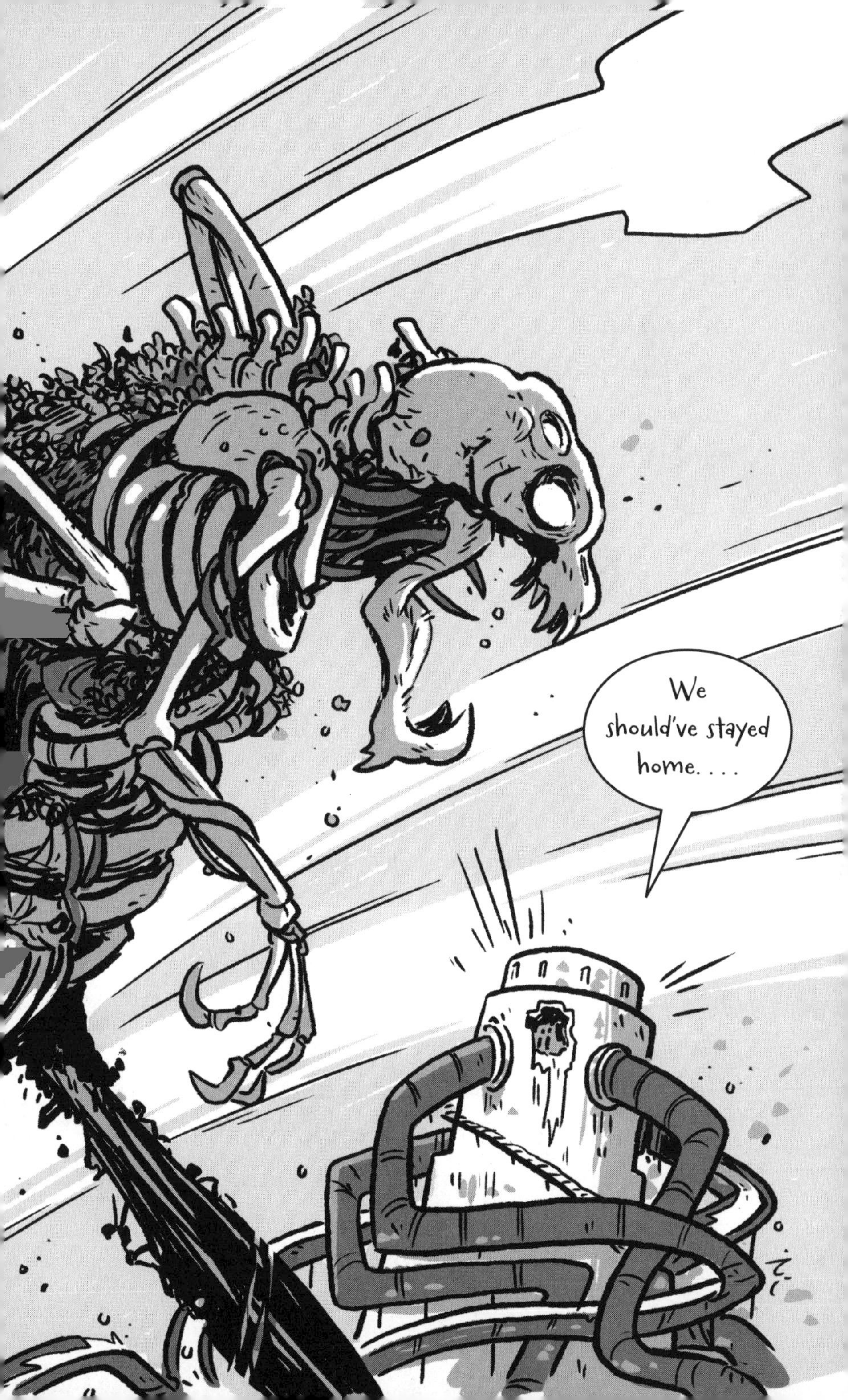
We should've stayed home. . . .

With the next step, skeletons begin leaping off—hurling themselves toward the slide's deck. They're like rats abandoning a sinking ship—only they *are* the ship. Many of them miss, smacking into the railing or the stairs and then falling. Others land on the deck but quickly collapse as the Ultra-Slime melts their vines.

But they keep coming, tumbling lifeless to the deck and sinking into the slime. More and more follow, until the deck is carpeted in bone.

"Uh-oh," I say as I realize what they're doing.

"Yep," Quint says. "Next wave will be able to march right over the backs of their bone-buddies."

More fling off the pyramid. This wave marches directly across the backs of their fallen comrades.

"Up and at 'em, guys!" I shout. "We got company!" I swing the Slicer, and the nearest skeleton dunks into the Ultra-Slime like a fry in a milk shake. Quint snaps his staff out—two skeleton soldiers drop to their knee bones. The air soon reeks of burning plant.

"DIRK! JUNE!" I holler. "WE GOTTA GO BEFORE IT'S TOO LATE!"

Then I hear it—and I realize it may be too late already. It's Thrull, whispering my name: *"Jaaaaaaaack . . ."*

I spin around. Blargus's massive, spindly hand is there, reaching for the railing. Skeletons sprint along his wrist, then bound onto the deck. But they stream past Quint and me. "They're trying to kill Drooler!" Quint says, but I barely hear him.

Blargus's bony hand opens.

He reaches for me.

I watch the swirling vines behind his eye sockets tighten, forming two gnarled neon globes. They almost seem to exhibit life, flickering with something like triumph.

Our eyes are locked for a sustained, seemingly endless second—and then those same eyes flash with surprise.

And then fury.

His bone-fingertips scrape the railing. Wood cracks. Splinters fill the air and splash the slimy ground.

He didn't make it. . . .

He won't reach us. . . .

He's falling, falling, falling. . . .

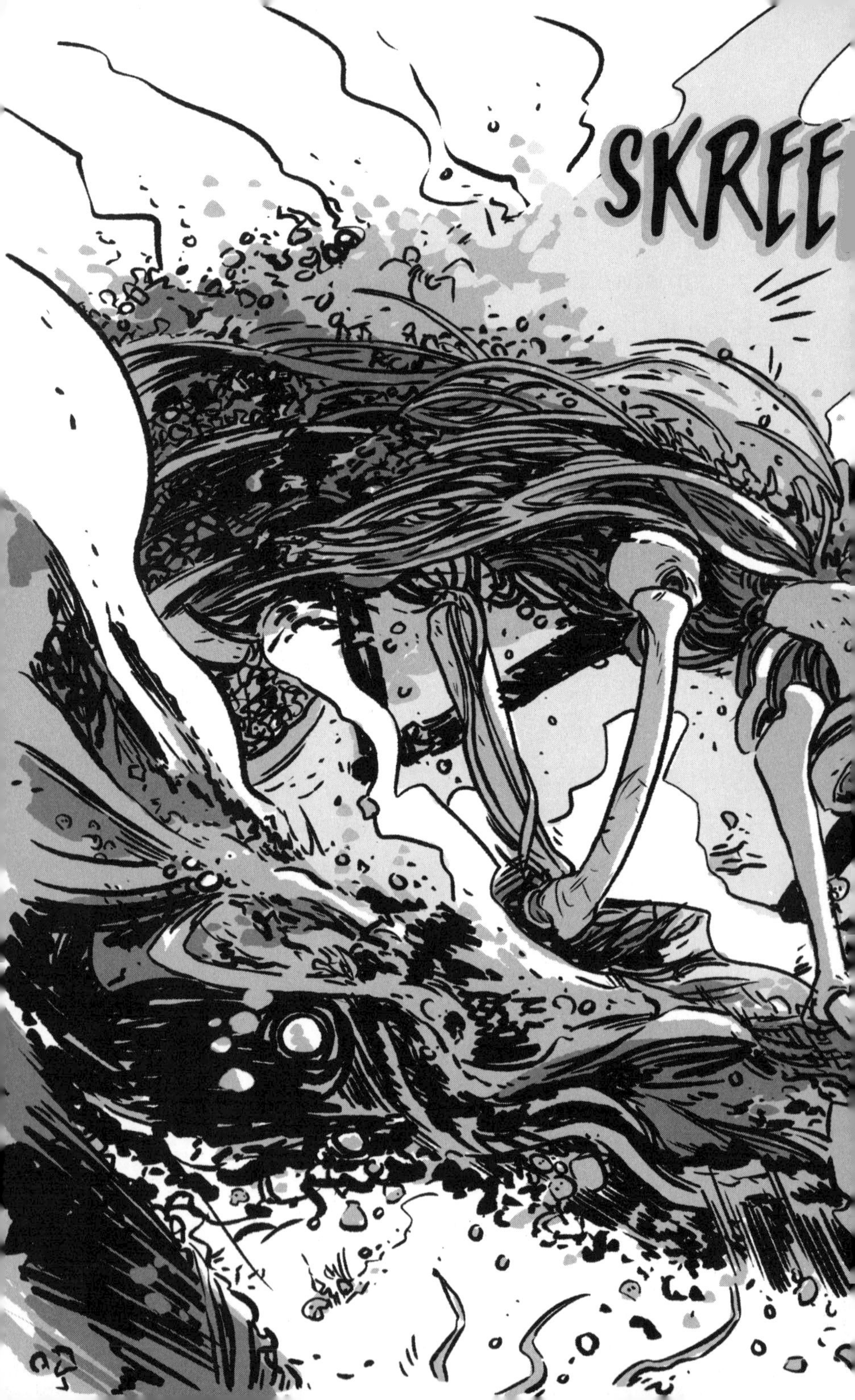
SKREE

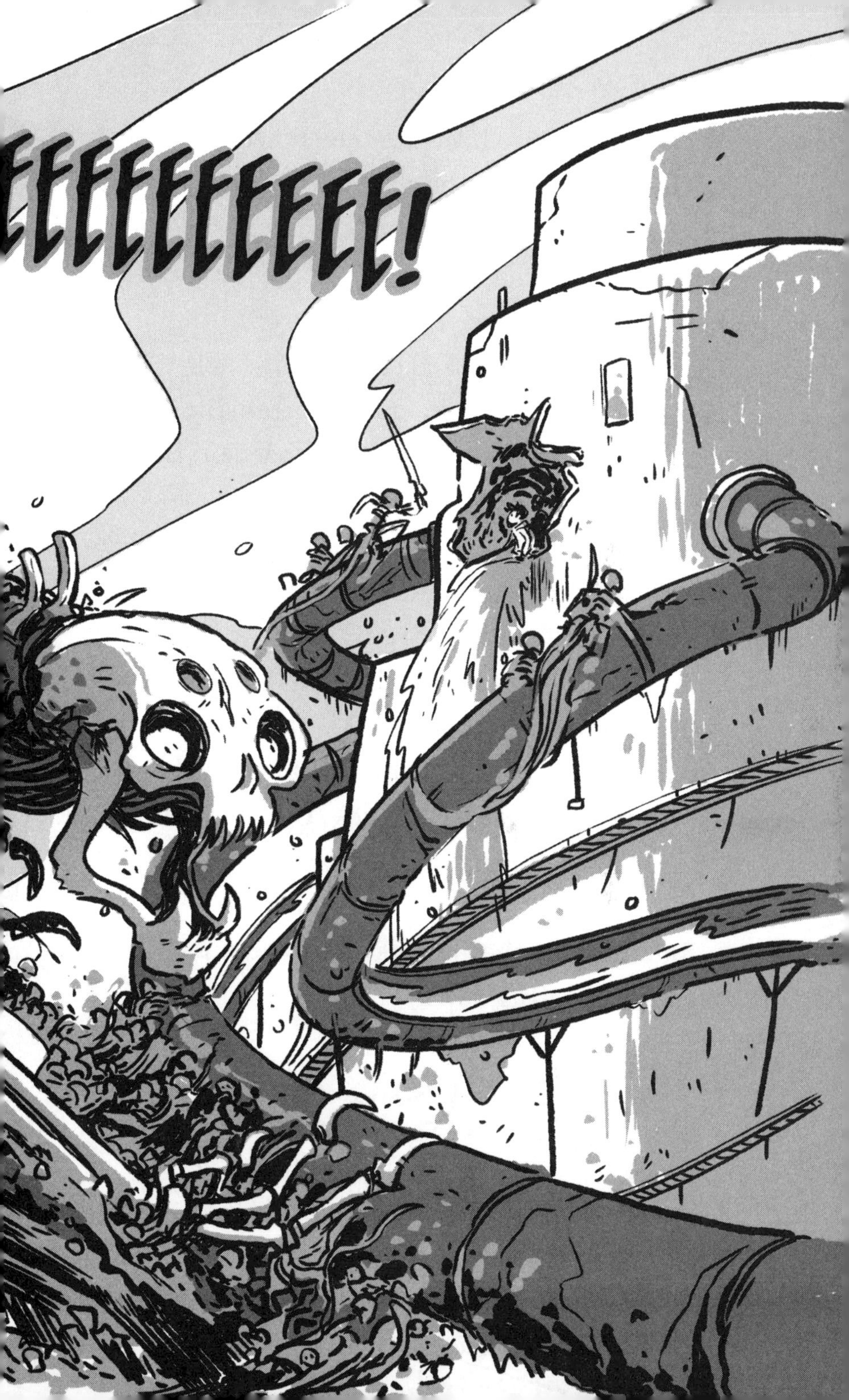
EEEEEEEEEE!

I don't get to see him plummet down. Don't get to see him splash into the slime. Because the clang of steel clashing against bone spins me around.

Dirk swings the Dagger, deflecting blow after blow from skeletons—all the while cradling Drooler. June is knocked back, back, back—then finally unleashes a furious boom from Blasty's barrel: a dozen skeletons are exploded off the deck.

Meanwhile, the Gargantulax is in the corner, frozen—the monster must now realize that we're no friend of Thrull, Blargus, or the army of bones. But it doesn't leap in to help us, either.

Most of the skeletons on the platform are going after Drooler. Thrull must know what he is, must fear what he can do—and now we've led Thrull right to him!

"You can't have him!" Dirk barks.

But at once, they attack—six skeletons, weapons coming down. . . .

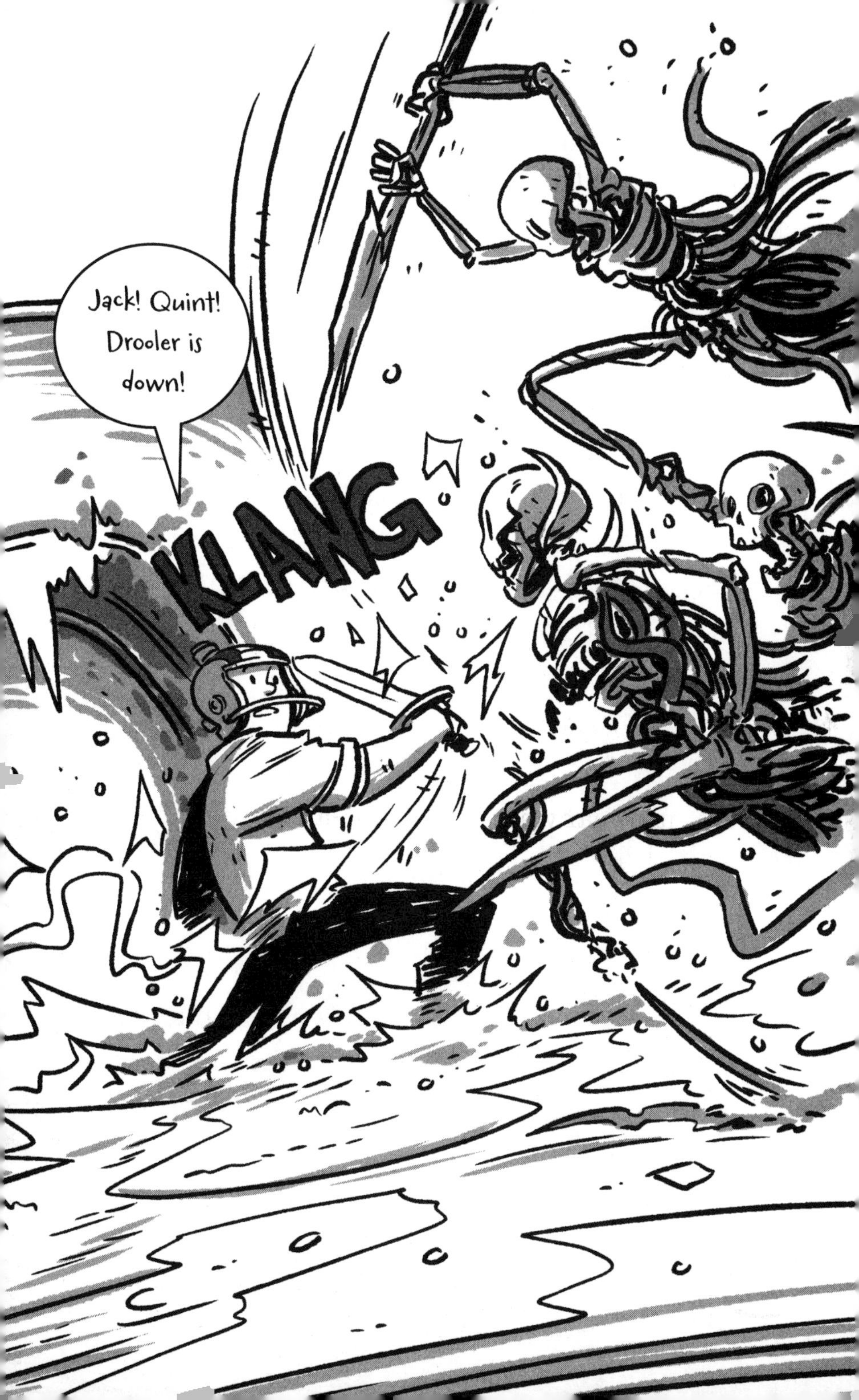
Jack! Quint! Drooler is down!
KLANG

Drooler splashes to the deck! Ultra-Slime kicks up as the little guy spins and slides across the platform like a hockey puck.

In a flash, the scene turns from combat to chaos—everyone is trying to grab hold of Drooler. Swarms of skeletons splash into the Ultra-Slime, disintegrating instantly. Skeletons slam their swords downward, trying to skewer Drooler like a kebab—but he continues gliding.

"Quint, he's coming your way!" Dirk shouts.

Quint lunges for the sliding Drooler. A bone blade whips over his head while Drooler slips between his legs.

"Slide for freedom, little buddy!" Dirk cries.

RAWWWRR!

The Gargantulax apparently understands now—because it goes into a crazed, skeleton-smashing rage. Cracking blows send skeletons spiraling through the air.

There's a foul hissing sound—and half of the remaining skeletons swarm the Gargantulax, while the others continue trying to get hold of Drooler.

In moments, the Gargantulax is overwhelmed. It's like one of those nature documentaries, where a bunch of vultures descend and devour a hunk of beef in, like, nineteen seconds.

"Watch out!" I cry. "The Gargantulax! It's gonna go over!"

And then—like it's happening in slow motion—the Gargantulax crashes through the deck's barrier, plummeting over the side, taking a dozen skeletons with it. . . .

"Where's Drooler?!" Dirk cries out.

We all spin, searching, then—

"There!" June says, pointing. I turn, just in time to watch the tiny monster slip into the mouth of the Double Trouble Dynamo slide, and then—

GLOOP!

It plunges down.

"DROOLER!" Dirk wails, barreling through two soldiers. "I'm a-comin'!"

Dirk dives into the tunnel first—and we follow, plunging into the darkness. . . .

The Double Trouble Dynamo is made for riding on huge round rafts, so it's super thick. All four of us, together, are sloshing around. "At least the skeletons can't follow us down the slide! Am I right, guys?" I shout.

"Jack, look behind you," June deadpans.

"Did the skeletons follow us down the slide?" I ask.

"The skeletons followed us down the slide."

I don't get it. They should be inanimate, lifeless heaps of bone. Their vines should have all melted by now!

But soon, I see it—they're riding skeleton rafts . . . using the bones of fallen soldiers as makeshift inner tubes.

Suddenly, we're bursting into sunlight as the slide goes from a full funnel to a half-pipe.

GOTCHA!

The slime is slicker than butter, and we're all blasting down way faster than regulation, that's for sure. If anyone from the World Waterslide Safety Commission—which is definitely a thing, I assume—saw what was going on right now, they'd shut this place down, *stat*.

"What's the plan?" I shout.

June hollers back, "We get to the bottom! We get to the BoomKarts! We get outta here!"

Suddenly, I hear the snarl of a skeleton. I raise the Slicer as—

WHAM!

Dude! Not cool! You wanna tango— let's wait until we get to the bottom, huh?

Ahead, the slide drops and turns. We slosh into a huge, long curve—and the slime has us going at *ludicrous speed*. The turn pushes me into the skeleton, and then we're both speeding, up, up, along the inside wall of the slide.

"Guys!" I cry out. "This is not gonna end well for me!"

My friends look back. There's nothing they can do. Dirk covers Drooler's eyes.

The skeleton and I go up the side, even higher, and then—

Oh no.

We're launched, up and over the slide's edge, propelled *out* into midair. . . .

I don't look down—but I can sense it, somehow: the concrete platform, far, far below.

But something else is below us, too.

A familiar shape emerges, a massive paw reaching out—a web of bone and vine . . .

Blargus, clinging to the side of the slide like King Kong hanging from the Empire State Building. . . .

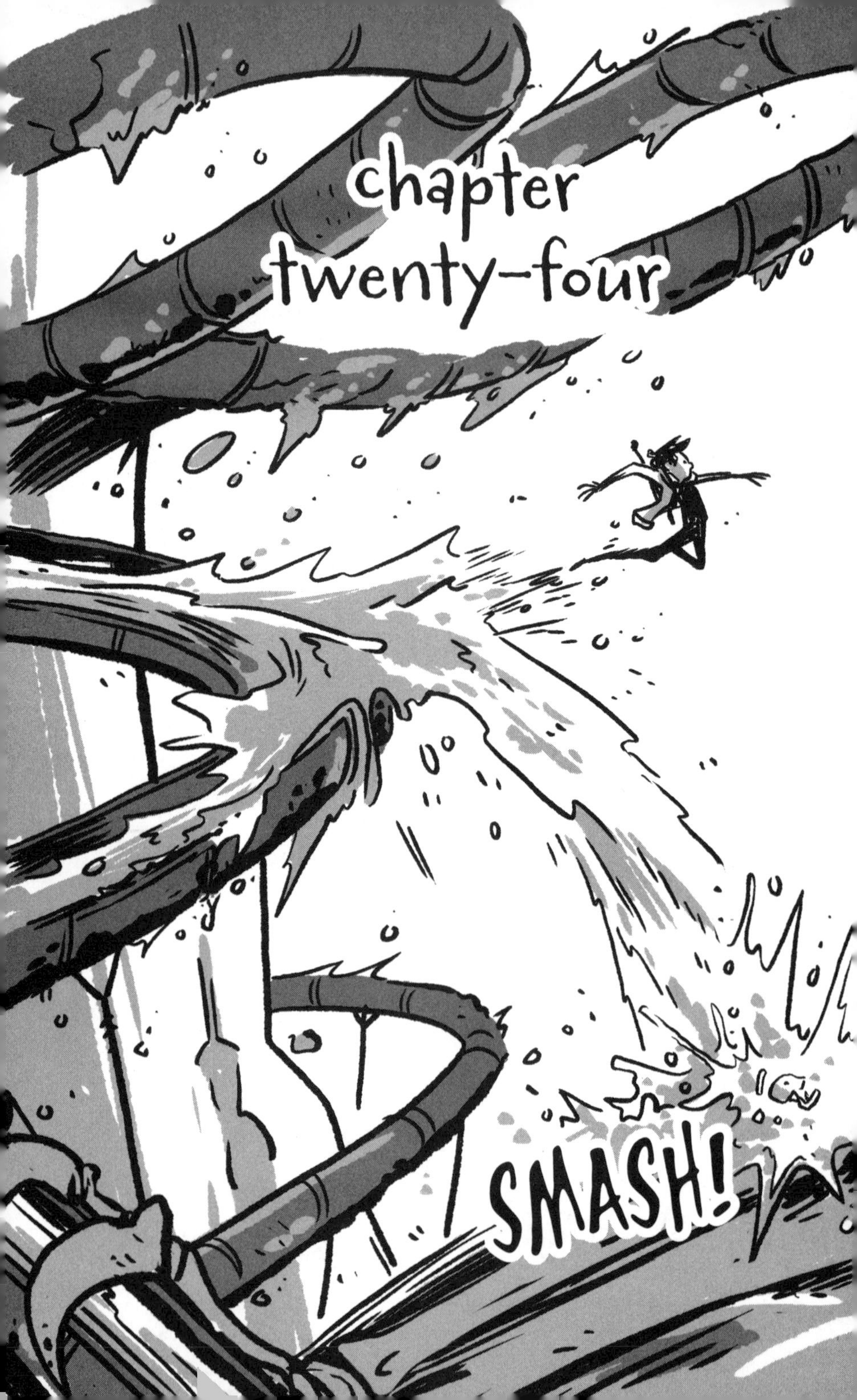
chapter
twenty-four
SMASH!

It's the only time it'll happen.

Ever.

It's the only time I'll be happy to see Blargus. Because grabbing him, hanging on to him, is my only chance. So, as I fall, I actually reach out to him with my Cosmic Hand.

My fingers swipe at his cold, bony body. The
Cosmic Hand grazes his side, and then—

YANK-SNAP!

The Cosmic Hand's tiny suckers latch on to
the bone. Pain shoots through my arm, and my
lower body swings into him. The Slicer drops
from my hand.

For a second I just hang there, catching
my breath. I peer down just in time to see the
skeleton splashing into the Ultra-Slime below.
My arm howls in pain.

Then the calm is over, because Blargus is
trying to rip me in half—and being ripped in
half is not conducive to calm. Using the Cosmic
Hand, I'm able to clamber up Blargus's back,
leaping from bone to bone. He swats at me
like he's trying to scratch an itch he can't
quite reach.

Too slow!

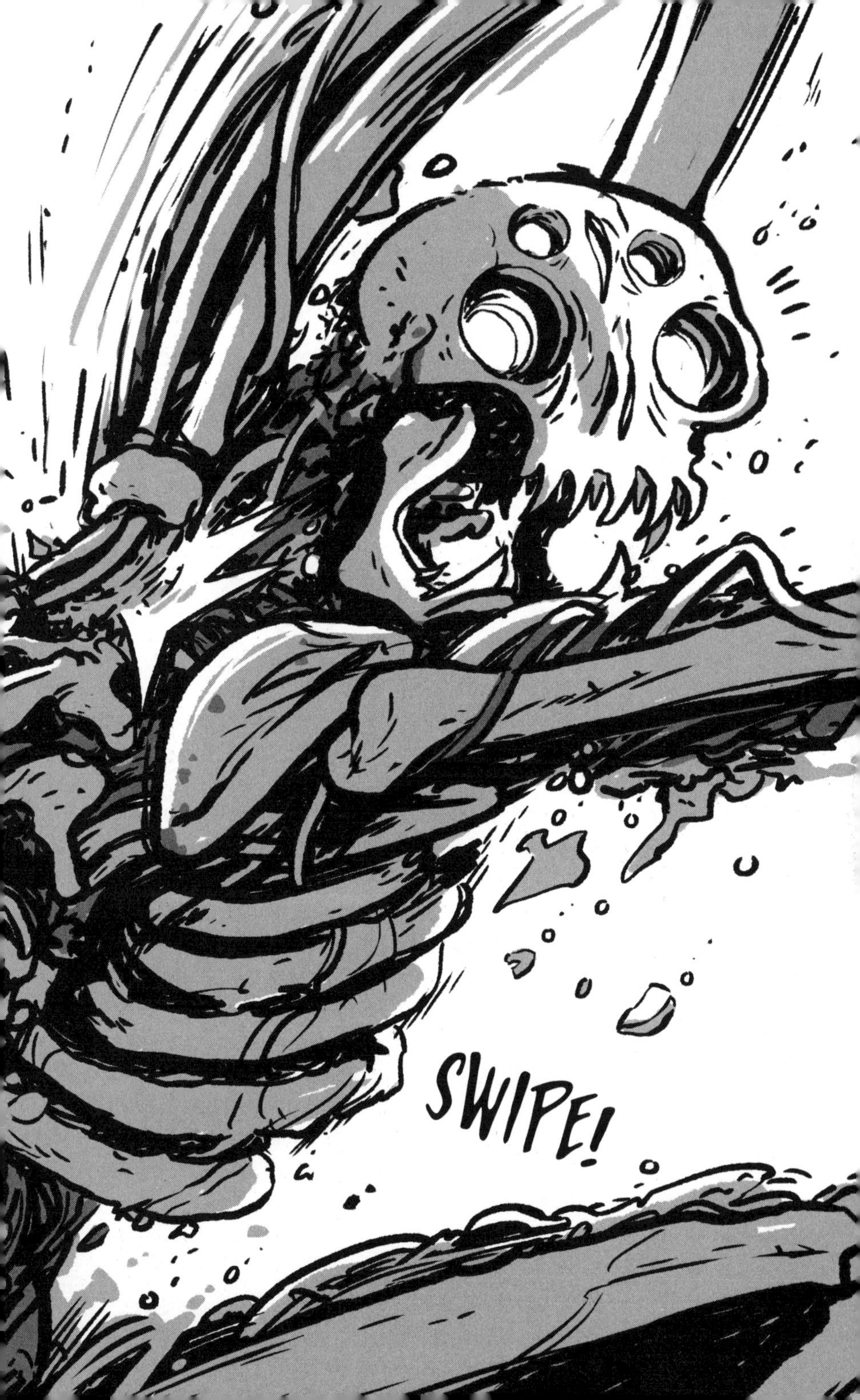
SWIPE!

Then he's swaying and jerking back and forth, trying to lob me off. But the Cosmic Hand holds like superglue.

I'm searching the ground below, still dodging Blargus's furious flailing, when I spot Quint, June, and Dirk erupting out of the mouth of the slide. They're greeted by a swarm of skeletons.

Nearby, I spot my zombies—doing nothing. They're like computers that aren't powered on. Without the Slicer, I can't control them.

And without the Slicer, I can't defeat Blargus.

My eyes scan the ground, searching. Blargus's thrashing doesn't make it easy. But then I spot it—

I need the Slicer.

But I've never controlled a zombie without the Slicer. I've never tried.

Could I do it now?

I've known Alfred the longest. It's a long shot at best, but I don't have time for anything else. Not with Blargus about to flatten me.

Alfred.

I concentrate, reaching out with my thoughts, toward Alfred—saying the words silently:

Alfred. I need the Slicer. Retrieve it. Please.

Alfred doesn't budge. He doesn't move one single, stinking, undead appendage.

Come on, Alfred! I think desperately. *You got this!*

I roll left, avoiding another of Blargus's attempts to grab me. I grip with the Cosmic Hand and scramble farther up his spine.

Alfred! Please!

Suddenly, Alfred looks up.

The Slicer. I need it.

Our eyes connect.

Listen to me, Alfred! That's Blargus! He speaks for Thrull! You saw Thrull, in the clearing— trying to bring Reżżőch here! The tree! The tree was going to swallow you, suck out your brains— but we saved you!

Alfred's eyes narrow.

Please . . . the Slicer. The Slicer!

And then he moves.

One slow step. Then another. And then—YES!—Alfred is staggering toward the Slicer. He reaches out, wraps his thin fingers around it, and—

YES AGAIN! He pulls it free from the Ultra-Slime, like some lowly squire destined to become the King of England. He's done it! He has pulled the sword from the slime!

Now I just need to get it from him.

I concentrate again. Letting the thoughts fill every corner of my brain. It works—and Alfred goes from butler to total, complete barbarian! He raises the blade high above his head and *jams* the blade into the tangle of vines that flow through Blargus's foot—

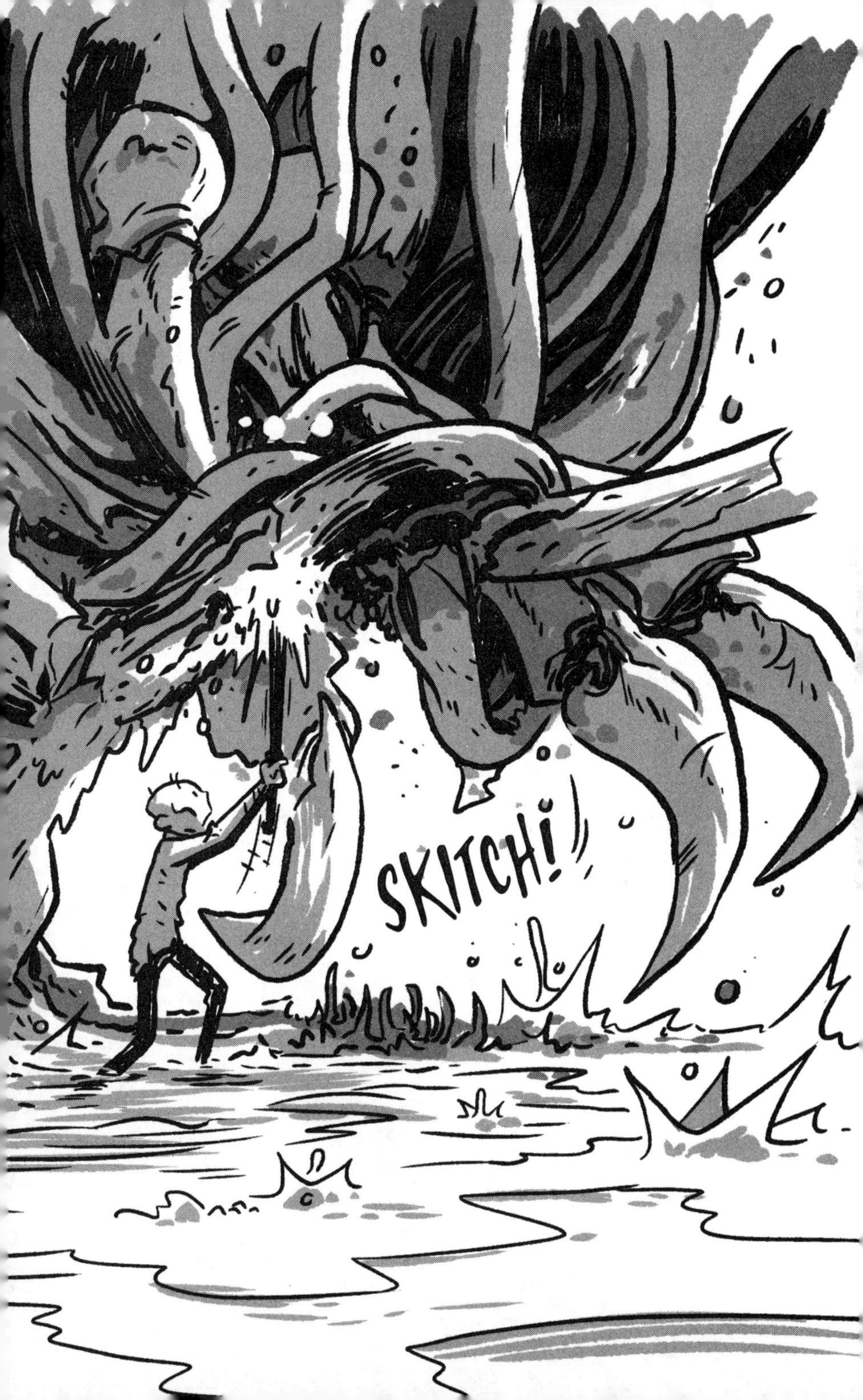
SKITCH!

Blargus howls, clawing at the slide to keep from slipping. *Good job, Alfred. Good job.*

I spread my fingers, loosening the grip of the Cosmic Hand, and slide down Blargus's cold, smooth spine. I dive off, skidding across the slime and completing the Slicer handoff from Alfred. "Thanks, buddy!"

I cock back the goo-coated Slicer, but—

GRAB!

"Oof! Vine sneak attack!" I groan as tight tendrils wrap around me, lifting me into the air. Blargus's mug forms a triumphant smirk.

The vines grow hot.

Oh no. It's happening again. Like at the motel.

I'm being ripped, pulled—somehow carried through Thrull's network of vines, transported into the throne room. I'm sure it's so he can taunt me before he kills me.

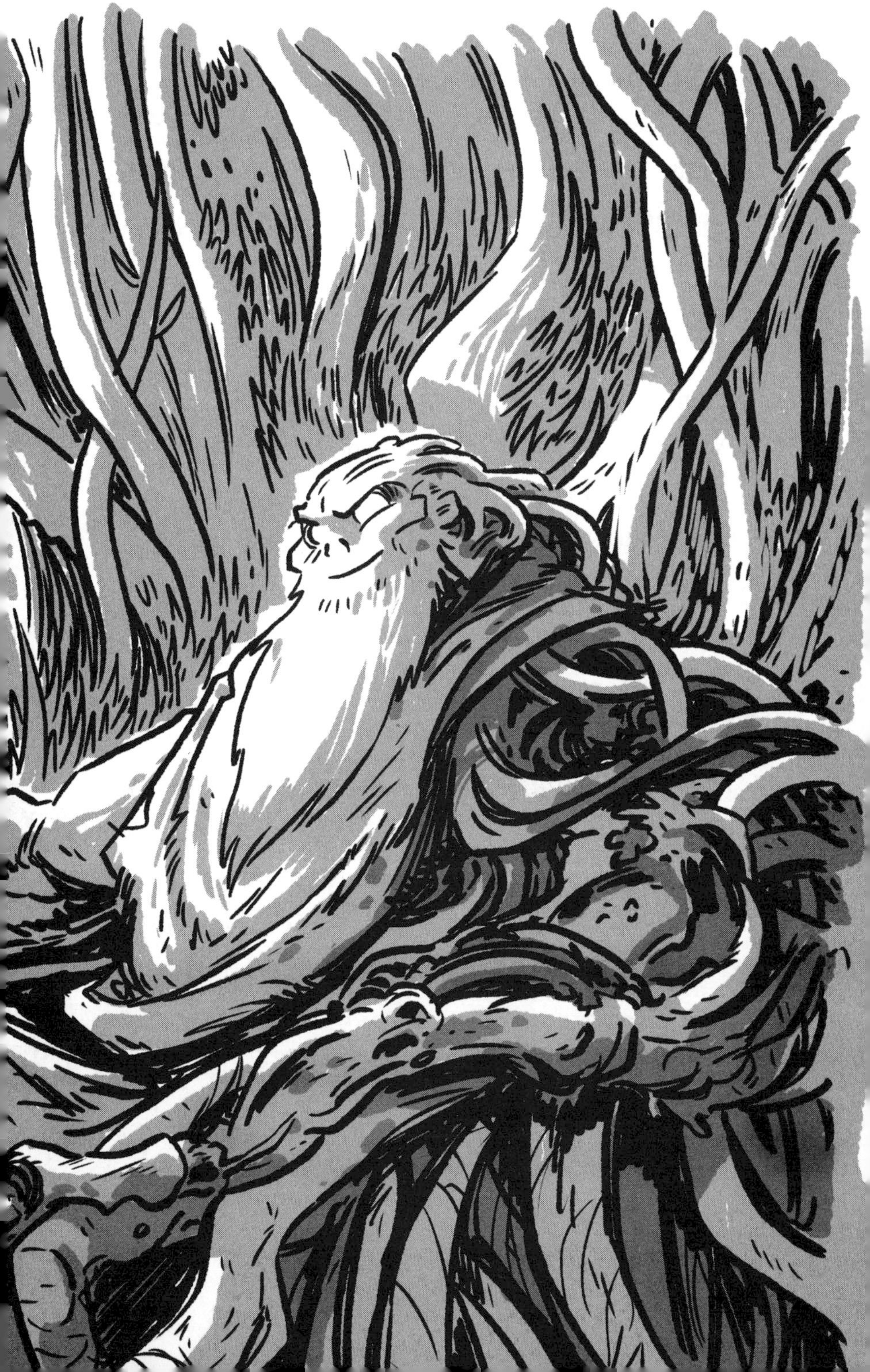

I stare into the villain's eyes.

"If you're gonna kill me—just do it, dude," I manage. "But don't act like it's so cool—we already know the location of the Tower. We *found it*, Thrull. And my friends are gonna finish the job— with or without me."

Blargus's head pulls back.

Thrull is surprised.

No—not just surprised: *enraged*.

And in that sliver of time, he could have crushed me. Blargus could have broken me. But the two villains—they waited a moment too long, because—

SKREE!!!

The Gargantulax lands on Blargus, caging him in with its sharp legs. The Gargantulax is soaked in slime, and it pours off its body, seeping between Blargus's bones. Steam pours off him.

Blargus scales the slide structure, going up, up, up. . . .

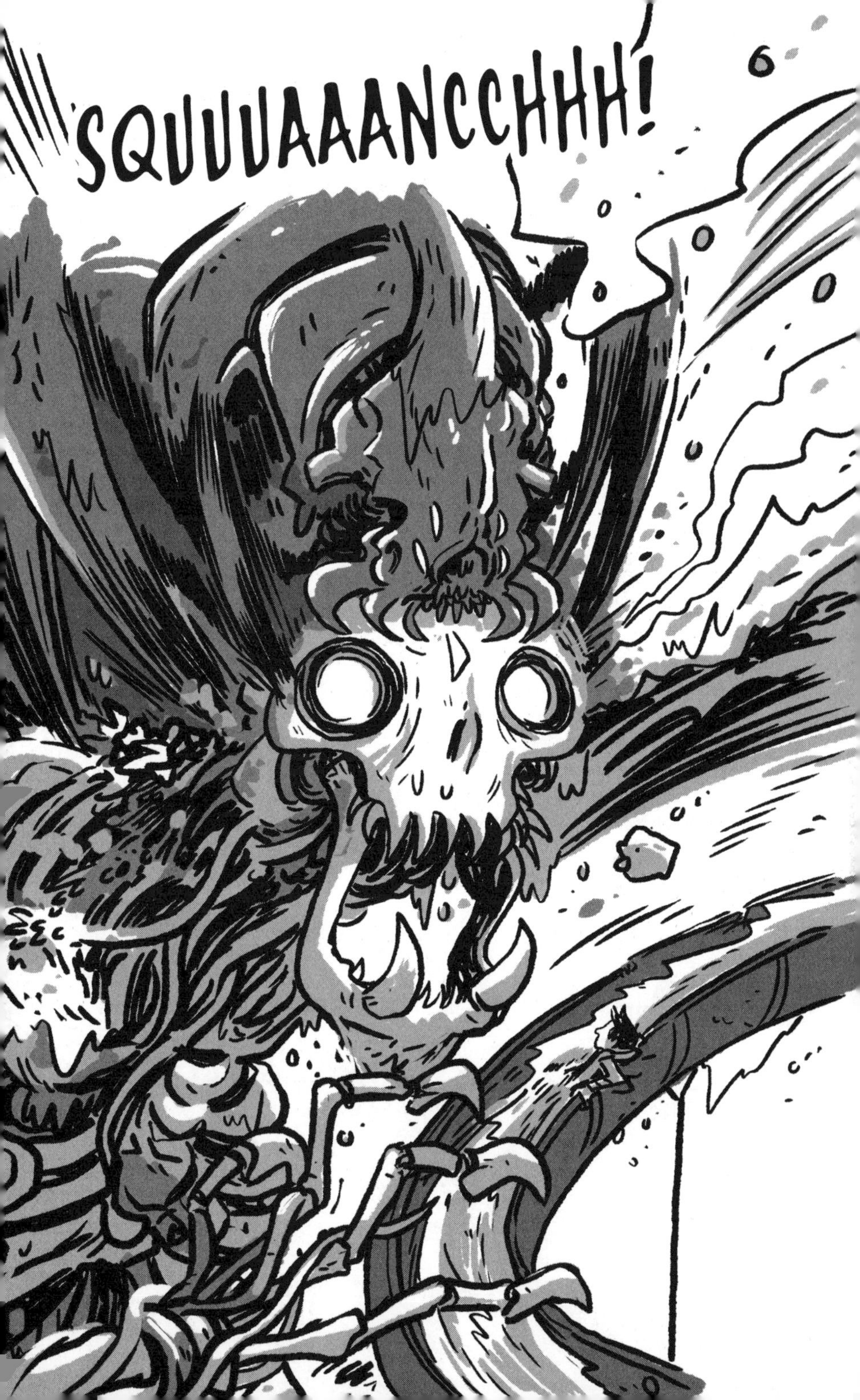
SQUUUAAANCCHHH!

But the Gargantulax doesn't let go.

Blargus clings to the bending, breaking slide.

Down below is the massive pool of Ultra-Slime.

He reaches up and grabs the Gargantulax.

Oh no you don't, I think. *You're not getting out of this one.*

SLICE!

Blargus's hand opens!

And he falls. A long, slow-motion descent, and then—

SPLASH!!!

He smacks into the pool of Ultra-Slime. Once the slime hits his body, he begins breaking— the connective tissue holding him together is disintegrating.

There's a wail—and I can't tell if it's Blargus or Thrull or both. But the voice fades away to nothing as Blargus slips into the pool of slime.

"HEY!" June cries out. "Little help over here!"

I throw a final glance at Blargus. One hand still grips the base of the slide. But the hand doesn't move.

He's done. For now.

The Gargantulax leaps down to help finish off the rest of the skeletons. It's got several injured legs and many wounds but is still fighting fiercely.

Fiercely enough to send every last skeleton into the slime . . .

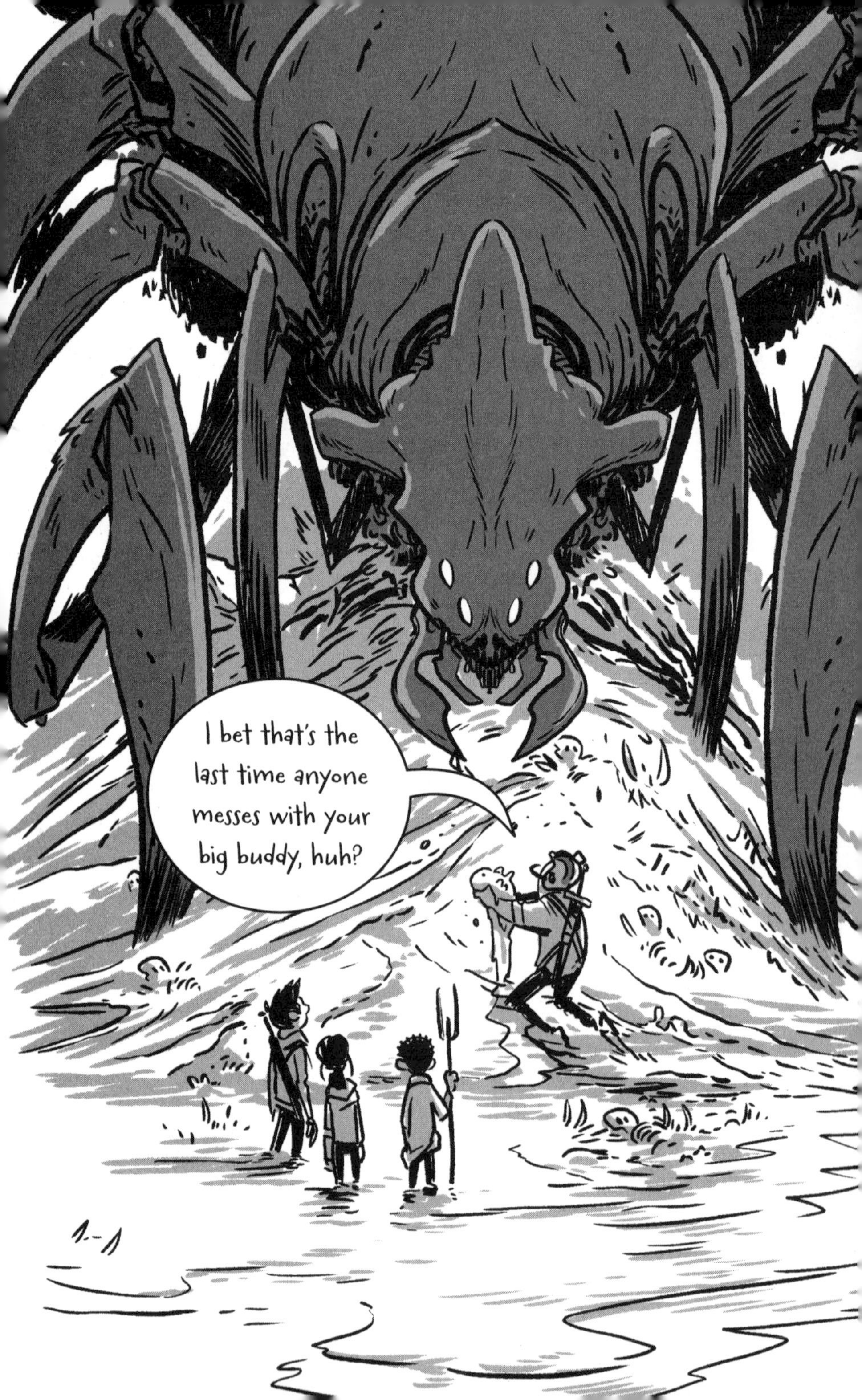
I bet that's the last time anyone messes with your big buddy, huh?

We look up at the Gargantulax anxiously. It looms, not attacking, but not backing away, either.

Dirk gives it a meaningful look and then kneels beside Drooler.

I have no idea if you can understand me, but here's the deal, Drooler.

You can help us defeat a very evil monster. And if you come with us, then I promise I will look out for you.

I will protect you, no matter what.

Drooler sort of just looks up at him blankly.

"I won't make promises I can't keep," Dirk goes on. "And when I say we're taking a road trip together, we'll actually do it! I won't make up ridiculous lies and I won't let anything happen to you."

The Gargantulax hisses, but it sounds more sad than angry.

"I will protect him with my life," Dirk says to the Gargantulax. "I'll be the best dad to this thing."

The Gargantulax lifts one wounded leg—and, very gently, taps Dirk. So he leans over and, slowly, picks up Drooler.

The Gargantulax lets him.

It finally knows we're the good guys. That we're on their side. That, in fact, we only want to stop evil. And more than all that—it knows Dirk means what he says.

"We got him!" June says. "We now have the source of the Ultra-Slime."

"Thrull is going down," Quint agrees.

Moments later . . .

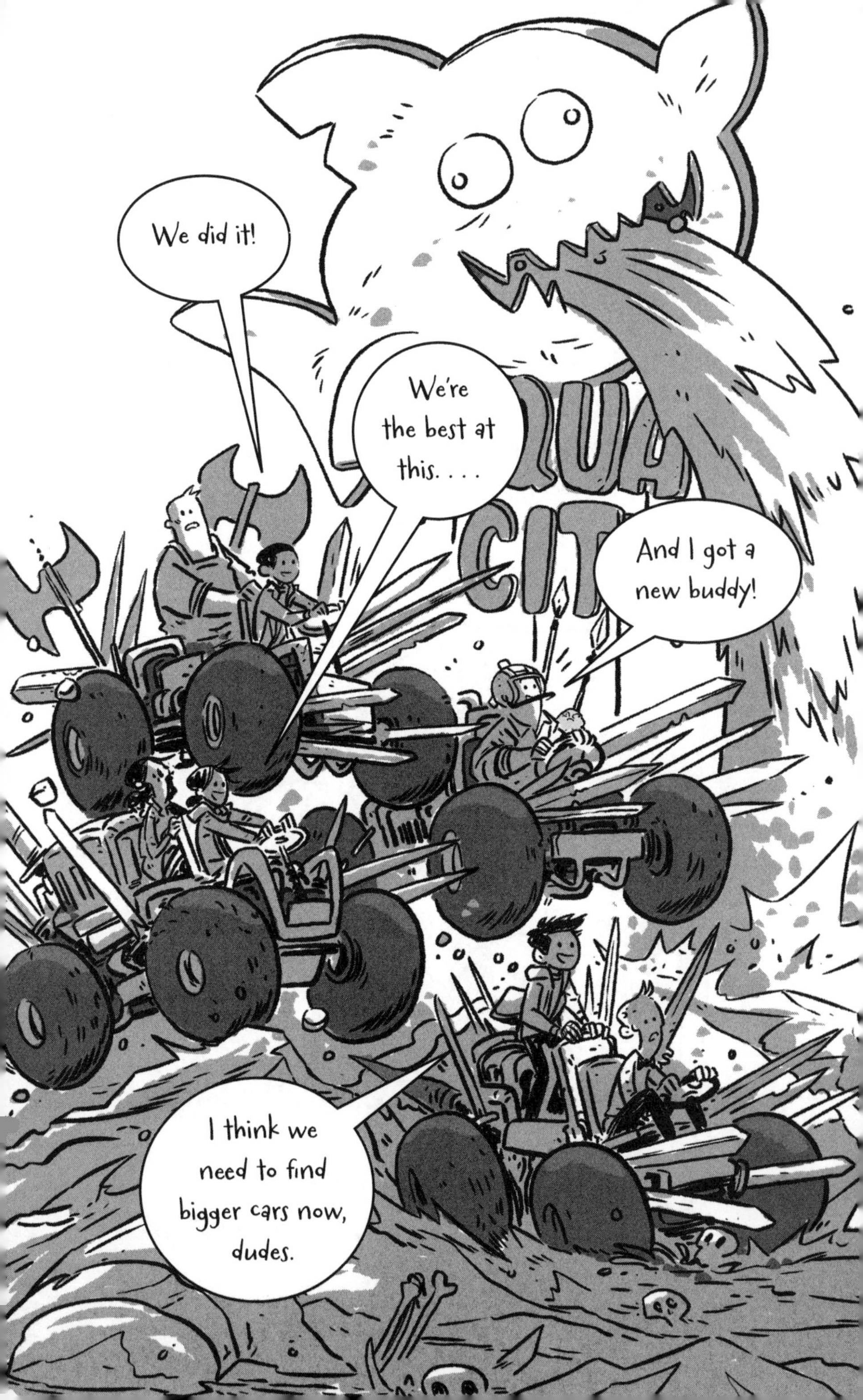

We did it!
We're the best at this. . . .
And I got a new buddy!
I think we need to find bigger cars now, dudes.

chapter
twenty-five

We stop at a gas station outside of town, once we're sure no skeletons are following us.

And the first order of business is to get a final road trip photo of all of us in super-cheesy souvenir shirts.

After the photo, June tries to get the fuel pump working so we can refill the BoomKarts.

"We kinda really kicked butt," June says. "Crushing this road trip thing."

"Not gonna argue," I say.

She says. "Not only did we get Drooler, but we also figured out a lot of stuff."

"Indeed," Quint says. "First and foremost: that Thrull views Drooler as a threat."

"Good point," I say, nodding. "But we also found out the Tower is WAY bigger than any of us expected."

"Not only that," Dirk adds, "but we know Thrull's army is nearly endless."

"You guys are being too negative!" June says. "We've got an Ultra-Slime machine now! Not to mention a massive army of zombies at our disposal back home!"

"We did achieve some victories," Quint agrees. "But it's important to recognize how far behind we still are. We're going to need more followers, more survivors, if we want to defeat Thrull and Rężżóch. It's a simple numbers game."

"I bet there are lots of monsters on the Mega Mallusk thing!" June says. "We just need to catch up to it!"

"Perhaps," Quint says before an easy silence settles among us.

And then I find myself sort of staring off into the distance, back toward the museum. A place I very much wish to never visit again.

"I can't believe Big Mama's really gone," I eventually say. "So many memories."

Quint smiles. "I did manage to save one memento from the wreckage. . . ."

He holds up the fuzzy dice that hung from Big Mama's rearview mirror ever since our first end-of-the-world day together.

I smile.

"Thanks, Quint."

We bump fists.

But then we're immediately distracted by someone making a squeaky baby voice.

Who's a good little Slime-Drooler? You are!

Yes, you are!

You're SO cute!

We're gonna take so many pictures together this trip! Yes, we are!

I'm gonna find you fun outfits and everything!

"Uh, should we be worried about this?" I ask.

"Worried?" Quint asks. "I'm delighted!"

I watch for another moment. Dirk hugs Drooler so hard that slime spurts out, splattering all of us.

"Yep," I say. "'Delighted' is the right word."

"I'm sorry, Dirk," June calls out. "I didn't mean to totally lose it back there. With Drooler and everything . . ."

Dirk looks up and shrugs, not seeming too worried about it anymore.

"No, really," June insists as she fiddles with the gas pump. "I never should have thought about stealing him from his guardian thing, or whatever. I was being selfish. We're all in this together, and I know that."

"You're good, June," Dirk says.

June finishes filling her BoomKart's tank and wipes her hands on her jeans. She walks over toward Dirk and says, "So . . . this is Drooler, huh?"

Dirk nods. June clumsily pats Drooler on the head and pulls her hand away to find it covered in slime. She laughs, and I think I even see Drooler crack a smile.

They are good.

And so am I. That's what I tell myself as I look back at the World's Largest Donut Hole. It's only a speck on the horizon now.

I've done Bardle proud. We honored his sacrifice—and we're gonna keep on doing that.

As I stare out at the strange, wrecked, beautiful landscape—I think about Rover.

"He's OK," Quint says. "He's with Skaelka." I turn as Quint comes up behind me.

"How'd you know what I was thinking about?"

He shrugs. "Best friend powers. Also, you were staring into the distance pensively, which means there's an eighty-six percent chance that you're thinking about Rover."

I sigh. Yeah, I miss Rover. But he's out there fighting the good fight. Just like us.

And now that we have Ultra-Slime AND know the location of the Tower, it's all gravy from here. We will march up to that Tower and show it who's boss! And we'll do it all heroically and stuff, and snap photos of how cool we are for sharing with people after!

NOTHING CAN STOP—

"Uhh, we got a problem!" June shouts, interrupting my thoughts.

"Big one," Dirk says from the pump. "Barely any gas left. Don't think there's even enough to make it to the next town, let alone New York."

"We'll find a way," I say confidently. "That's sort of what we do-o-o-o-o-o-o. . . ."

My voice begins quavering as the ground beneath our feet rumbles. And we all immediately recognize that rumble.

I quickly realize June was talking about a different problem altogether. In a second, we're eclipsed by a massive shadow.

The Mega Mallusk.

It towers so high it blocks out the sun. Each one of the monster's hundreds of legs is the size of a jumbo jet. Its head is in the ground, digging up everything as it thunders toward us.

It's so big, so powerful, that the air around it seems to swirl and change. The wind whips toward us.

And the smell of evil is thick in the air. . . .

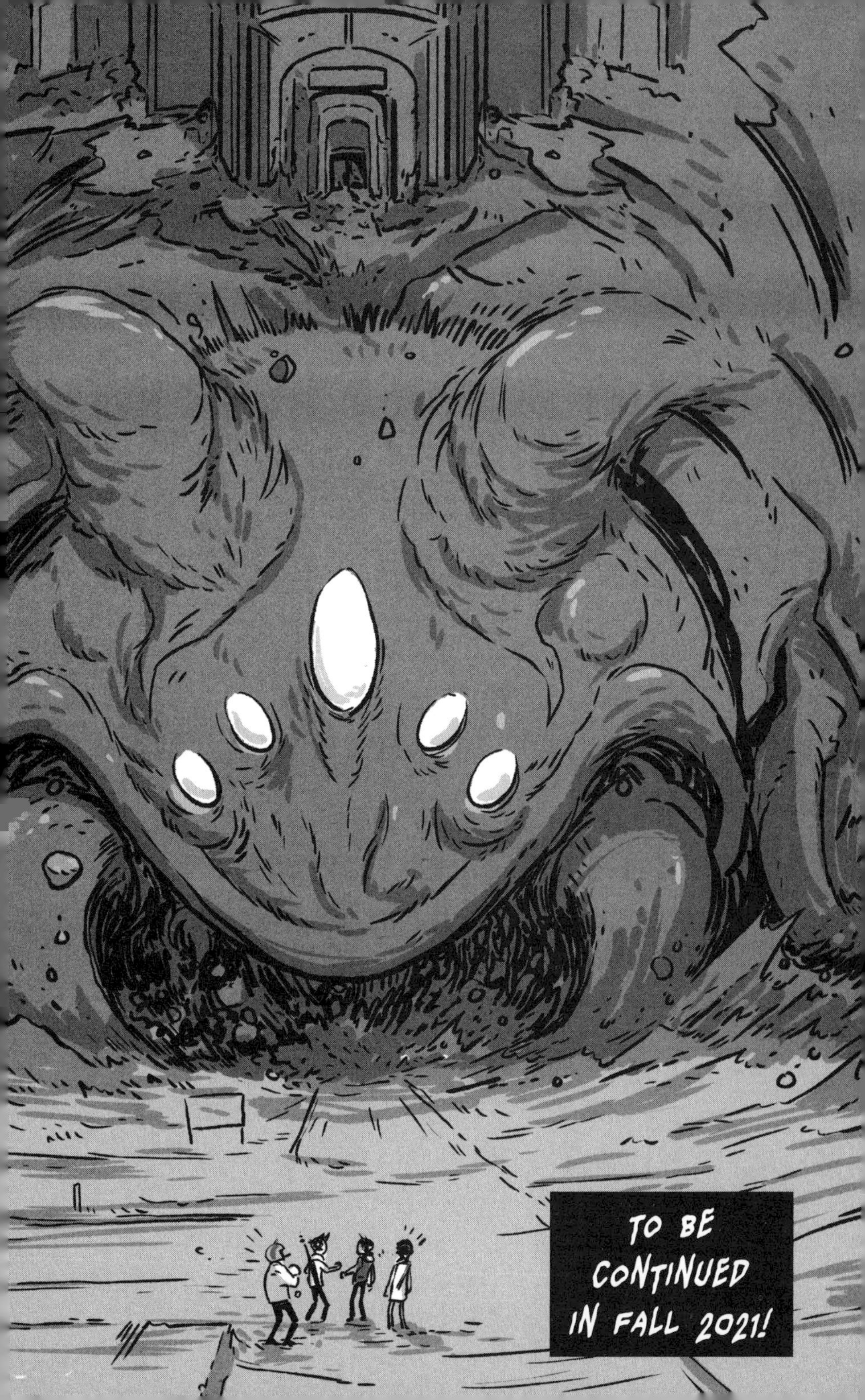
TO BE CONTINUED IN FALL 2021!

Acknowledgments

A million billion thanks to Douglas Holgate for joining me on this ride. Dana Leydig, you make this all bearable. Jim Hoover, you do what you do so darn well—thank you! Jennifer Dee, for keeping your sanity and working magic in the weirdest of times. So grateful to the army of copy editors needed to save me from embarrassment. Emily Romero, Carmela Iaria, Christina Colangelo, Felicity Vallence, Lauren Festa, Elyse Marshall, Sarah Moses, Kara Brammer, Michael Hetrick, Alex Garber, and everyone in Viking's marketing and publicity departments—thank you for doing the impossible, again and again. Kim Ryan and Helen Boomer in subrights, and the team at Listening Library—you rock. Ken Wright, for *everything*. Robin Hoffman and all the good people at Scholastic—thank you for endless support and bringing books to kids. Dan Lazar, I value you more than I can put into words. Cecilia de la Campa and Alessandra Birch, for taking Jack and the gang around the world. Addison Duffy, for taking this where I dreamed. Matt Berkowitz and Scott Peterson and all the folks at Atomic Cartoons for bringing this to wonderful life. And Josh Pruett—the best sounding board and the best person. Alyse—I love you.

A monster-sized thanks to everyone who preordered *The Last Kids on Earth and the Midnight Blade!*

Henry D.	Naomi H.	Hank M.	Annabelle W.
Tristan C.	Nathaniel P.	Gavin A.	Caroline W.
Charlee P.	Amarion D.	Loki B.	Manning W.
Sebastian M.	Lillian D.	Jovanni C.	James L.
Marcus V.	Spicer J.	John M.	Kaleb L.
Alden B.	Hudson C.	Mila M.	Henry L.
Ryan K.	Carter A.	Olivia M.	Jack D.
Jacob N.	Brayden A.	Marshall B.	Trex A.
Leo G.	Malcolm A.	Colin F.	Percy P.
Nick N.	Matthew A.	Xander B.	Vincent P.
Van H.	Chance C.	Aiden W.	Keegan N.
Devin L.	Henry B.	Bradley C.	Isaac O.
Sebi C.	Austin B.	Matthew R.	Jude R.
Heather B.	Jonathan M.	Aiden S.	Braxton M.
Mason H.	Max F.	Keira B.	Jameson L.
Ruby L.	Elisai V.	Ethan M.	Blaise M.
Emmaline L.	Cooper Z.	Luke A.	Owen M.
Ethan B.	Caleb H.	Avery C.	Lukas L.
Keiran J.	Beckett L.	Seamus M.	Benjamin M.
Aiden J.	Jack C.	Lincoln M.	Zeke R.
Dash G.	Henry B.	Justin R.	Toby R.
River B.	Kingsley W.	Ben R.	Brandt C.
Eli HG.	Brianna M.	Logan C.	Korrine C.
Kai L.	Jaden C.	Carson H.	Alysse Z.
Cataleya L.	Paden J.	Greisyn L.	Tristan L.
Roan T.	Stefan L.	William R. B.	Brenden K.
Path T.	Nicolas S.	Dorren T.	Evan M.
Quinn W.	Noah W.	Gavin B.	Oakley P.
Andre (AJ) W.	Gabe B.	Thor S.	Kiara T.
Kai K.	Mireya M.	Jake Z.	Lennox R.
Lucas W.	Samuel L.	Justin F.	Arvid T.
Griffin W.	John O.	Jake H.	Gael N.
Ryan "Iron" F.	Carson O.	Vitty P.M.	Rhiannon M.
Brion J.	Hunter K.	Jude B.	Riley K.
Ryker S.	Aaron P.	Brandon G.	Jonah C.
Ava Q.	Brandon S.	Atticus Z.	
Brady M.	Hayden M.	Alaric Z.	

© Ruby Brallier

MAX BRALLIER!

is the *New York Times* and *USA Today* bestselling author of more than thirty books for children and adults. His books and series include the Last Kids on Earth, Eerie Elementary, Mister Shivers, Galactic Hot Dogs, and *Can YOU Survive the Zombie Apocalypse?* Max lives in New York City with his wife, Alyse, who is way too good for him, and his daughter, Lila, who is simply the best. Follow Max on Twitter @MaxBrallier or visit him at MaxBrallier.com.

DOUGLAS HOLGATE!

(skullduggery.com.au) has been a freelance comic book artist and illustrator based in Melbourne, Australia, for more than ten years. He's illustrated books for publishers such as HarperCollins, Penguin Random House, Hachette, and Simon & Schuster, including the Planet Tad series, Cheesie Mack, Case File 13, and *Zoo Sleepover*. Douglas has illustrated comics for Image, Dynamite, Abrams, and Penguin Random House. He's currently working on the self-published series Maralinga, which received grant funding from the Australian Society of Authors and the Victorian Council for the Arts, as well as the all-ages graphic novel *Clem Hetherington and the Ironwood Race*, published by Scholastic Graphix, both co-created with writer Jen Breach. Follow Douglas on Twitter @douglasbot.

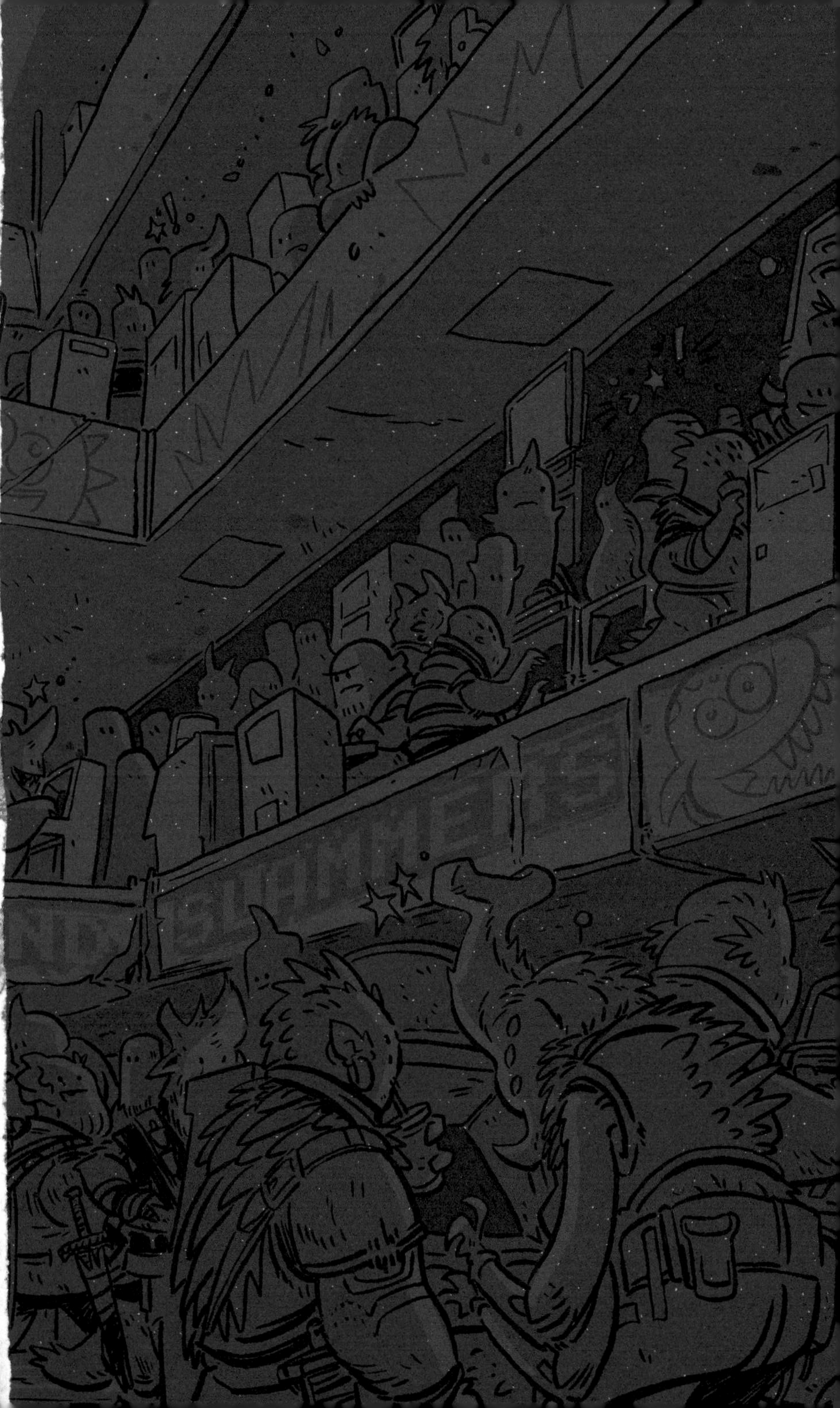

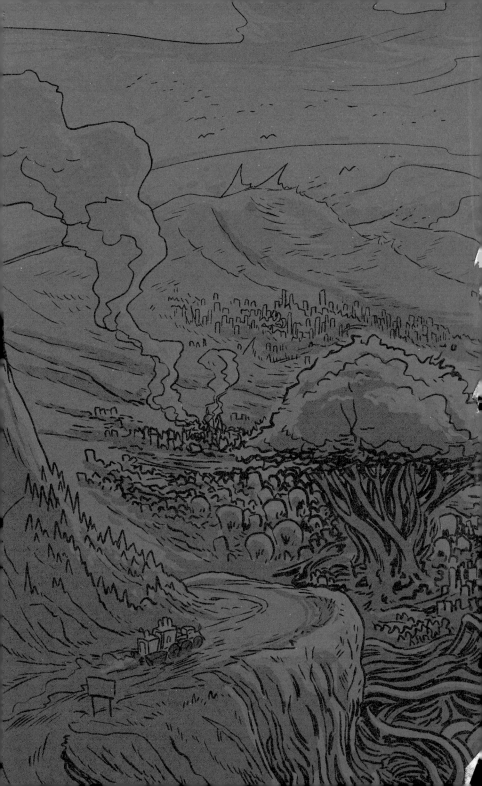